Yellow Death

ALEX LETTAU

This book is dedicated to medical missionaries worldwide, who accomplish so much with so few resources to better the lives of people with the greatest health needs.

ACKNOWLEDGMENTS

The author gratefully acknowledges Ellen Clair Lamb for her skilled editorial review and comments, as well as my agent/publicist Erin Mitchell for her invaluable advice and guidance through the publication process, and finally my wife Lisa for her patience, love, and support.

Chapter 1

Junior Murphee had been a big kid. Now he was huge. His abdomen was bloated and his arms and legs were massively swollen with edema. His eyes were only visible as canary yellow slits between puffy upper and lower lids. Dark blood filled his nostrils and tracked down from the left corner of his mouth. His skin was grayish-green and mottled with purple blotches from skin hemorrhages. Three large dragon tattoos covered the front of his chest and shoulders. A dry ulcer was present on his left shoulder and dense linear needle injection scars marked the former veins of his forearms.

Dr. Kristen Jensen completed her inspection of the body and turned to the Corham County coroner beside her. "Fulminant liver failure is never pretty. I can't believe he was only twenty years old, with needle tracks like that. Northern Mississippi boys must start injection drug use early."

Jeb Sloane cocked his head. "What kinda drug use?"

"Injection. I mean a drug abuser by self-injection. That's our Public Health Service's latest politically correct name for junkie, shooter, whatever. I suppose next year we'll be calling them non-traditional mood pharmacologists. So this guy's hepatitis B antigen was negative and the hepatitis C antibody was positive?"

Sloane nodded. "Yup. Same as the Herman kid from Millerville. Doc Calhoun signed that death out as acute fatal hep C, and I had to agree. But Doc did notify the state health boys in Jackson who called y'all in." As Kris leaned over to get a closer look at the dragon tattoos, Sloane said, "You know I was kinda expectin' CDC woulda sent someone, ah... a little more senior. With all due respect, Dr. Jensen, how long you been out of medical school?"

She stiffened and turned toward him. Stifling a retort with a quick breath, she just said, "Wisconsin, four years out. Mr. Sloane, you've got a real problem here. Acute fatal – or fulminant, as we call it – hep C, *if* that's what this is, is one rare bird. Two cases in a single county in less than a week is almost unheard of. Something other than hep C wiped out their livers."

"So how we gonna find that out?"

"We start by overnighting a sample of this man's blood to Atlanta, so our lab guys can run the hepatitis alphabet on it."

"I dunno if the lab saved any."

"Then to be sure we have one, I'm going to draw a heart blood specimen right now. I'll need two pair of number seven gloves, a six-inch 21 gauge needle, a 20 cc syringe, and four red top serum separator tubes. By the way, any leftover blood or serum samples from the first drug user who died?"

Sloane opened a cabinet to retrieve the supplies. "I dunno about that either, but you'd need a six-foot needle to get at Billy

Herman now. Oh, and I did hear this boy's girlfriend LaDonna is feeling puny. You want to test her too?"

"Most definitely. And ask her questions about Junior here." After she put on the second pair of gloves, she took the syringe with the attached six inch needle in her right hand, and carefully pierced the head of a dragon overlying the fourth left intercostal space. The needle easily penetrated the skin, fat and muscle layers of Junior Murphee's anterior chest wall, straight into the left ventricle of his heart. As she pulled back on the plunger, dark blood filled the syringe. She removed the blood-filled syringe and needle from the body and held it in her right hand in front of her with the needle pointing toward her left hand.

Standing to her left, Sloane had placed the empty serum tubes on Murphee's abdomen. Just then, the tubes began to roll off to the floor and as Kris reached for them, Sloane lurched forward to grab them. Their arms collided. The bulk and force of his right arm knocked her left arm and hand toward the needle and syringe in her right hand. As her left index finger pad contacted the needletip, she felt a slight sting.

"Damn it! I think I just got stuck."

The coroner's mouth dropped open. His eyes bulged. He stammered, "I'm s-so sorry Ma'am! W-what can I do? W-what can I get you?"

She shook her head in response and quickly set the needle and syringe down on a table. When she removed the gloves, the sight of blood on her left index fingertip intensified the queasy ache in her stomach.

His blood or mine?

She washed it off, and squeezed her fingertip to try to purge any of Murphee's blood out of the wound. A bead of her own blood welled up. She wiped it away with an alcohol swab. She was glad it stung. She squeezed and wiped again, and then a third time.

Sweaty and weak, she sat down and asked, "What's his HIV status?"

"I – I dunno," the coroner said, still shaken. "But here comes someone who should know." He was pointing at two men who had just entered the morgue: a balding, chunky, middle-aged doctor in surgical scrubs and a tall, graying man with deep smile crinkles next to his eyes.

The coroner introduced them, starting with the doctor in scrubs. "Mike Sandusky, the hospital pathologist, and Dan Stevens, our County Public Health Director." He swept his hand toward Kris. "Gentlemen, meet Dr. Kristen Jensen, an epidemiologist with the CDC Hepatitis Division, who, ah – we think just now had a needlestick exposure to Junior here."

Sandusky frowned. "You're kidding. What happened?"

As the visiting hepatitis expert, Kris was upset and embarrassed. She reluctantly recounted the incident as she applied a Band-Aid to her finger. "I'd call it a minor exposure but it never seems minor when it happens to you. It'll be all right. I've had the vaccines for hep A and B, and the risk of C from this should be less than two percent. Right now I'm more concerned about his HIV antibody status."

"Negative on hospital admission three days ago," Sandusky replied.

"Wonderful," Kris said. "I'm going to overnight this blood sample to Atlanta, but we'll still need an autopsy done."

Sandusky ignored the issue of a post-mortem examination and said, "Any idea yet about what might have caused these two deaths?"

"It could be the start of another New Bern–type outbreak."

"New Bern?" asked Stevens.

"1979. New Bern, North Carolina. Nine drug users developed fulminant hepatitis and seven died. Wasn't type A or B. They were shooting up MDA – that's methylene diamphetamine – which the CDC could only determine as a possible lethal co-factor. Any MDA used around here lately?"

Dan Stevens turned to Sandusky. "I don't think we've seen any in years."

The pathologist nodded. "I agree."

"So, what about an autopsy?" Kris asked again.

"Yes. An autopsy." Sandusky cleared his throat. "All our forensic stuff and the – ah – complicated cases are sent up to Al Stone at University of Tennessee in Memphis. I'd like him to handle this one."

"Then let's get the body on up to Memphis. Have Stone get more serum and freeze fresh liver at minus 70 degrees. Our lab guys at CDC will probably want to inject both tissue and serum into small animals."

Sandusky looked relieved. "I'll get on it right away."

"And sometime soon," she added, "I'd like to see the hospital charts of both Mr. Murphee here and the first case, Billy Herman."

"Their medical records are in my office," Sandusky said. "You can use my desk."

"Thanks." She nodded at the Pathologist and then turned to Stevens. "I'll need you to help me find local drug abusers that these two partied with, to interview and to get blood samples for hepatitis testing. I have a feeling we're going to see more cases."

Stevens rubbed his chin. "I expect we could find some of those boys out where Junior and LaDonna lived, at the Dixie trailer park, one of our finer neighborhoods. We might want to pay our respects to LaDonna first and see what she can tell us."

"Sounds good. Give me an hour to review the records and to check in with my supervisor at CDC."

Jeb Sloane spoke up. "So Dr. Jensen, are you thinking these kids died of hep C or not?"

She looked back at Murphee's corpse and shrugged. "I'm not sure. More likely C was only a co-factor along with a drug or toxin, or maybe even hepatitis X virus, a new one we haven't seen before."

"Sounds like something out of 'X-Files.'"

"Don't it, though?"

Chapter 2

Kris sat alone in Sandusky's office and felt her left index finger throb. She peeled off the Band-Aid to look. It was a little red and puffy around the puncture wound, but that was probably from the repeated squeezing and alcohol rubs. The image of Junior Murphee's corpse flashed in her mind. She put her hand to her forehead. *I'm 30 years old. My sense-of-immortality gene has long since switched off, but I can still conjure up good old-fashioned denial. Fulminant hep only happens to other people, not to me.* She gave Sandusky's wooden desk a couple of knocks.

After taking a deep breath, she paused and shook her head. *No question that I was exposed to Murphee's blood. I need to be rational about what I do about it. First possibility: if a toxin killed his liver, there's no risk to me or anyone else. Second possibility: if he had fulminant hep C, my risk of getting it is likely 2% or less. No effective preventive treatment for hep C but there would be no risk to anyone else if I did get it. Third possibility: hepatitis X virus. Needlestick transmission risk to me is unknown –would depend on how viremic he was. My risk to others? –unknown but it's zero right now since I'd only be incubating the infection. Drugs for prevention or treatment of hep X? – totally unknown. So do I tell CDC? They wouldn't know what to do and until they figured it out, might order me back to Atlanta with a pretty darn good chance I'd be taken off this investigation unnecessarily. The bottom line? A lot of unknowns but I'm not putting myself or anyone else at risk by carrying on at least until we find out more about a possible hep X.*

She flipped open the chart of Billy Herman from Millerville, Mississippi, a 21-year-old white male at the time of his death the previous Wednesday. She studied the typed admission histories of both charts, but skimmed through the mostly illegible daily progress notes and cursed the attending physicians more than once for their bad handwriting. *A cursory review*, she thought and smiled at the double meaning. She went over all lab results and read Billy Herman's typed death summary. After a glance at her watch, she decided it was time to check in with her chief in Atlanta.

Mike Bauman was Chief of the Epidemiology Branch of the CDC Division of Viral Hepatitis. In that position he supervised Kris Jensen and Jim Phillips, the other Epidemic Intelligence Service officer assigned to Hepatitis. Bauman was a career Public Health Service epidemiologist who had once been an EIS officer himself, and was an extremely knowledgeable field investigator. Following the usual CDC practice, his skill and experience had gotten him promoted to a supervisory and administrative position and away from direct participation in field investigations. Kris was glad to hear his voice.

"Hi, Kris. How's it going so far?"

"There're now two fulminant hepatitis deaths. A second drug abuser died a couple of hours ago. I got a look at him in the hospital morgue and drew twenty cc's of heart blood that I'll overnight to Charlie in the lab. Both were white males in their early twenties, known heavy IV users. Not sure yet which drugs, but both tested positive for cocaine and opiates on their admission urine drug screens. Best as I can tell from the records, they were both only sick for a week or less before death from liver failure with multi-organ shutdown, hemorrhage and shock. Both had hep C antibody and were completely negative for A and B except for B surface antibody. Both had had hep B vaccine. Give them credit for that."

"Huh. That is a *fulminant* course." The normally unflappable Bauman sounded excited. "These two have got to be connected. They died only five days apart, so either it's a common source for both, or maybe the first case infected the second early in the incubation period. Acute hep C isn't likely because antibody to C never shows up so fast. We could fingerprint their C viruses if we can dig up serum from the first case."

"You don't literally mean dig up his body?"

"No. Not yet, anyway. Check with the serology reference lab. They might have kept some of his unused serum. Any chemicals, *Amanita* mushrooms, or MDA that might've been a hepatotoxic co-factor?"

"Nothing in their charts about those, but I'll try to interview their family and friends, and hopefully some local drug abusers later today and tomorrow. I told the hospital pathologist and the County Public Health Director about New Bern, but they weren't aware of any MDA use around here for years."

"Autopsy?"

"Case Two will be autopsied at U.T. Memphis by a Dr. Al Stone. I asked to have him get us more serum, and to deep freeze liver tissue."

"Good work. On the blood we get tomorrow, Charlie can run the virus alphabet, including D,E,F and G. Maybe we'll inject a few rats, hamsters, and a couple of macaques if there's enough material."

"I drew twenty cc's of heart blood that I'm sending."

"That's probably enough to get started," Bauman said. "Hey, be *really* careful packaging and handling specimens. This sounds deadly. Use gowns, double gloves, masks, goggles, safety needles, the whole works."

She swallowed and her voice quavered a bit. "Don't worry. I will. The hospital has already mobilized the ten-foot poles and stocked up on hotcakes and flounder."

"Hotcakes and flounder?"

"Meals you can slide under the patient's door."

Bauman laughed. "Kris, you're something else. Don't forget to call a report to Jeff Wilson, the state epidemiologist in Jackson. You need any help yet?"

"Not yet. There's no one else sick, except maybe Case Two's girlfriend. I can handle the interviews."

"Okay. By the way, even drug abuser deaths can send the media into a frenzy. Try to keep them out of it. It'll be easier to get your work done. Keep me posted. Bye."

She had just hung up the phone when Sandusky's secretary Emma poked her head through the door. "There's a newspaper reporter from the *Memphis Flyer* on line two. He wants to talk to you about the hepatitis cases."

Kris rolled her eyes. "Please take his number. I need to call a report in to Jackson first."

After her report to the Mississippi State epidemiologist, Kris stopped at the hospital lab to pick up supplies to draw and store blood. She met Dan Stevens in the parking lot for the drive out to the Dixie trailer park.

She sighed as she climbed into his white Ford Explorer. "I just talked to a reporter from the Memphis paper. So much for working undercover."

Stevens nodded. "Yeah, I talked to him earlier. Someone from the hospital probably tipped him off about the second death and CDC coming to investigate. Folks around here are scared, but mainly that this hepatitis will spread to someone other than drug abusers."

"How big a drug problem do you have in the county?"

"There's marijuana and crack cocaine use in the black community, but IV drug abuse is pretty much limited to low-income white kids who mostly shoot up cocaine, sometimes heroin. There're probably only a dozen regular users around, but a lot more weekend-only types. There's not a huge demand for 3 liter soda bottles in and around Corham."

"What do you mean?"

"The regular users have the notion that IV drugs dehydrate the body and make them crave sugar, so they try to drink a three-liter soda bottle every day. My niece works at the grocery store in town. She swears she can tell who's shooting up regularly and who isn't by the three-liter soda bottle sales."

She raised her eyebrows. "We need to alert the Drug Abuse Warning Network – DAWN, as it's called – about this new way of monitoring intravenous drug abuse. If we have trouble tracking down drug abusers, maybe we could tie a three-liter Pepsi bottle to the back of our car and troll through the trailer park for them."

"Good idea." Stevens chuckled. "The trailer park's another mile or so." He slowed the Explorer and turned onto a washboardy dirt road.

"Tell me about LaDonna. Were she and Junior married?"

"I don't believe so. LaDonna Fry is only about 20. We've seen her at the health department clinic a couple of times. Nice kid. Doesn't do drugs. She's – ah – real country. But not nearly as clueless as she comes across. Her parents were killed in a tractor-trailer accident on I-55 three years ago. After that's when she moved in with Junior."

"What's the story on him?"

"Junior was a bright kid, but he started using years ago and stayed hooked. Believe it or not, he was a health nut otherwise. Even came to the health department last year to get hepatitis B vaccine and brought a few of his drug-using buddies in with him. I remember Junior telling me at the time that he once tried to sell his blood and was rejected for having had hepatitis, so he never wanted to get it again."

"I'll bet he was rejected for having hep C. Health nut or not, he got hepatitis again. I'd like to know where he got the dragon tattoos done. Could even be the source of his infection. Any local parlors do that quality work?"

Stevens shook his head as he turned the Explorer into the trailer park. "You'd have to go at least to Memphis or Jackson. LaDonna might know. I called earlier. Hers is lot number 39. Should be down this way."

Junior and LaDonna's home was a single-wide at the end of a row of similar trailers. When they drove up to it, eight yapping yard dogs of indeterminate breeds announced their arrival and quickly surrounded the Explorer. Kris hesitated to open her door. "Whoa. Four more mutts and they'd have a twelve-pack."

LaDonna Fry appeared at the trailer door. She shooed off the hounds and beckoned the doctors to come in.

Kris's first impression was that LaDonna could indeed be the poster girl for "country," with her curly brown hair, freckles, wide eyes, and dirty bare feet. But up close, as Stevens introduced her, Kris could see that she wasn't well. LaDonna looked tired and depressed, with bluish circles under her eyes and a sallow hue to her skin.

They sat in the small but tidy living room. Kris spoke first. "I'm sorry about Junior. I'm a specialist in hepatitis from Atlanta and I came to help figure out what made him and Billy Herman so sick. Then maybe we can help keep other people from getting this hepatitis."

When LaDonna did not respond, Kris said, "You don't look well. Have you been sick?"

"I've been feelin' bad since the end of last week. Real tired, and I can't eat for puking. Maybe I got the bug that's been goin' round the park. Y'all got something for that?"

"Not with me," Kris replied. She was concerned that LaDonna's symptoms represented acute hepatitis. "Your eyes look a little yellow. Does your urine, I mean your pee, look dark?"

"All I know is my tushie is hurtin' for certain when I pee. It does look a little dark, but Auntie Flo is visitin'," she said with a conspiratorial wink at Kris.

Stevens looked quizzically at Kris, who mouthed the word *period.* He nodded.

Kris turned back to LaDonna. "You need to come down to the clinic for a check-up and blood tests."

LaDonna nodded. "I'll come. I can't go on like this."

"Right now I need to ask you a few questions about Junior and his use of drugs."

"I'm telling y'all that I don't do drugs," LaDonna said. "Never have, never will. Junior did 'em with Billy Herman and Frankie, and Bubba, and sometimes other boys I seen come to the trailer. I wouldn't let them do it in here. And I know Junior always used clean needles, – for a fact."

"How did you know for sure?"

"He was scared of catching hep. He always brought plenty of clean needles back from his trips. *Never* shared his works – his needles and syringes – at least, not since we been together."

"Where did he go on these trips? Is that when he got the tattoos?"

LaDonna shrugged. "He never told me where. He leaves on Friday and comes back Sunday night with new needles and sometimes another tattoo. I didn't like them dragons. Too creepy looking. He came back with a new one a week or so ago just before he took sick."

"So that trip when he got the new dragon was the weekend of Saturday the 13th. Left Friday, came back Sunday?"

LaDonna closed her eyes and shuddered. "That's right."

"Looks like you hate for him to be away."

She nodded.

Kris leaned forward. "Miz Fry," she said, "it is really important that we find out *exactly* where Junior was getting the dragon tattoos."

"I dunno," LaDonna said. "Really!"

"Did he bring back drugs too?"

"I dunno about that either. Maybe. I know them other boys never went along. They'd come sniffin' around here, especially that Billy, but I'd run 'em off with the dogs. I never saw any receipts from the trips. Junior always paid cash, even for his computer."

Kris raised her eyebrows. "Can we have a look at his computer? It might give us some answers."

LaDonna nodded as she got up and led them to a back room. "Junior never let me touch it. I guess it's okay now that he's gone."

Kris sat at a desk and turned on the power switch. The screen came up but further access required a password. Combinations of Junior's initials, birth date and Social Security numbers didn't work. She turned to LaDonna. "What else was important to him?"

"Me," she said. "Want me to do it?"

"I thought he wouldn't let you touch it."

"He didn't, but I watched him work it. Try L-a-d-o-n-n-a."

When that password worked, Kris smiled at her. "Bingo! We're in. Good for you." She hoped to find clues about Junior's trips, but the e-mail file, documents file, and trash bin were all empty.

As Kris brought up the list of bookmarked websites, LaDonna asked, "What's in there? The guys who sold Junior needles?"

"I doubt it. I'm looking for where he got his tattoos, which could be where he got needles and maybe drugs. Here we go – King Dewey's Castle of Tattoos, in New Orleans." She brought up the website and clicked on the advertised dragon special. The image on the screen matched Junior's chestwork. "Now we know where the dragons were done."

"New Orleans? Junior said he was gonna take me to Mardi Gras next year. Guess not now." LaDonna hung her head. A tear trickled from the corner of her eye. She wiped it away and sighed. "Hey, I'm tired. Unless y'all got more questions, I gotta get some sleep. I'll catch a ride to the clinic in the morning."

"I do have one more," Kris said. "When was the last time you and Junior had sex?"

LaDonna blushed. "You mean the last time we did it?"

"It's important for me to know."

"It's been about two weeks. I got mad when he came back with that new dragon and I wouldn't do it. Then he took sick and – ah – didn't want it no more." She hung her head in regret.

Kris stood and gave her a hug. "LaDonna, I am so sorry about Junior. You've been a big help to us. You be sure to come in tomorrow or we'll come out to get you, okay?"

"Yeah, thanks, LaDonna," Stevens said. "We'll see you in the morning. I have one more question. Where we can find Frankie Howell and Bubba Watkins?"

"Frankie lives in lot 51. I don't have no idea where Bubba is. Maybe Frankie knows," she said. "One last thing for y'all – watchit. Those boys got guns they ain't afraid to use."

Chapter 3

As the trailer screen door squeaked to a close behind them, Kris turned to Stevens. "I'm worried about LaDonna. She looked jaundiced. Don't know what the tushie pain is about, but she needs her liver tested at your clinic and a serum sample sent to Atlanta. I tend to believe her about not doing drugs, but I've been wrong before."

Stevens nodded as he unlocked the Explorer. "I doubt she does drugs. And maybe Junior intended to not share his works, but after getting drugged up, coulda been he got careless. I suggest we go see Frankie Howell before it gets too late. We never go knocking on doors around here after dark. She wasn't kidding about the guns."

They found trailer 51 and were relieved to see no dogs around. After several unanswered knocks, they were about to leave when the door opened. A disheveled young adult male who looked like he hadn't slept in a week, greeted them with a slurred "Yeah?"

"Are you Frankie Howell?" Stevens asked.

"He ain't here," was the mumbled reply.

"We're doctors from the Health Department. We need to talk to him about Junior Murphee and Billy Herman and the hepatitis that's been going around."

"Uh – okay. I'm Frankie. I thought you was bill collectors. Come on."

The mess in the trailer's living area matched its owner. Empty pizza boxes, cigarette butts and crumpled beer cans littered the room. The smell of stale beer and cigarette smoke was almost overpowering. Kris saw a monster cockroach scurry under the couch and sidled over to sit on a wooden chair instead. Stevens sat on the couch and asked Frankie, "You heard about Junior?"

"Yeah. Too bad. What's crazy is he was so spooked about getting hep and then he got it. But I don't care that much and I ain't been sick."

Kris asked, "Did you two party together much lately? I mean, do drugs together?"

"Yeah, every couple of weeks we'd do coke. That's about it. Excuse me a minute." Frankie got up and stumbled into the kitchen. He returned shortly, carrying a three-liter bottle of Mountain Dew. He sat again and took a big drink.

Seeing something Kris had been sure was a joke play out in real life was almost too much to bear. She managed to only partially stifle a belly laugh, which exited her nasal passages as a snort. Frankie didn't notice, but it made Stevens smile. She collected herself.

"So did you and Junior shoot up the coke or sniff it?"

"Junior never put stuff up his nose."

"Did you two ever share needles?"

"Junior would never share works, even when he was shitfaced. He always had plenty of clean needles for both of us. It's not like we had to be blood brothers or somethin'."

18

"Did you two ever do heroin or MDA?"

"I heard Junior scored some heroin, but I ain't seen it. Dunno about MDA."

Suddenly, Frankie's head jerked and his eyes widened, as if struck by a lightning bolt of awareness. He looked back and forth at them and jumped to his feet, knocking over the bottle of Mountain Dew. "Hey! You guys ain't the cops, are you?"

They shook their heads and said no in unison. "I told you we're from the health department," said Stevens, pulling out his ID card.

Frankie looked at it. He lit a cigarette and sat down again. "Okay. Just checkin' you out."

"What about Billy Herman?" Kris asked. "Did he party with you and Junior?"

"Billy was a leech. Never had his own works or nuthin'. I dunno why Junior put up with him. He even gave him some of that sparkle shit he scored."

"What's the sparkle shit?"

"Some stuff Junior picked up on a trip. Billy said it was hot new heroin."

"Did Junior and Billy ever use the same needles?"

"I told you Junior never shared works. Not with Billy, not with anyone."

"If they didn't, how did one of them give hepatitis to the other?"

"I dunno. Maybe the shit had hepatitis in it."

Kris paused to consider the suggestion. "If the drug had germs in it, they would have had to snort it to get infected. Did they?"

Frankie shook his head. "Nah, all of us always cook our stuff, then suck it up through a filter with a needle."

"But melting down heroin or coke should kill any germs in the drug. Could Junior and Billy have had sex with each other?"

"You mean were they queer? They'd shoot you for even askin' that."

"I guess that's a 'no'. Any of this sparkle stuff still around?"

Frankie shrugged. "I never seen or had any."

"Know where we can find Bubba Watkins?"

"I ain't seen him in weeks. He mighta left town."

"One last thing," Kris said. "Can I draw a blood sample from you to test for hepatitis? It's free." She hoped she'd be able to find a vein.

"Forget it. If I get sick, then you can *try* to draw my blood." Frankie laughed as he showed them out.

Back in the Explorer, Stevens shook his head. "Trashy trailer, messed up kid."

Kris turned to him. "Did you see that uber-roach the size of a Cadillac? I don't know how it fit under the couch you were sitting on."

Stevens laughed. "I thought I felt something moving around underneath me. They do grow big in these parts."

"I hate huge bugs like that." Kris shuddered. "It's the one thing I can't get used to here in the South." She paused and shook her head. "LaDonna seems like a nice sweet kid and keeps a neat and tidy little trailer. Now she's sick and Frankie's not. Where's the justice in that?" She watched the passing farms, then shrugged. "Anyway, even though he refused the blood draw, Frankie was still the catch of the day." She rubbed her forehead. "But there're pieces missing here that would help make better sense out of when

20

and how these kids got this hepatitis. Let's talk to LaDonna again tomorrow. Otherwise we may yet be trolling the streets with a three-liter bottle of Pepsi."

Back in her motel room, Kris checked her cellphone messages and noted a voice mail from Mike, asking her to call him at home in Atlanta. Jeannie, his wife answered the phone, and got him on the line.

"Congratulations. You're the star hepatitis detective, according to the Associated Press wire. They picked up the story from the Memphis paper."

"Swell. Maybe this is just my fifteen minutes of fame."

"Not a chance. You can expect more and more media interest. Get the hospital and the Health Department to handle them as much as you can. Listen, we got a call today from a George Schmidt, who's the hospital epidemiologist at Parish General Hospital in New Orleans. Seems they have an injection drug user in their ICU who's dying of non-A, non-B, maybe C fulminant liver failure, and a nurse got stuck with a needle used on the guy. Sound familiar?"

Kris's jaw dropped.

"I mean the liver failure, not the exposure," Bauman added. "Schmidt mainly called for our recommendation for hepatitis prevention in the nurse. I suggested high dose interferon and a lot of prayer."

"Interferon? You think that would work?" she asked, eyeing her wounded finger.

"I have no idea. I don't know that the patient is infectious for anything other than HIV and hep C. They're sending us a serum sample to run our hep A to G panel."

She took a deep breath and summarized the interviews with LaDonna Fry and Frankie Howell. "Even before you mentioned that case at Parish General, I was suspecting Junior brought this hepatitis up from New Orleans. I'm just not sure how he got it, or how Billy got it from him and managed to die five days earlier."

"Maybe this sparkle stuff is MDA or another drug that's a hepatotoxic co-factor with hep C. We need to find a sample to analyze. Maybe Junior gave some to Billy to try a week before he used it himself."

"That's a good thought, except I'm pretty sure that LaDonna is sick with this hepatitis and she denies doing drugs. Call it feminine intuition, but I don't think she was lying."

"Then," Bauman said, "if it's a virus, another possibility is that Junior brought back virus-contaminated used needles that someone had only wiped clean and then repackaged as supposedly sterile. Wouldn't be the first time it's happened. Try to get a supply of Junior's clean needles and we can look for traces of blood contamination."

"Okay. I'll check with LaDonna tomorrow," Kris said and hesitated. "Mike, I want your blessing to drive down to New Orleans tomorrow to investigate the tattoo parlor and the hep case at Parish General Hospital. Right now there's not too much else to do here. Dan Stevens can follow up with LaDonna and can interview any more local drug abusers that he finds. I want to stay on top of this."

Bauman hesitated, then said, "I hear the Louisiana EIS officer *is* totally tied up right now with a monster salmonella outbreak in Baton Rouge, so okay, go for it. You sure you want to drive?"

"A Memphis to New Orleans flight would take me two hours longer. Besides, I like driving. I could stop in Jackson to update the state guys in person."

"All right. I'll talk to the Orleans Parish Health Department about having one of their people go around with you. I'll also want you to meet with the DEA's New Orleans Field Division about this sparkle stuff and the regional drug scene. I'll arrange that and we'll get you a hotel room near the Tulane-LSU-Parish General medical complex. Call me on your cellphone mid-day tomorrow, but not while you're driving."

"Great. Talk to you tomorrow." She smiled and raised a fist in the air. "Road trip!"

That night Kris Jensen had trouble sleeping. Her finger throbbed.

The wake-up call came at 6:30 A.M. Kris bumped her left index fingertip returning the receiver to its cradle, and winced. She rubbed her eyes and examined the wound again under the bedside light. It looked a little redder and more swollen than it should. She wondered if a staph or strep bacteria had gotten into it. She made a mental note to beg an oral antibiotic from the Health Department.

She called Dan Stevens at home. He answered on the first ring. "I'm glad it's you," he said. "Two TV stations called last night looking for you."

"You're going to have to handle the media. I'm driving down to New Orleans, leaving this morning. There's a drug user dying of fulminant hepatitis at Parish General Hospital and I'd like to pay King Dewey a visit."

"Going to get a tattoo?"

"That crossed my mind. I'll have to see how well he cleans his instruments first. Mike Bauman, my boss at CDC, is setting up a meeting with the New Orleans DEA office about the sparkly– ah – stuff. I'll ask them about King Dewey. Anyway, make sure LaDonna comes in this morning. Send someone out after her if you have to."

"I was already planning to send a nurse."

"Good. Have her check if LaDonna can find any of Junior's clean needles. Bauman suggested they might actually be used needles that were repackaged as sterile. If it looks at all like she has hepatitis, save twenty cc's extra serum. I'll drop off supplies for express shipment to our lab at CDC. I'll call you this afternoon for an update. I'm stopping in Jackson, but I'd like to get to New Orleans before supper."

"That shouldn't be a problem. It's a straight shot down I-55, then east on I-10. We'll take care of LaDonna. You coming back up here?"

"Not sure. Depends on what I find in New Orleans. If this turns out to be a multi-state outbreak, I may need to go back to Atlanta to help plan strategy and get reinforcements. I'll keep you posted."

A half hour later, Kris started up her rented Jeep Cherokee and left for the Health Department, unaware that she was under surveillance.

****

Two men had been waiting in a Lincoln Town Car in the motel parking lot since 6:00 A.M. As Kris Jensen walked out to her car, the man in the driver's seat clicked off his cellphone and glanced at a photo in his hand. "That's her. Word is she's headed to the

24

Health Department and then New Orleans with a stop in Jackson. They want a KO. We'll follow her down I-55 and pick a spot between Jackson and LaPlace."

The second man picked up the photo. "Too bad. Nice lookin' woman."

Chapter 4

Kris dropped off the shipping supplies at Stevens' health department office and begged samples of Keflex from a clinic nurse to treat her finger. A weak smile was her only response to the nurse's finger-wagging chastisement: "The doctor who treats herself has a fool for a patient and a physician."

Forty-five minutes later, after leaving a message for Sandusky to request return of any unused reference lab serum on Billy Herman, she was headed south on Interstate 55. The road surface was an unusual tan color, but it was smooth and traffic was light. As on many interstates in the southeast, a monotonous green wall of trees on both sides of the roadway obscured the view of the countryside.

She set the cruise control for 65 and mulled over the information that she had gathered so far. *Junior must've brought this up from New Orleans, especially if there's another case at Parish General. If LaDonna is infected, it's got to be a virus and probably sexually acquired – or by close contact.* She shook her head and dismissed the possibility of casual contact transmission. If that were the case, they should have seen a lot more people infected by now. *If Junior brought it two weeks ago and then somehow gave it to both Billy and LaDonna, the incubation period from exposure to symptom onset might be only a day or two. Billy and Junior both died after less than a week of illness so that would mean this virus can kill you a week to 10 days after exposure. Scary, more like Lassa fever or Ebola than any hepatitis virus. The Special Viral Pathogens people might need to get involved, but that'd be up to Mike and Carl Essex. Whatever this is, it hits the liver first, so for now it's our outbreak and I'm a big part of it... hmm... the lead field investigator. That sounds better.*

As the interstate bridged a small river, she caught a glimpse of a southbound Amtrak train in the distance. "All right! Has to be the 'City of New Orleans,'" she said, and sang a few bars of the song made famous by Arlo Guthrie.

Trains had been her father's passion. If he hadn't become a family practitioner, he would have been a train engineer. Their basement had been filled with his HO gauge model trains. Family trips had been by train whenever possible. Gunnar Jensen had collected books, movies, and songs about trains. As a small child, she had listened to him read "The Little Engine That Could" and sing "I've Been Working on the Railroad." But her favorite had always been "The City of New Orleans."

For her father, the steam locomotives at work in the railroad yards of Bulawayo, had been a highlight of their family's mission trip to Rhodesia. Kris, at eight, had been more impressed by the wildlife, especially the elephants and giraffe, and the thundering waters of Victoria Falls. But the defining memories of the trip to Africa were the vivid images of her father's illness and death. He had developed a fever two months after their arrival at the mission hospital in the northern district near the Zambezi river. He deteriorated rapidly, first becoming pale and sweaty, and then swollen and lethargic. Then came the bumpy ride to the big hospital in Salisbury where the doctors and nurses in white uniforms wore masks and spoke in whispers. Kris, Eric and their mother had to stay in a special room where they cried a lot. Her mother told her years later that a sample of her father's blood had been sent to CDC for testing, but they never determined a specific cause of death.

Kris' older brother Eric was to have gone into medicine but decided on business school instead. Their mother was disappointed that Kris hadn't become a medical missionary after she finished her internal medicine residency training. Shortly after starting her position as an EIS officer at the CDC, Kris searched the archives of the Special Viral Pathogens laboratory and was able to establish that her father had tested negative for Ebola and Marburg viruses 22 years earlier. *Maybe he died of this disease*, she thought, *this hepatitis. Maybe I will too.* She shook her head. *Nope. Not going to happen.* She smacked the steering wheel to punctuate her determination.

In her father's memory, she sang every verse of every one of his railroad songs that she could remember, all the way to the outskirts of Jackson.

She met with Jeffrey Wilson, the Mississippi State Epidemiologist, in his office at the State Department of Health. He was graying at the temples, and the goatee completed the image of the southern gentleman. He was as polite and friendly in person as he had been on the telephone. He listened intently as she summarized her investigation.

He shook his head slowly and said, "Almost all of the illegal drugs in Mississippi come up through New Orleans. It's totally out of control. We've already had almost as many heroin overdose deaths in the first three months as we had all last year. We're seeing high potency heroin coming up from South America, mostly from Colombia. I would be pleased if you would relay my sentiments to the DEA in New Orleans, to get on the stick and shut it off. I shall pass the word along to our department to look out for this sparkle drug."

"It would be great if we found a sample to analyze, although I'm thinking more and more that the cause is a virus rather than a toxic drug," Kris said. "And by the way, I've really enjoyed working with Dan Stevens."

"Dan's one of our best directors."

"I'd better get on the road. I want to make it to New Orleans by suppertime."

"New Orleans is about a three-hour drive. Ever been there?"

She shook her head.

"The wife and I really like a little Italian restaurant called Gambino's on St. Charles Avenue. Try it if you get a chance."

"Okay, thanks," Kris said. "I'll keep you posted on what we find out."

She left the office and decided to call the Hepatitis Division from the parking lot to keep her promise to Mike. *He's so hung up on cellphone use causing car accidents. I guess I would be too if my brother had died with one in his hand.* Gina, the Hepatitis Division head secretary answered, and quickly got Mike Bauman, Jim Phillips, and Charlie Sable from the lab, and the Division Chief, Carl Essex, on a speakerphone.

Kris spoke first. "Not much new from Mississippi. LaDonna Fry gets tested for hepatitis today. I just left Jeff Wilson's office here in Jackson. Nice guy."

"He is indeed," Essex said. "Known Jeff for twenty years. We did EIS together in Special Pathogens. Ah, Kris – Mike's kept me posted on the Corham outbreak. It is reminiscent of New Bern, but rather than a drug or toxin-induced hepatitis, it's likely a virus, possibly with a relatively short incubation period and a high attack rate of fulminant hepatitis. If you can confirm a short incubation, we'll have to move all work with blood, tissue, and animals to a P3 biosafety level of containment. That means out of our lab and into Building Four. So information you can get on incubation period is urgently needed. Good work so far."

"Thanks. I thought this outbreak might be important enough to inject a chimpanzee."

"Kris, it almost now takes an act of Congress to inject anything potentially harmful into a chimp," Essex said. "And our Division has the track record of maybe killing off a chimp with an MDA overdose after New Bern. So forget about a chimp, but here's Charlie with our current plans for testing."

"Hi Kris," Charlie said. "We're running rapid viral assays on the blood sample you sent, and should have results tomorrow. I talked with Dr. Stone in Memphis, who was going to do the autopsy this morning. He'll be sending us fresh frozen liver and more serum on a flight arriving into Hartsfield at 6 tonight. I'll pick it up, and we may even inoculate a few mice and a couple of rhesus monkeys yet tonight under cover of darkness."

"Cover of darkness?"

"Mike, here. The story in yesterday's *Journal Constitution* mentioned our plans for animal inoculation. Just our bad luck that the WAR people – Watchdogs for Animal Rights – are meeting in

Atlanta all this week. They're animal rights extremists and are promising loud and aggressive action, whatever that means, targeting us over the next couple of days, so we've decided to work late tonight."

"I've heard of them and their WAR-path raids," Kris said. "They're crazy. Think I'll stay in New Orleans an extra couple of days."

"We may need you here for a strategy meeting if this outbreak gets much bigger," Bauman said. "The media publicity prompted about a dozen phone reports from around the country about injection drug users dying of hepatitis, although a lot of that is background noise. Unrelated sporadic stuff. Jim's been handling most of the calls. A hospital in Tampa did report concurrent severe hepatitis in two drug users who shared needles. We're trying to get more information on them. We'll need to come up with a working definition of an outbreak-related case by tomorrow, after you review the situation at Parish General."

"By the way," Bauman continued. "the Orleans Parish health department has assigned a Dr. Eduardo Beaufain to help you. In fact, he's ready to go with you over to Parish General yet tonight if you don't get in too late and aren't too tired. Gina has his pager number and the info on your hotel."

"I hope to get there by six or so. I'll grab a bite and we'll go over. Want me to send a serum sample out tonight?"

"George Schmidt should have already sent one that we'll get today."

"And what about the DEA?"

"You're scheduled to meet a Dennis Foster at the DEA office at 9:00 a.m. tomorrow," Bauman said. "Dr. Beaufain should know where it is."

"Anything else? I need to get on the road. Haven't been talking while driving, you know."

"I know," Bauman said. "I've been listening for road noises. I'll put Gina back on. Talk to you tomorrow."

Back on I-55 southbound, traffic was light. She decided to call Dan Stevens, who she didn't think would object to her talking while driving.

His secretary answered. "He's anxious to talk to you. I was about to call Dr. Wilson's office in Jackson to see if you were there. Here he is."

"Hi, Kris," Stevens said. "How's the driving? The forecast is for thunderstorms in southern Mississippi and Louisiana."

"So far so good. What's going on in Corham?"

"We sent a nurse out to get LaDonna, but she didn't answer the door or the phone. Once animal control cleared out the dogs, Jean, our nurse, went in and found LaDonna confused and definitely jaundiced. Took her straight to the hospital."

"Probably all symptoms of hepatitis, but I'd get a urine drug screen on her anyway."

"I believe they did and it was negative. She was admitted to ICU in strict isolation and her liver transaminases were in the 8,000 range. Protime was 28 and ammonia was 90."

Kris winced. "Bad stuff. Liver failure. Did you send a blood sample to Atlanta?"

"It left here about noon. One more thing. She was having vaginal bleeding, so the ER physician examined her and found a single large labial ulcer. They asked me to take a look, since I run our VD clinic. Never really seen anything like it. Too painful for a syphilitic chancre. Didn't look like herpes or chancroid and I've seen plenty of those."

"So that's what caused the tushie pain. Genital ulcers predispose to getting HIV. Maybe the ulcer was the entry point for sexual acquisition of this hepatitis virus. How long did she have a sore bottom?"

"I don't recall her ever saying," Stevens answered. "By the way, they're thinking about transferring her up to U.T. Memphis Medical Center."

"I don't think I would be much help with her clinical care anyway. Anyone else sick?"

"Not yet. Earlier this morning I interviewed two drug users locked up in the county jail, but neither one was sick. They knew Junior and both independently confirmed Frankie's story that Junior never shared needles, and that Billy Herman was totally parasitic off him. Got blood samples from both and shipped them to Atlanta along with LaDonna's."

"Good work. The two jailbirds know anything about the sparkle drug?"

"Supposedly super new heroin that Junior got in New Orleans, like we suspected. They'd never actually seen it and didn't know who might have any."

"The media found out about LaDonna yet? I think the fact that only drug users have died has dampened their interest so far."

"You're right about that. The hospital staff is in a tizzy over LaDonna's admission, so someone's bound to tip off the media," Stevens said. "By the way, how's your finger? Betty Cochran in our clinic squealed on you about the antibiotic."

"Still a little red and swollen. Hurts less when I keep it elevated. I'll give the Keflex a little more time to work."

"You're breaking up. Must be getting out of range of a tower."

"Okay. Talk to you tomorrow." She clicked the phone off and put it away.

That LaDonna had the hepatitis was not unexpected, but the confirmation of it and the severity was disheartening. She sighed, shook her head, and whispered, "Nice kid. Awful disease." It was especially depressing because she admired LaDonna's spirit and because Kris thought they had connected a bit during the interview.

Kris figured it was a virus destroying LaDonna's liver and killing her, and probably without hepatitis C or a toxic drug as a co-factor. *Do I still need to chase after the sparkle drug?* She nodded yes to herself. Wherever Junior got the drug could be the source of the virus. *Is this the next AIDS?* She shrugged and concluded only that viruses were still at the top of the food chain.

She looked ahead at the dark sky to the south. She couldn't shake the feeling that things were going to get worse for a lot of people, and maybe for Kris Jensen, before they got better.

Chapter 5

The rain began as a sudden downpour just past the Louisiana state line and continued heavy after Kris turned the Jeep Cherokee east onto Interstate 10. It was already getting dark as the interstate passed through miles of swampland just south of Lake Pontchartrain between Laplace and New Orleans. No lights were visible other than the few cars headed east and the increasing traffic coming from New Orleans, which was still 15 miles away. Kris looked out the side window into the gloom and tried not to think about spiders, snakes or alligators – the creepy swamp creatures that had been the stuff of her early childhood nightmares.

It started to rain even harder. Kris slowed to 50 mph. She was trying to find some zydeco music on the radio when she noticed that the car that had followed her for a while was passing on the left. "Moron," she muttered to herself. The car had barely pulled in front of her Jeep Cherokee when it swerved hard into her lane. She reflexively braked and turned to the right to avoid a collision, but the car kept on moving into her lane and forced her off the roadway. The Jeep Cherokee skidded and slid down a grassy embankment, flattened two low bushes and jolted to a hard stop in the swampy muck.

Kris was momentarily stunned. "You bastard! This is a rental." The words erupted from her mouth while her brain was still engaged in gathering damage reports from the rest of her body. She sensed that she wasn't seriously injured, but the mental shock of the near-disaster kept her from being sure. She whispered, "Thank God for seat belts and not rolling over."

After a minute, she had calmed down and was satisfied that she had no injuries. She was feeling around in the dark for her cellphone, which had been thrown to the floor along with everything else, when she remembered the ceiling light. As she reached up for the switch, a light and a face blurred by the wetness of the glass loomed in the driver's side window. In response to the unexpected appearance of a goon who maybe wanted to finish her off, she slammed at the door lock and groped frantically for her phone to call the police. *And where's the gun? All these southern car rentals are supposed to come with one!*

The stranger shone his light in at her and knocked on the window. "Y'all okay in there?"

She realized that he could actually be trying to help so she opened the window enough to speak out. "Yeah, I think so. I hope you're not the bastard who ran me off the road."

"No, ma'am. We're Rhett and Brett, LaFitte Brothers towing. We saw you go off the highway and we can pull y'all up out of here for 100 bucks."

She began to feel better. "You can? Out of this swamp?"

"Yep. We's got a heavy duty winch on our truck that's pulled out much bigger rigs."

Fifteen minutes later she was in the cab of the tow truck next to Beauregard, the LaFitte brothers' "world-famous Cajun coon dog" watching the Jeep Cherokee being pulled back onto the interstate shoulder. She wondered if she'd been the victim of a premeditated "woe and tow" scam but didn't feel like waiting around for the highway patrol to find out.

"Mr. LaFitte," she asked, "will the engine run okay?"

"Rhett will check it out for ya."

She felt lucky. Out of possible catastrophe, she had lost only 45 minutes and some money, and had gotten only a little wet.

"Should be good to go," announced Rhett as he closed the hood. He wiped the headlights clean and said, ""There's marks from the brush, but I don't see no dents."

"That's great. And no creepy crawly swamp critters in there to hitch a ride?"

Rhett and Brett smiled near-toothless grins and shook their heads. "No, ma'am."

"Okay. I'll need a receipt. Thanks a lot for your help."

She still felt shaky as she started the Jeep. Giving herself a pep talk, she drove back onto the interstate in the direction of New Orleans. She wondered if anyone would believe what had just happened to her. *I could use a beer*, she thought, *with a shot of peppermint schnapps. Chased by another beer.* It had been the preferred alcohol loading method of her college days in Madison, ten years earlier. *But I'll settle for iced tea and a hot shower.*

Kris stopped for gas in Metairie and was suddenly hungry. Against her better judgment, she bought a shrimp and oyster po'boy sandwich at the gas station's hot food counter. She found the hotel on Canal Street just three blocks off the interstate and felt much better after she was cleaned up and ate the sandwich. The minibar tempted her; a drink would further settle her nerves and numb her finger. It hurt more than ever and she wondered if she had bumped it in the accident.

She removed the Band-Aid and inspected the wound under the bedside light. Looks blistery. Did I get Herpesvirus into it? She sighed. This finger is turning out to be a major reality check. She glanced at her watch. Only 6:45. Plenty of time to go over to Parish General. She made coffee and paged Dr. Beaufain.

Chapter 6

Kris had been waiting outside her hotel only a few minutes when a tan-colored Orleans Parish Health Department van drove up and stopped at the curb. Dr. Beaufain stepped out and greeted her with a shy smile. He was about six feet tall with black curly hair and dark but friendly eyes.

"Dr. Jensen? Ed Beaufain. Welcome to New Orleans."

She smiled and shook his hand. "Pleased to meet you. Call me Kris."

"Ánd I'm Ed," he said. He opened the van door for her, then climbed into the driver's seat. "I brought the van because it has a designated parking spot at Parish General. Did you have a good trip down from Mississippi?"

"Let's just say it wasn't boring. Did Mike Bauman fill you in on what's happened up in Corham?"

"He did. I'm excited to help out."

"What do you know about the hepatitis case at Parish General?"

Ed shook his head. "Not much. His name is Homer Renk, and he's not expected to survive. I talked with his senior attending physician earlier today. She okayed a visit to see him and to discuss his case with the house staff. Fortunately, they're on duty tonight – Doctors Binghamton and Sanchez."

"How far is the hospital?"

"Only a few blocks. Parish General is our main public hospital. Stays very busy. A lot of the resident doctors from LSU and Tulane train there."

"What's your job with the health department?"

"I'm Assistant Director. Been with OPHD for four years since I got my MPH here at Tulane. Went to medical school at Galveston. How about you?"

"Medical school and residency at the University of Wisconsin."

"Heard it's a good school. Okay. Here we are," Ed said as he steered the van into the designated OPHD parking spot. "We'll housepage the doctors to meet us, and then go see Mr. Renk."

The medical resident Carson Binghamton and the intern Art Sanchez met them in the doctor's lounge. Binghamton looked to Kris like one of those eternally neat and tidy, bow-tied residents who never got mussed or flustered, while Sanchez presented as a grubby, facial-stubbly type who wasn't afraid to get down and dirty to get the job done.

Sanchez seemed a bit in awe as Kris summarized the status of her investigation. "You know I've never met a live CDC person before," he said.

"Just dead ones," added Binghamton. It was the natural order of things for attending physicians or upper level residents to "pimp" lower level interns or students, teasing or harassing them with snide comments or difficult questions. "So what can we tell you about Homer? Got no home, no friends, no relatives. It's sad, but we're the closest thing he has to family."

"How bad is he?"

Binghamton shook his head. "Beyond bad. He's been here about a week and gotten worse every day. He's now in a coma, with his liver rotting away and multi-organ failure on a blower. AIDS on top of all that. He's about ready for his pine tuxedo."

"Treetop level and all engines out," added Sanchez.

"I'd still like to take a look at him, along with the hospital chart," Kris said. "And I was wondering if he has any tattoos."

Binghamton smirked and raised his eyebrows. "Yes, he does." He turned to Sanchez. "Art, you found it. You tell her."

Sanchez hesitated and then blushed. "Ah...he's got a dick on his sword. I mean, a sword on his dick. His penis, you know what I mean."

Binghamton rolled his eyes.

Kris tried to keep from laughing. "Maybe like a medieval sword?"

"I dunno," Binghamton said. "Could be medieval. We've been kidding the nurses that he's a member of a gang called the Knights of Amour."

"One of the Mississippi cases had dragon tattoos done at King Dewey's Castle of Tattoos here in New Orleans. Ever heard of it?"

Sanchez and Binghamton both shook their heads.

"Actually, King Dewey's is not too far from here," said Ed. "When we go there tomorrow, we can ask them about penile sword tattoos."

"I'll leave that question to you." She turned back to the housestaff. "Was Mr. Renk an active IV drug user?"

"You've got to be kidding," laughed Sanchez. "When they found him, he was passed out with a needle and syringe hanging off his arm. We thought he'd overdosed. Giving him Narcan didn't wake him up much though."

"What drug was he shooting up?"

"His urine screened positive for opiates, so I assume heroin," Binghamton said.

"What happened to his clothes?"

"Probably still in a plastic bag in his room," said Sanchez. "The hospital confiscated his wallet, but if I remember right, his undershorts should be good for dried blood, urine, and stool samples. Maybe even semen. What are you looking for?"

"None of that," Kris said. "I was wondering if he might have carried drugs on him that he hadn't finished shooting up yet."

Binghamton said, "His clothes are easy enough to check out. Let's go up and see."

The sights and sounds of the Medical ICU brought back memories from her own internal medicine residency training at the University Hospital in Madison. They passed room after room of immobile patients lying spread-eagled with a variety of tubes inserted into various natural and unnatural body orifices, accompanied by the hiss of the ventilators and the beeping and flashing of monitor alarms.

When they came to Homer Renk's isolation room, Binghamton asked the nurse for the plastic bag that contained Renk's clothes. As Kris expected, Sanchez was handed the bag and assigned the duty of searching the contents.

"Better wear gloves," she advised.

"Woof! And a mask," exclaimed Sanchez as he got a noseful of the pungent vapors that escaped from the bag as he opened it. "Nothing in the shirt. Pants pockets empty. Wait, hold it. There's a lump in the coin pocket." Sanchez reached into the pocket and pulled out two small glass screw-topped vials. Each was half-full of a white powdery substance that seemed to glitter when the intern held it toward the light. "What's this?"

Kris leaned forward to look at the vials. "It's probably a drug." She put on gloves and held them for a closer inspection. "It might be the sparkle stuff the Mississippi drug users told me about. It does seem to have little sparkly bits in it. I'm meeting with the DEA tomorrow, and I'll see if they can ID it. You guys mind if I take these vials with me?"

Binghamton waved his hand toward her. "Finders keepers. All yours."

She double-packed the vials in small plastic biohazard bags normally used for blood specimens and put them in her purse. "Okay. Let's go take a look at Mr. Renk. What kind of isolation is he in?"

"Respiratory with gowns and gloves," answered Binghamton. "He wasn't in any special isolation until infection control talked to someone at CDC the other day. Now everyone's spooked, especially after the Mississippi deaths and B.J. getting sick."

"Who's B.J.?"

"Betty Jo Miller. She's the nurse who got stuck by a needle used on Mr. Renk. I think Dr. Schmidt, our bug specialist, wanted you to talk to her sometime while you're here."

Kris nodded. "I'll be glad to. When did she get stuck?"

"Last Sunday morning, I think."

"What kind of symptoms is she having?"

"Vomiting, fever, aches. I haven't actually seen her. That's all secondhand from the nurses."

"I was told that she's being treated with high dose interferon plus meds for HIV prevention. She might just be sick from drug side effects. Health care workers don't tolerate HIV drugs well at all," said Kris as she cleaned her hands with a dollop of alcohol rub from a wall dispenser. She took a blue isolation gown out of a box and said, "Okay, then. Let's get dressed and see your patient."

After putting on gowns, gloves, and masks in a small anteroom, they entered the isolation room. Homer Renk was on his back and intentionally paralyzed to allow more effective artificial ventilation via an endotracheal tube in his mouth. The only visible movement was the rise and fall of his chest with the tidal inflow and outflow of oxygen enriched air from the MA-1 ventilator. His skin was a yellow-green mottled with purple blotches, and his face, arms, and legs were puffy and swollen.

As she examined him, Kris thought he looked remarkably like Junior Murphee with one exception. So far only Renk's hands and feet were dusky and cold.

His nurse, Carla, looked to Binghamton. "Blood pressure's only 70, tops, and he's maxed out on Dopamine and Levophed. I gave the Lasix but over the last four hours, he's only put out five ml of urine."

"Bladder sweat," Binghamton said, shaking his head. "Catheter's not obstructed?"

"I flushed his Foley just now. Nothing." She turned to ask Kris, "What is this hepatitis? Is there any effective treatment? We're all really worried about B.J."

"We don't know the cause, and treatment is only supportive care. Doesn't look like Mr. Renk will survive much longer," Kris said as she inspected two skin ulcers on Renk's left arm. "Did he skin-pop drugs?"

"He had at least one of those arm ulcers on admission," Sanchez said. "They're right on top of veins, so I thought maybe he misfired drug into skin. Haven't healed up, but most of our shooters keep skin sores. Would you like to see his sword?"

Kris nodded. The nurse pulled back the cover sheet to reveal a tattoo of a silver sword with a green handle on the shaft of Renk's penis.

Kris inspected it. "No KD signature trademark in sight. Let's go look at his chart."

They left the room, took off the protective clothing, washed their hands, and walked over to the nurses' station. Kris had just sat down to review Renk's chart when one of the ICU nurses approached her. "Excuse me, Dr. Jensen?"

"Yes?"

"I'm Dana Johnson. My roommate Jill works in the ICU over at the Tulane Medical Center. She told me they had a teenage boy die of hepatitis there last weekend and from her description, he ended up looking a lot like Mr. Renk does now."

Kris closed Renk's chart and put it down. "Oh, really? Was he a drug abuser?"

"I don't think he was a known drug user. His father is a prominent businessman in New Orleans."

"Probably why the health department didn't hear about it," said Ed.

"Thanks for letting us know," Kris said. "We'll definitely check it out. Do you have his name?"

"It's Girardeau," the nurse said. "Jill said they did an autopsy. Please don't tell anyone how you found this out. I just want to help B.J."

"Don't worry." Kris turned to Ed. "Girardeau?"

"Old New Orleans family, very rich. Johnny Girardeau's obit was in the Sunday *Times-Picayune* but no cause of death was listed. Rumor had it he was into drugs. Maybe if he didn't have hep A, B, or C, they didn't feel they had to report it. Or it got squelched."

"Upper class kids have no special immunity to IV drug abuse," Kris said. "Might even be more susceptible, in some ways. You know anyone over at Tulane?"

"I know the infection control director pretty well. I'll call her first thing in the morning."

"Actually, we should contact all the hospital infection control practitioners and epidemiologists, as well as the GI and ID specialist docs in the metro area," Kris said, "to see if there've been more unreported cases of non-ABC hepatitis, whether drug related or not and whether severe or not. The more cases we look at, the better our chances of figuring this out. There may be milder cases that we're missing. I pray to God there *are* non-lethal cases."

"I'll get someone on it tomorrow," Ed said.

Binghamton and Sanchez had been stat-paged away to the ER, so Kris returned to Renk's chart while she chatted with the assembled nurses about fulminant hepatitis and its causes.

Another nurse approached Kris. "I called Rhonda Addison in dialysis and told that you were here. She's B.J.'s best friend, and she wanted to come up and speak to you for a minute, if that's okay."

"Sure."

Rhonda Addison was a plump but pleasant-looking redhead who arrived flushed and breathless in the ICU. "Hi. Whoo. I ran up the stairs. Has anyone told you that Dr. Schmidt wanted you to see B.J. tomorrow?"

Kris nodded.

"Where should she meet you? She's feeling so sick. Much longer and it might have to be the ER."

"I heard she was quite ill. I'm sure Dr. Schmidt wants to be there when I talk to her, so how about 11:00 a.m.in his office?"

"That's on 2 West. Great. I'll let her know. One more thing."

"Hmm?"

"The needlestick wound on her palm. What would make it blister up and ulcerate?"

Kris swallowed hard. After a moment she answered, "I – I don't know. I'll just have to look at it tomorrow."

"I'll tell her. Thanks. Bye."

Kris began to feel nauseated, weak and sweaty, which was exactly how she'd felt right after the needlestick on Monday. Her mind raced with the implications of Rhonda Addison's question. First Murphee and Renk's skin ulcers, then LaDonna's tushie ulcer, and now the news of one on the hand of the nurse B.J. Together they indicated that the skin entry site of this virus blistered and ulcerated as an early sign of established infection. She stared at the Band-Aid on her finger and wondered how much time she had left.

She felt a hand on her shoulder. She looked up at Ed, who had a worried expression on his face.

"Kris, Are you sick? You look pale and awful."

Wait till you see how I look a few days from now, she thought. She took a deep breath and let it out slowly to collect herself. "My stomach got upset all of a sudden. Maybe it was that shrimp and oyster po'boy sandwich. Right now, here in the Big Easy, my stomach is the Big Queasy. Let's go. I think we're finished here." She returned the chart to the rack and waved good-bye to the ICU staff.

Kris wasn't ready to tell Ed or anyone else that she would almost certainly be dead in less than a week.

Chapter 7

In the van on the way back to her hotel, Kris said, "I didn't want to say it in front of the nurses, but now I'm sure this virus causes an ulcer at the point of skin entry."

"So you think the nurse is infected?" Ed asked. "I'll check if the Girardeau kid had any skin ulcers. What hepatitis virus would do that?"

"None that I know of. Bauman and Carl Essex, our Division chief, will probably ask for help from the Special Viral Pathogens Branch. We don't even know the incubation period. It might be as short as a couple of days. The nurse B.J.'s course should help define it. I'll get Schmidt to test her liver tomorrow."

"Good idea."

"I still can't figure out how Billy Herman got infected and died five days before Junior if they really didn't share works or have sex with each other." They rode in silence for a moment. "Maybe Junior's clean needles weren't actually sterile, or maybe the drug was contaminated with virus after all," Kris said. "But Junior would've had to have gotten contaminated needles or drugs before his last trip to New Orleans because Billy got sick before that trip was made. Maybe it is the drug, though the virus would somehow have to survive the drug heating process."

"If virus were in the drug, maybe Junior had Billy try it before he used it himself," Ed said.

"Mike Bauman suggested that. But why would Junior do that?"

"Maybe he was suspicious of it and used Billy as a guinea pig, but then didn't wait long enough for the result of his experiment."

"That would be a stretch," Kris said. She opened her purse and took out the biohazard bag to look at the two vials of drug again. "You know what? These look the same. I'm going to have the DEA analyze one and send the other vial to our lab at CDC. Maybe Charlie Sable, our lab chief, can bioassay it, or maybe even inject a chimp. When's the last flight to Atlanta?"

"I think around 8:30. Too late for that one. There's a Delta flight departs at 6:00 a.m. Took it once to catch a morning meeting at CDC."

"That'd be okay, but can we stop at my hotel to pick up a labeled shipping box? The airline people freak when they see these biohazard bags."

"No problemo."

They dropped the package off at the airport for the 6:00 a.m. Wednesday flight. On the way back, Kris felt exhausted and fell asleep. Ed felt sorry for her and gently awakened her only after they had arrived back at her hotel. "You better get some sleep. Tomorrow will be a busy day for both of us. I'll pick you up at 8:30 to go over to the DEA office."

"Okay," Kris yawned. "Thanks for all your help. It's been a long day. Good night."

Back in her room, Kris flopped on the couch to think. She peeled off the Band-Aid and looked at her left index finger wound. It was definitely ulcerated. There was no doubt that she was infected. She drew a deep breath which she exhaled slowly and then whispered to herself, "Okay, so I've got it. First order – am I putting anyone else at risk?" She shook her head. "Every case so far got it from either contaminated needles or sex, so transmission is by blood and body fluid, just like hep B, C and HIV. Thank God that this is not transmitted casually. I can't have transmitted it to anyone else, and I won't." She nodded in affirmation and took another deep breath. "Next order – do I tell anyone?" She shook her head again. "If I'm not putting anyone at risk, there's no obligation to tell. If I do tell Mike Bauman, he'll pull me off the investigation for treatment even though I'm not sick yet and there's no known effective therapy. He'd ship me to the NIH where they'd stick me in the Clinical Science Center, scratch their heads, and poison me with toxic anti-virals until I croaked. No thanks. It's my life. There'll be others for them to experiment on." She vowed to keep investigating the outbreak as long as she was able. "And who knows? Maybe with a little luck and help from my friends, we can solve it."

It was 10:30 p.m. Kris had promised to call her roommate in Atlanta, Janie Jaskwich, every couple of days to say hi. Janie was only 23, but they had become good friends. She was like the younger sister that Kris had never had. Janie would likely still be up at 11:30.

Janie answered on the second ring. "Hi, Kris. Where are you?"

"New Orleans. I drove down from Mississippi today."

"I read about those drug users dying. They quoted you in the Atlanta paper. I cut out the story."

"Thanks. I have a bad feeling about this outbreak. Going to get a lot worse with maybe a lot of deaths."

"You be careful," Janie said. "I just couldn't do what you do. You know how I pass out at the sight of a needle."

"I know. How're things in Atlanta?"

"My dumb brother Ryan's being a pain in the butt again. He left his Corvette here for me to get serviced at my job while he flies off to Cancun with his Dixie-Louise bimbo of the week."

"Didn't you do it for him before?"

"Yeah, but just because I work at a tire and brake place –" Janie said. " –Oh, never mind. I just won't do it. That'll teach him. When are you coming back?"

"Not tomorrow. There's too much to do here yet. Maybe Thursday to help plan and co-ordinate a multi-state investigation."

"At least you get to see New Orleans for a day," Janie said. "–French Quarter, Riverfront, Preservation Hall. Met any cute guys?"

"Janie, I'm not here for tourist stuff. So far I've only seen the inside of Parish General Hospital. Tomorrow I get to see the DEA office, maybe the Tulane Medical Center, and a tattoo parlor."

"Cool. Are you going to get a tattoo? A scorpion on the butt like mine?"

Kris laughed. "No, I won't have time. Anyway I think they specialize in medieval designs."

"Then, a black rose maybe?"

"Not that, either. We're thinking the parlor could be where the hepatitis virus was transmitted by tattoo needles, or maybe where a virus-contaminated drug was distributed."

"Oh wow. Hep central. You better put one of those space suits before you go in there."

"Thanks for the advice," Kris said. "Listen, Janie, I just called to let you know I'm all right. I'm really tired. Got to get some zz's."

"You don't sound okay. You sound major stressed out. Go on to bed. I hope sleep is all you need."

"Thanks. Talk to you soon. Love you, bye."

Kris hung up the phone and shook her head. She wondered how Janie, with all her ditsy tendencies, could somehow always sense her mood and almost read her mind. It would remain one of her life's mysteries. Kris went to bed.

Sleep was fitful as it often was when she was under stress. She lay awake thinking about Janie, her mother, her brother, her dead father, and various ex-boyfriends. She dreamed about finding and hugging her little dog Lukie, who was lost and "gone to doggie heaven" when she was eight years old. In another dream she met Junior Murphee and was just telling him how terrible he looked when the clock radio alarm went off. It was 7:30 a.m. She awoke and realized that she had been dreaming. She smiled as she thought, *Darn, I had questions I wanted to ask Junior.*

She sat up and felt a wave of nausea followed by a grumbling in her lower abdomen. The possibility of diarrhea crossed her mind. Soon there was no further doubt about it.

After washing up, she felt a little weak and sat down. She wondered if this was just the New Orleans version of *turista* or early symptoms of the hepatitis. If traveler's diarrhea, she would have to think of a name with more local flavor. "The Big Queasy" had been clever, but that was a name for upper GI misery, not lower. She decided on "Canal Street Waters" and was wondering about where to get Kao-pectate or Imodium when the telephone rang.

"Hi, Kris." It was Mike Bauman. "I hope I didn't wake you up. Things are popping here. Late yesterday, we got ten more reports of severe viral hepatitis with a couple of deaths, mostly drug users in Florida or the Gulf coast states, Alabama to Texas. I need your input on the outbreak case definition and the incubation period. But before we get to those, we really need to set up a strategic planning meeting to organize formal surveillance, to coordinate multi-state investigations, and to define preliminary control measures."

"When and where?"

"I was thinking here, either late today or more likely tomorrow morning. I wish I could avoid tomorrow, because a big, noisy WAR protest will likely be on our doorstep all day. Some dickhead already leaked it out that we injected animals last night. How much do you still have left to do in New Orleans?"

"A lot," Kris said. "I have to meet with the DEA, visit the tattoo parlor, go back to Parish General to talk to the nurse who got exposed, and check out a possible case at the Tulane Medical Center, just for starters. I'll be busy. I could fly out early tomorrow morning. Who are you inviting?"

"Most of the Hepatitis Branch, including the lab guys. Probably someone from the local DEA office, and one or two people from Special Viral Pathogens. The Director's office is pushing to include a WAR representative to try and defuse the protest. I'd like to go ahead and plan for 11 tomorrow morning. Can you make that?"

"I think so. Will I need my Groucho mask to get past the protesters?"

"I don't think they'll recognize you."

She made a pretend pouty-face. "Shoot, I was hoping for an excuse to wear it. Want my suggestion for an outbreak case definition?"

"I do."

"Case – known or suspected injection drug user, or sexual or other direct contact, who has acute, severe non-A/B hepatitis without an alternative etiology for acute liver disease such as drug toxicity or mushroom poisoning. Possible case – same, but not a known or suspected injection drug user, or direct contact. I'd leave hep C out of it because it's so rarely severe. I'll let you define 'severe.' Got all that?"

"Yup. I'll work with it a little more."

"One more thing. I'm almost positive a skin ulcer forms at the site of initial inoculation of this virus. Murphee and Renk each had at least one ulcer. LaDonna Fry had a vaginal ulcer and last night I found out that the ICU nurse developed one on her hand where she got stuck. I don't know about Billy Herman or the possible case at Tulane, but I'll find out. If it holds up, it will help further differentiate this infection. One thing I'm not sure about is how long anyone had the ulcer before they developed systemic symptoms of hepatitis."

"Fascinating. Have any of these ulcers been biopsied?"

"Not that I know of. Maybe you or Charlie could ask Dr. Stone in Memphis whether he noticed and sampled Junior's ulcer. I think it was on his left arm, near the shoulder."

"Really? That's not the usual place to self-inject."

"You're right about that." Kris paused to visualize the ulcer on Junior's arm. "You know what? I think it was right over the tail of one of his dragons. That makes me wonder if he got infected by a tattoo needle."

"Tattoo needles *can* transmit hep B and C. See what you can find out at the tattoo parlor today. So, do we add skin or mucous membrane ulcer to the case definition?"

She glanced at her left index finger. "Yeah, include it. If no ulcer, only a possible case. By the way, I sent you a present, a package that should have arrived on the early Delta flight into Hartsfield this morning. It contains what I think is a drug in a vial that we found in Renk's clothes at Parish General. I'm wondering if it's the heroin that Junior's friend Frankie referred to as the 'sparkle stuff'."

"Why send it here? The DEA needs to identify it."

"We actually found two vials of it. I'm giving them the other one this morning. Mike, this stuff looks weird with little sparkly bits that reflect light when you hold it up. I've got a hunch it might be contaminated with the hepatitis virus. I was thinking Charlie could examine it under a microscope, or test it for blood, or inject lab animals. Please get him to look at it this morning."

"Wait a minute," Bauman said. "We just added transmission by tattoo needles and now you're also proposing contaminated drug as a vehicle?"

"But Renk's tattoo had no ulcer on it. His skin ulcers were on his arms."

"All right, I'll talk to Charlie. Maybe we could dissolve some of the drug and inject rats and rhesus monkeys. I doubt we could tell if it's contaminated with a virus short of doing that, at this point. And I'd just as soon get it done this morning. The animal rights crowd won't protest any louder, but it'll beat any temporary freeze on animal work from the Director's office to get WAR off CDC's doorstep."

"But lots of people at CDC do animal studies. You think the Director would do that?"

"He might," Bauman said. "He's so politically correct. Kris, one last thing – what about the incubation period? If it's just a few days, we need to upgrade all lab work to at least a P3 level of containment, which would mean out of our lab for sure and probably into Building Four. It would affect animal work and the handling of all blood, tissue, and specimens like your vial of possible drug. It'll slow everything down, but would be safer for the lab guys."

"Not sure yet about the incubation period. The nurse at Parish General has the best defined exposure, which was last Sunday morning. She's already sick, but I think it's from the interferon and HIV drugs that she's been given. She'll have her liver function tested today, so I'll have a better idea by tomorrow's meeting."

"We need to decide by then at the latest. Kris, listen, I've got to go. I'll talk to you again later today. I'm drafting an article on this for next week's MMWR."

"Okay. Bye." She heard Bauman hang up, followed by a distinct second click. *What was that?* she wondered, but another urgent call from her lower intestine interrupted any further speculation."

Chapter 8

Kris was waiting in the lobby of her hotel when Ed arrived promptly at 8:30. He looked well rested and cheerful. As they walked out to the OPHD van, he asked, "Did you sleep okay?"

She shook her head. "Not great. My stomach's still upset and the Battle of New Orleans is being re-enacted in my colon."

"Uh-oh. Still from that po'boy sandwich? I could send one of our sanitarians out to inspect that food mart. A couple of the guys are real good at always finding something being done wrong."

"No, just find me a drug store where I can get meds to settle my stomach and to slow down the... ah...transit time," Kris said. "While I was waiting for you, I was trying to think of a cute, local name for my intestinal trouble. Like maybe I have a case of 'Canal Street waters' or how about 'Huey Long's revenge?'"

"Sorry, the Health Department is under a directive from the New Orleans tourism office that gastroenteritis cannot be locally acquired, much less named. But I will find a drug store for you."

"I might even be off base to blame New Orleans cuisine. This could be *Clostridium difficile*. You know, the colon bug that can activate when you're taking an antibiotic and then cause a toxigenic diarrhea. I had it once before, and I've been taking Keflex for my finger."

"I noticed the Band-Aid. What happened?"

She wasn't ready to tell him the whole truth. "Cut it last Monday and infection got into it."

They stopped at a pharmacy and she was already popping her purchases into her mouth as they walked back to the van. "I don't want to have to bolt from the meeting," she said.

Ed decided to change the subject. "I meant to tell you that Homer Renk died last night. The attending wanted to know how extensive of an autopsy we wanted."

"Just the abdomen and the skin ulcers on his arms. I don't want the pathologist unnecessarily exposed to the hepatitis virus, or to HIV, for that matter."

"Okay. I'll let them know." He started up the van and pulled out into traffic. "The DEA office is only a few blocks from here. Did you bring that vial of the sparkly stuff?"

She nodded. "I did. I think the DEA can even fingerprint drugs to determine the country of origin. Plus I'd like to know what those little sparkly bits are."

"Anything else we want from them?" Ed asked as he searched for a parking spot at the Federal Office Building.

"Maybe a sense of the heroin use patterns in the metro area, recent changes in suppliers, sources of clean needles, and whatever they can tell us about King Dewey and his tattoo parlor."

"Speaking of King Dewey, I got background info on him from Pete Diamond who's a police detective friend of mine. I'll tell you later. Let me call the Pathology Department at Parish General before we go in to see the DEA people."

They met Special Agent Dennis Foster of the New Orleans Field Division of the DEA in his office at 9:00 a.m. Foster was chubby and rosy-cheeked. He came across as a relaxed, folksy family man and just the opposite of Kris' stereotype of a veteran narcotics agent. He introduced himself and his colleague, who was exactly the grim-faced, humorless type Kris had expected.

Foster waved his hand at the other agent and said, "This is Agent Bill Swanson of the DEA's X-Operations Force. He was in town and wanted to sit in on our meeting. We mostly work with law enforcement but we're glad to help you public health folks out when we can. I expect we're all working toward the same goal. Dr. Jensen, I understand from your boss at CDC that you're investigating lethal hepatitis in drug users in Mississippi and here at Parish General. Why don't you give us an overview and then tell us how we can assist you?"

She nodded and briefly summarized the Mississippi cases and that of Homer Renk. "Since these cases were all self-injectors of narcotics, I'm interested in current heroin use patterns in the New Orleans metro area, the suppliers and sources, and what, if anything, has changed in the last month or two."

"Heroin is becoming a much bigger problem for us especially in the last six months. I will give you a copy of our quarterly report, which just came out last month. I think it summarizes our current regional situation quite nicely." Foster went on to describe their active control programs and their limitations, and finished by saying, "and that's why Agent Swanson of X-Ops is in town – to help us explore new initiatives that I'm not at liberty to discuss further at this time."

Kris had taken notes while Foster was talking. When he finished, she turned to Ed. "Do you have any questions?"

He shook his head.

"I have another question. Two hepatitis cases had had tattoos, and at least one of them had it done at King Dewey's here in New Orleans. Do you know if he has ever been involved in drug trafficking?"

"Who?"

"Dewey Duarte, aka King Dewey," Ed said. "Runs a tattoo parlor over on Airline Highway. Big fat guy."

"I seem to recall the name. I'll have to review our files, but I'm pretty sure he's not been arrested for distribution. I can run a check on him and let you know."

"I'd appreciate it," said Kris. "One last thing. Take a look at this." She took out the plastic biohazard bag containing Renk's vial and handed it to Foster. "We found this in Homer Renk's clothes at Parish General. I think the white powder is a drug that he was self-injecting that may have made him sick. And see those little sparkly bits? What are they?"

Foster was holding up the bag to inspect its contents when Swanson spoke for the first time. "Any reason you have it in a biohazard bag?"

"Routine precaution. We don't think the hepatitis is transmitted by casual contact or through the air. But we have wondered whether this drug or supposedly clean needles, might be contaminated with the virus."

"Why?"

"It would help explain the timing of the first two Mississippi deaths."

Foster looked at her and shook his head. "I've never seen this before. The powder could be heroin except for the little bits that reflect light. Bill, what do you make of it?"

Swanson briefly examined the vial and shrugged. "It's new to me, too. Might not even be an illegal drug. I can get it analyzed."

Foster nodded. "To speed up the process, why don't we do the ID and, if it's a drug, the purity assay in our lab here. Bill, maybe you could take a sample to the X-Ops lab, investigate those shiny little bits and do the fingerprinting for country of origin if it's coke or heroin. Okay with you, Dr. Jensen?"

"That sounds good. But be sure to handle it as a potential biohazard. When might we at least get an ID?"

"Should be sometime this afternoon. Here's my card. Call me after 3:00 today. Bill, what about X-Ops results?"

Swanson frowned. "Don't know what this is, so I can't promise anything right now."

"I'll follow up on their results for you," Foster said. "The X-Operations people are hard to reach sometimes. Anything else?"

"Not right now. I'll think of something as soon as I'm out the door, but I'm sure it can wait until this afternoon. Could you please check your file on King Dewey between now and then, too? We really appreciate your co-operation."

As they returned to the van, Kris looked back at the DEA building. "I had hoped to get more out of that meeting. Foster seemed receptive, but the other guy looked like he'd just swallowed a pickle the whole time."

Ed laughed. "I agree. Pickle-puss looked interested enough, but didn't come across as being too anxious to help us out." He glanced at his watch. "It's only 9:30. Shall we pay King Dewey a visit?"

"I have to be at Parish General by 11:00 to meet with George Schmidt and the nurse B.J., so we should have time. Let me call first to make sure they're open and that he's there." She looked up the number, and confirmed King Dewey's availability. "The King is in his court. Tell me about him."

Chapter 9

On the way to the tattoo parlor, Ed told Kris what he had learned about its owner. "His full name is Dewey Alonzo Duarte. He pronounces it do-art. Don't ask me why. Maybe he wants to emphasize his artistic talents. Anyway, he's a late 50-ish white male. All-state football player in high school in Metairie back in the '60s. Went to LSU on scholarship but had a career-ending knee injury. Got hooked on pain pills and then moved on to hard drugs. Dropped out of school and was drafted. The Army shipped him to Vietnam and there he got into big trouble involving drugs. Almost got court-martialed. Pete didn't know any of the details. Drifted around, went to art school, and eventually found his niche in the tattoo business. Always been a big guy but in the last ten years he's blimped up to around 500 pounds."

"Is King Dewey still doing drugs?"

"Let me put it this way. When they call him 'your highness,' they usually really mean it. He does them all, but his favorite is mainlining heroin."

"If he's so fat, how does he find a vein?"

Ed nodded. "I wondered about that, too. The suspicion is that he's had a port-type device implanted under his skin somewhere. You know, one of those venous access reservoirs that cancer patients get when they run out of veins."

"I know what they are, except no ethical surgeon would put one in an injection drug user for that purpose."

Ed shrugged. "I doubt any local surgeon would. He could've gotten it put in somewhere in Mexico or the Caribbean. Who knows? Anyway, he's also one of the strongest local advocates for free clean needle exchanges for drug users."

"Oh really? So then he could have been Junior's contact, or even his source for clean needles. But how are we going to get him to talk? If he's been using, and especially if he's been trafficking drugs, he'll clam up. Any arrests on any drug charges?"

"Pete said NOPD has only busted him once, for marijuana possession. Maybe the DEA has more on him." He considered their options. "You know, I'm pretty familiar with the infection control regs for tattoo parlors. Maybe I can find a violation and threaten to shut him down."

Kris shook her head. "Let's not play the infraction card unless we have to. We'd have a stronger case for a shutdown if we could link another hepatitis case to his parlor."

"But he's smart enough to know that drug abusers are much more likely to get hepatitis from shared injection needles than from tattoo needles."

"You're right. We need a tattoo-associated case who's not a drug user."

"A few more tidbits. He loves to say things that have a double meaning. 'Damn double talk,' Pete called it. And he's got this big booming laugh that's always loudest after one of his own jokes."

"I can't wait to meet his royal highness."

"You won't have to wait much longer. There's his castle."

King Dewey's tattoo parlor had a false medieval castle front complete with watchtowers and flags on both ends. On the windowless front wall, a painted mural showed shining knights on horseback battling fire-breathing green dragons. Over the entrance, a red neon sign blinked "Tattoos" on and off in the morning sunlight.

They parked the van and entered through a creaky metal door. Inside it was cool and dim, with only two flickering lights intended to simulate torches. A short hallway led to a waiting area that was much better illuminated. Hundreds of tattoo designs covered the walls. The only persons present were a black-leathered biker couple arguing over whether their serpents should be black or green.

As they approached the reception counter, Ed nudged Kris and pointed out a sign that read "Payment expected at time of service or we take it out of your hide." He raised his eyebrows and whispered, "Tough place." He tapped the service bell to announce their arrival.

A pimply-faced kid who looked about 20 emerged from a back room. He was dressed like a medieval page, but had a New Age hairstyle consisting of a row of 5 multi-colored clumps of spiked hair across the top of his forehead. He gave a slight bow and said, "Welcome to King Dewey's Castle. I am Micah. How may I serve you?"

Ed handed him his ID. "I'm Dr. Ed Beaufain with the Orleans Parish Health Department and this is Dr. Kris Jensen of the CDC. We're investigating fatal cases of hepatitis in Mississippi and here in New Orleans. At least one of the dead men had recently had a tattoo done here. We have a few questions we'd like to ask King Dewey."

Kris thought she saw a flicker of fear in Micah's facial expression when Ed first mentioned "health department" and again when he said "hepatitis."

Micah returned Ed's ID. "I will relay the message that you seek an audience. Please wait here."

After he left, Kris pulled Ed close and whispered, "Did you see him flinch when you mentioned health department and hepatitis? I think he's afraid of something."

Ed shook his head. "I missed it."

Micah returned and beckoned them to follow him down another dimly lit hallway. As they walked past a room where a tattooist was working on a body builder's biceps, Kris thought she smelled marijuana. She sniffed again and was sure of it. It was a distinctive aroma, unforgettably imprinted onto her nasal receptors as a college student. They continued to the end of the hallway and entered a large brightly lit, colorfully decorated room. In the middle of it, in a king-sized gilded chair, sat Dewey Duarte.

He was huge. He was covered from the neck down in a full length royal purple gown. The phrase "purple mountain majesty" popped into Kris' head. His massive head was bald and his face was fleshy and yeasty-looking, with a sparse gray beard. His face lacked expression and his eyes seemed glazed-over. He didn't seem to acknowledge their entry into the room. Kris wondered if he was stoned on marijuana or something stronger.

She glanced sideways at Ed and moved directly in front of King Dewey. She said a loud "Good morning," and waited for his response.

King Dewey slowly turned his head to stare at her. Suddenly he reached out to her with both arms and said, "Allow yourself to come closer. I know you are attracted to me."

The gesture and request caught her off guard. "P-pardon me?"

"Elementary astrophysics. The greater the size and mass of a body, the stronger is its gravitational pull. I am, therefore, very attractive." He reared his head back and a burst of raucous laughter erupted from his throat.

She couldn't help laughing a bit with him. "Yes, you are most attractive, but I think I'm going to try to stay in orbit around your heavenly body."

He nodded. "May I inquire as to the reason for your visit?"

"We're investigating a cluster of lethal hepatitis cases among drug users in Mississippi and New Orleans. This particular hepatitis causes rapid liver failure and death in less than ten days. Three people have died so far."

King Dewey patted the right side of his belly. "Yes, I've always believed that whether life is worth living is determined by the liver." He punctuated his wit with a staccato "Hah" and paused to see if they got it.

Kris acknowledged it with a slight smile and a quick upward roll of her eyes.

"So, why do you come to King Dewey's Castle?"

"One of the Mississippi cases, a Junior Murphee, had a large dragon tattoo done on his chest here a week or two before he died," Kris said. "He did shoot up coke and heroin, but supposedly never shared his injection needles. We're looking into the possibility of his hepatitis coming from a tattoo needle."

"Chasing the dragon may be a dangerous game. Would not the self-injection of drugs by needle be a much more likely source of hepatitis?"

"Maybe not in his case. Who might've tattooed his chest dragon about ten days ago?"

"That would have been Hugo. He does all the large dragons."

"Can we talk to Hugo?"

"If you can find him. He's not been in to work for over a week. We called his residence, but his number was disconnected. We gave up and hired a replacement yesterday."

"Was he sick his last day of work?"

"I don't recall that he was."

"Why did he leave?"

King Dewey shrugged.

"Did he use drugs?"

Another shrug.

"If you don't mind, we'd like his full name, address, social security number, and whatever else you have to help us find him."

"Micah will give you what we have."

"And maybe a list of all of his clients over the last month?"

"We can provide a list, but many clients give a false name. Cash payment is our only requirement. We ask for an ID only if they appear underage."

Kris was trying to think of a way to bring up the subject of drug trafficking when Ed asked, "Do you do tattoos on penises here?"

"Yes, that is Ramon's specialty. It's not easy work, but for Ramon...ah...the harder it is, the better he likes it." Dewey Duarte smirked.

Ed forced a smile. "I'd like to see Ramon. Is he here today?"

"He only works evenings. Would you be interested in a missile in the 'pocket rocket' series, or a serpent in the 'trouser snake' series, or perhaps a medieval sword or battering ram? We have a catalogue with prices that you may peruse."

Kris watched with amusement as Ed's face reddened with embarrassment.

"I'd like to see the catalogue, but it's not for me. The hepatitis case who died at Parish General last night had a sword tattoo on his penis. Name was Homer Renk. Know him?"

Kris thought she saw King Dewey's face twitch ever so slightly.

King Dewey turned both palms up and shrugged again. "No. Maybe you should ask Ramon? He doesn't do many of those. Was it recent?"

Kris said, "We're not sure. By the way, how many tattooists do you employ?"

"Seven, but only one working right now. Morning is our slow time."

"Any of them close friends with Hugo?"

King Dewey shrugged again.

"Any use drugs?"

"Illegal activities are not tolerated on the premises."

"I hear you're an advocate for clean needle exchanges for drug users," Ed said.

"Yes. Sterile, single-use needles for both tattooing and self-injection of drugs. Cuts down on the spread of infection, don't you know."

Ed didn't let the sarcasm bother him. "Do you utilize single-use pigment cups?"

"Yes, always."

"Mind if I look around and talk to the tattooist who's working?"

"Not at all."

Ed turned to Kris. "I'll take a quick look around while you get the info on Hugo and his client list."

He left and King Dewey asked, "Anything else, Dr. Jensen? Perhaps a tattoo as a memento of your visit? You look perfect for one we call 'Maiden Heaven.'"

"Thank you, but I'll pass. We'll probably need more information from you in the next couple of days. I appreciate your time."

King Dewey nodded and pulled a cord that rang a bell. Micah reappeared.

"Micah, please pull Hugo's employee file and his client work log for the last month for Dr. Jensen to review."

"Yes, your highness."

Kris left with Micah and made a copy of Hugo's employee record as well as his list of recent clients. She looked through the penis tattoo catalogue and identified Renk's sword tattoo. When Ed returned, she pointed it out and said, "Maybe we should have a chat with Ramon."

"Definitely."

She turned to Micah. "Could we get Ramon's home phone number also?"

Micah hesitated, then nodded and wrote down a telephone number. He handed it to her and said, "Call after four today."

"Are you two friends?" she asked. "You knew Ramon's phone number without looking it up."

Micah shook his head as sweat beads glistened on his peach fuzzed upper lip.

Kris sensed fear and urgency in Micah's demeanor, but she also suspected it was not the time or place to ask questions. "I'm leaving my business card, and Dr. Beaufain will give you his. Call us if you hear from Hugo, or if you hear about any staff or clients with hepatitis."

"Or if you have any questions or concerns," Ed added as he handed Micah his card. He turned to Kris. "Ready to go?"

They were walking back to the van when Kris said, "I want your opinion on Micah and King Dewey, but first you need to find me a ladies' room."

Ed stopped and pointed back to King Dewey's. "We can go back. You can learn a lot about a place by visiting their restroom."

She grabbed his arm and pulled him toward the van. "The hepatitis wasn't transmitted in their restroom. Move it, Bub."

****

Dewey Duarte sat alone brooding over his morning visitors. He pulled out a cellphone and dialed a pager number. Within a minute his cellphone rang for an incoming call.

"Yeah?" the voice on the line said.

"It's me, Dewey."

"I know."

"A guy from the parish health department and a woman doctor named Jensen from the CDC were just here snooping about hepatitis."

"I know."

"They're thinking transmission from tattoo needles."

"Good. Let 'em. They'll never prove it."

King Dewey wiped the sweat off his brow. "And Hugo is dead, right?"

"He'll tell no tales."

"They don't know about the stuff, do they?"

"Yeah, they do. They found some because you, you stupid shit, gave that homeless scumbag too much of it."

"I wanted to be sure the bastard died. I only wish I'd had someone cut off his dick. The parish health department guy asked about his sword tattoo."

"They know it was Ramon's work?"

"Yeah, but Ramon doesn't know squat about Renk paying for it with funny money. They'll have trouble finding Ramon anyway. He's usually out partying with his gay boy friends. Hasn't even been in to work for three days."

"Anything else?"

"Don't you think that if they have the stuff, they're going to figure out what's in it? I want these health department spooks off my back."

"We have plans to eliminate all of our problems *very* soon. So just keep your fucking mouth shut. Get it?"

Chapter 10

A few blocks from the tattoo parlor Ed turned the van into the parking lot of a fast food restaurant. He looked at Kris and said, "We shouldn't stay too long. After 15 minutes, the manager of these places usually starts to whine about an OPHD van in their lot scaring off customers."

She nodded and headed for the ladies' room. Ed bought a cup of coffee and sat down in a booth to wait for her.

"Do you want coffee or something to eat?" he asked when she rejoined him.

"No thanks. Too irritating to my GI tract. I'll stick to water, along with my Imodium," she said as she searched her purse for the anti-diarrhea pills.

He got her a cup of water, sat down, and took a sip of coffee. "So what did you think of King Dewey?"

"I about had a heart attack with that opening line about my attraction to his heavenly body."

Ed grinned. "I thought I was going to have to pry you out of his clutches."

She grimaced. "Not a pleasant thought." She started to giggle. "But it is funny now."

He nodded and they laughed together.

She sighed and said, "Feels good to laugh. Milton Berle once said 'Laughter is like an instant vacation,' and it's true. Anyway, I do think King Dewey knows a lot more than he lets on, but he won't talk unless we can pin something major, either on him or on his parlor. Did you find any violations?"

"From just a quick look around, it's actually one of the cleanest and safest-run tattoo operations I've seen. Single-use, sterile supplies and good technique all the way."

"Okay, but something went wrong." She tapped her fingertips on the tabletop. "I'm sure of it. Tell me, how could one of King Dewey's clients have gotten infected from the tattooing process anyway?"

"Maybe if a client came in with the hepatitis, and then, if a single-use cup or needle accidentally got re-used, that could infect a later client." Ed paused to consider other possibilities. "Maybe a more likely scenario would be if Hugo himself had the hepatitis while still tattooing. He then could have contaminated a needle tip from an open wound on his hand, or maybe if he tested the needle sharpness on his own skin. That practice is now a major no-no, but old habits may be hard to shake."

She frowned. "Our problem is the major players in that scenario are either dead or missing. You think the other tattooists would rat on Hugo about bad technique?"

Ed shrugged. "I don't know. Probably wouldn't, but they might tell us if he looked sick when he last worked there."

"You know who might be willing to talk is what's-his-name – The Statue of Liberty – with the hair."

"Micah?"

"Yeah. He's scared about something. But we need to get to him alone. I had a feeling the reception area was bugged. You may have to go back there and get to him somehow if he doesn't contact us."

A manager-type approached their booth. "Excuse me, but are you the folks from the health department?"

Ed looked up and nodded. He knew what was coming next.

"We do appreciate your business, but – ah – "

Ed interrupted. "I understand. We'll be on our way shortly." He turned to Kris. "It's 10:30. I need to drop you off at Parish General. I'm going to the Tulane Medical Center to meet with Jean Casper, who's the infection control nurse. I'll find out as much as I can about the Girardeau kid and his autopsy."

Ed dropped Kris off 15 minutes early. She decided to call the Hepatitis Division lab to get the latest results before her meeting with Dr. Schmidt and B.J. She sat down in the lobby and dialed the lab directly. Charlie answered the phone himself.

"Hi, Kris. You must be calling for results. The patient sera are just showing hep B and C antibodies so far. Nothing too exciting. The animals we injected with the sera all look well so far. We'll test their liver function later today."

"Did you get a chance to take a look at that sparkly drug?"

"I was just about to tell you. The little bright bits might be plastic beads. They were hard when I poked at them under an operating microscope, but when heated they melted down and appeared to release a bit of brownish material."

Kris sat up and covered her right ear with her right hand to hear better. "The brownish stuff. Stool? Or blood maybe?"

"Are you a mind reader? I was just trying to decide how best to assay it for hemoglobin."

"If it *is* blood, I bet there's virus in it. And if the powder really is heroin –" She paused to be sure of her logic. "Then somebody is deliberately killing drug users. I mean, these beads aren't natural, are they?"

"Of course not. I agree that it's provocative, but it's premature to call this murder or to notify the FBI about possible bioterrorism, before we either confirm viral particles by electron microscopy, or show that injection into an animal causes fulminant hepatitis."

"Let's get on with it then!" She was shouting into the phone. Several people stopped to stare at her.

"Calm down, Kris. We will. I'll bet it turns out there's a boring explanation for the beads, but I will talk to Mike about it. It's been a madhouse here. Everyone's on edge over the animal rights protest tomorrow."

"Charlie, I'm sorry I yelled. I'm getting a little stressed out myself. Listen, I've got to get to a meeting. Tell Mike that I'll call him later today."

George Schmidt was Parish General's hospital epidemiologist and the director of all infection control and employee health activities. Binghamton had referred to him as "the bug doc" because of his specialty training in Infectious Diseases. She found his office on 2 West and walked in a few minutes early.

Dr. Schmidt's secretary looked up from her computer monitor. "Good morning. I'm Margie. You must be Dr. Jensen. My instructions from Dr. Schmidt were to send you right on in whenever you got here."

When Kris entered his office, George Schmidt was sitting behind his desk staring out the window. Noting his suntan and sandy blond hair, she scanned his desktop for a picture of him holding a surfboard, but saw only a sign that read "The Bug Stops Here."

When he saw her, Schmidt lurched up from his chair and shook her hand with both of his. "Boy, am I glad to see you. We really need your help."

She smiled and pointed to his Bug sign. "Maybe you do. The bug stopped Mr. Renk last night."

"Yeah, it sure did. They're starting a limited autopsy about noon. Want to go down to Pathology later?"

"Absolutely."

Schmidt sat back down behind his desk and stroked his chin. "B.J. Miller and her parents aren't here yet. But I've got a number of burning questions."

"Her parents are coming? Oh Lordy. I won't have all the answers for them or for you, but go ahead."

"What do we know about this hepatitis that Renk had?"

"We think it might be a new hepatotropic virus, or at least one that's been previously unrecognized. Unknown incubation period. Infection results in rapid liver failure, then multi-organ failure and death from shock in a week or less from onset of symptoms. Could be 100% fatal. I pray to God it's not."

"Wow. That's scary." Schmidt drew a deep breath. "Transmission?"

"Contaminated needlestick and one probable sexual transmission to a girlfriend. There may be a virus-contaminated drug spreading it, but we don't know that for sure yet."

"Any estimate of the incubation period?"

"Really not sure. Your nurse has the only known defined exposure date. If she's having symptoms from hepatitis, that should tell us the incubation period, unless the drugs she's taking are working to delay or prevent the hepatitis."

"B.J. got stuck last Sunday about 10:00 a.m., so it's been just over three days. She's been sick for a couple of days, but I thought it was all side effects of her medications. I sent her down for a stat liver panel earlier this morning and we should have the results shortly."

As if on cue, Margie poked her head in the door and said, "Here're B.J.'s results from the lab."

Schmidt looked at the faxed report and pursed his lips. "SGOT 1475, SGPT 1798, total bilirubin 3.5, pro-time 16 seconds. Not good."

"Could any of her drugs be hepatotoxic?" Kris asked hopefully.

"I don't think so. I avoided nevirapine just for the potential. She's on Kaletra, D4T and 3TC plus 3 million units of alpha-2 interferon subcutaneously daily."

"Then she's almost certainly infected. Doesn't really surprise me."

Schmidt looked up. "Why do you say that?"

"It's looking more and more like the entry point of this virus ulcerates as an early sign of established infection. Renk and a Mississippi case named Murphee both had arm ulcers, and Murphee's girlfriend had a vaginal ulcer, maybe from sexual transmission. Last night I heard from her best friend that B.J.'s needlestick wound has ulcerated."

"Yes, it has. I was going to ask you about that." Schmidt sighed and stared at the floor. "I'll to have to break the news to her this morning – along with an action plan. If this progresses as fast as you say, we better get her in the hospital and stop the HIV drugs. The hepatitis is now the biggest threat."

"I agree 100%."

Margie buzzed the intercom and announced that the Miller family had arrived. Schmidt brought them into his office and introduced everyone.

It was obvious to Kris that the Miller family was in trouble. B.J. had walked in slowly being guided and helped to a chair by her father. She looked exhausted. Her sallow skin color and her drawn face with circles under her eyes reminded Kris of LaDonna Fry. Corinne Miller's puffy, red eyes and anxious expression bespoke of tears and sleepless nights. Gareth Miller was a wiry, 50-something whose facial expression and body language signaled toughness and hostility. Kris thought of a bantam rooster getting ready to fight. From his demeanor and crew cut, she guessed military vet and likely to make things more difficult for everyone.

Kris looked over at Schmidt. He motioned for her to speak first. "I'm sorry to have to meet with all of you under these circumstances." She turned to B.J. "Miss Miller, Dr. Schmidt and I can talk with you alone first if you like. And then talk later with your parents to answer everyone's questions."

B.J. kept her eyes on the floor and spoke softly. "Thanks, but I want my parents to stay. You'd just have to repeat everything for them. And you can call me B.J. – Everyone else does."

Kris nodded and made an effort to smile. "And please call me Kris. B.J., can you tell me about the needlestick incident last Sunday morning?"

"There's not a lot to it. I had just started a new IV access on Mr. Renk. I was wearing double gloves and used a safety needle. I was about to engage the plastic clip to cover the needle tip, when Mr. Renk moved and bumped my right hand, which was holding the needle, and I got stuck on the left palm."

"How deep did the needle tip penetrate, and what did you do next?"

"Just deep enough to make me bleed. I tore the gloves off and we flushed and wiped the wound with alcohol – I don't know – lots of times. I was shocked. My mind went numb. The charge nurse reported it right away. Everyone was worried about HIV, and I took the first dose of the drugs about 45 minutes later. I started the interferon Monday." She covered her face with her hands. "Oh God, why me?"

Kris bit her lip. She reached out and held B.J.'s hand, nodded slightly and said, "Something awful like this is only supposed to happen to other people, or just be a bad dream that you wake up from." She whispered, "I know." B.J. started to cry and Kris felt her own tears welling up.

Gareth Miller jumped to his feet, pointing fingers at both Kris and Schmidt. "Hey, why are you two torturing her? You already know all this. We're wasting time. That sonofabitch died last night. I want to know if my daughter is infected and what's going to be done about it."

"Gary," Corinne Miller hissed. "Stop it!"

"Daddy, please sit down," B.J. said. "You're making it harder."

Gareth Miller backed down. "Okay, but I want answers...soon." He glared first at Kris, then at Schmidt.

"Mr. Miller, we'll get to all your questions, I promise," Kris said. She took a deep breath and turned back to B.J. "Exposure to HIV is pretty scary, isn't it?"

"Scariest thing that's ever happened to me. Now this hepatitis looks even worse." B.J. began to sob. "I'm afraid – I'm afraid I'm not being a b-brave patient."

"You're doing just fine." Kris offered her a box of tissues from Schmidt's desk, then passed it on to B.J.'s mother. "B.J., your risk of getting HIV from this exposure is about one in 300, probably even lower than that given the drugs that you've taken."

"I know. Dr. Schmidt told me. But the meds make me so sick."

"It's common for health care workers to get sick on them, plus you're also getting interferon, which can make people feel like they have the flu all the time. The HIV meds are weakening you by compromising your nutrition. Dr. Schmidt and I think you should stop them. To keep you stronger."

"But they made such a big deal about taking them. Why not just switch to different drugs?" She then realized the implication of the recommendation. "Why? W-what did my liver panel show?"

Kris turned to Schmidt. He was B.J.'s treating physician, and the one who had ordered the test. Breaking the bad news was his responsibility.

Schmidt cleared his throat. "Ah – B.J., Your blood work showed your liver transaminases are significantly elevated. Bilirubin and pro-time are up a bit also."

"Translate that," demanded her father.

"When the liver is sick or injured, it releases protein chemicals called enzymes into the blood that we can measure. Hers are abnormally high. She has acute hepatitis."

"You mean she has what that man died of?" Corinne Miller's eyes were wide with apprehension. "Are you sure it's not something else?"

Schmidt glanced at Kris for support. "It's not the medication. We think she got Renk's hepatitis virus from the needlestick."

B.J. stared across the room. "I'm going to die," she said in a calm voice.

Kris had just opened her mouth to respond when Gareth Miller erupted. She heard a growling sound and saw him leap out of his chair toward Schmidt, as if he were going to physically attack him. She stood up, ready to bolt for the door for help.

Miller stopped at the edge of Schmidt's desk and spittle flew from his mouth. "You bastard! You let it happen to her. You left her helpless so that fucking junkie could stab her with that dirty needle. Why wasn't he in hard leather restraints?" Miller grabbed the "Bug" sign and held it up. "This is bullshit. The bullshit starts here." He threw the sign against the wall, where it struck and cracked the glass over Schmidt's LSU medical school diploma.

Schmidt buzzed Margie. "Call Security."

"Done," she said.

"Mr. Miller, please." Kris said.

He turned his wrath on her. "As for you and your phony, sorry-ass 'I'm here from the government to help you' attitude. You couldn't care less about nurses dying for you on the front lines. You don't have a fucking clue what it's like to be stuck by a dirty needle, do you?"

Kris stood silent.

Two burly hospital security guards appeared in the doorway. Schmidt pointed at Gareth Miller and said, "Please escort this man off the hospital grounds. He is not allowed to return until tomorrow."

Gareth Miller left without a struggle or another word. When he was gone, the only sound in the room was B.J. weeping softly. Corinne Miller bit her lip to keep from crying. She put her arm around her daughter and turned to face Schmidt, then looked at Kris.

"I sincerely apologize for Gary. He just loves his little girl so much." She shook her head. "There's nothing we can do when he gets upset like that. He'll calm down after he thinks things over. In my heart I know that you both care deeply and will do your best to help B.J. The two of you have every right to walk out, but I beg you to stay. I have more questions."

Kris wiped away her own tears. "Of course we'll stay. When patients or family get stressed out over a terrible illness, they're not the same people they normally are. I understand. I've got a pretty thick skin for this type of situation." She got up and gave Corinne Miller a hug. Then she hugged B.J.

The tears streamed down Corrine Miller's cheeks as she squeezed Kris's hand with both of her own hands. "God bless you, Dr. Jensen."

Schmidt watched in silence. He rose and picked up the "Bug" sign off the floor, then sat next to B.J. "You know you need to come in the hospital for hydration and nutrition, and so that we can monitor your liver function."

B.J. closed her eyes and nodded slightly. "I know."

"Here or Tulane or Touro Infirmary?"

"I have Health-Flyer HMO. I think they contract with Touro."

"Don't worry. 'Hell-fire' can deny all they want. This comes under workman's comp, so you can go pretty much anywhere."

"There are hepatitis specialists at NIH," Kris said. "The National Institutes of Health in Bethesda, Maryland. They may be interested in treating you with experimental anti-virals. I'll discuss it with my boss at CDC later today and get back to Dr. Schmidt."

Corinne Miller's expression brightened. "We'll take B. J. anywhere you think they can help her. I do have one last question." She looked Kris in the eye. "Does everyone who gets this hepatitis die from it?"

Kris hesitated. "The three who died all had livers previously damaged by chronic hepatitis C infection. B.J.'s starting out with a perfectly healthy liver, plus she's already had some anti-viral treatment. I think there's good reason to hope for a better outcome."

Corrine Miller pursed her lips and bowed her head. "I'll be praying for her and for God to be with you in your work."

Kris nodded. "We'll do our best for her."

B.J. turned to her mother. "I think I'll stay here at Parish General with Dr. Schmidt, and to be close to my friends."

"Okay," Schmidt said. "Why don't the two of you go on down to the admissions office, and I'll arrange for a private room on the sixth floor."

The Millers left after another round of hugs.

Kris put a hand to her forehead. "I don't know if I can take much more of this," she said. "I'm afraid it's going to get a lot worse for B.J. I really tried to put a positive spin on my answer to her mom's last question."

"You did good," Schmidt said. He reflected for a moment. "It *is* going to get rough. Think we should continue interferon?"

"I guess so. Unless I hear otherwise from the liver people at NIH. I don't think they'll know what to do, either."

Schmidt stood up and stretched. "Let's go down to Pathology and see what they're finding on Renk." He left instructions with Margie for B.J.'s admission, and they headed downstairs.

The Pathology Department was in the basement. Just outside the autopsy suite, they entered a small anteroom to put on gowns, double gloves, goggles, and tight-fitting masks as protective barriers against Renk's multiple blood infections, and because the autopsy procedure could aerosolize unrecognized infection, such as tuberculosis. As they were putting on the protective clothing, they heard rock music over the intercom system.

"That music. It's by a rock band called 'Autopsy.'" Schmidt chuckled at his own joke. "There actually is, or at least was, a rock band named 'Autopsy,' but I don't really know if that's a recording of theirs or not."

"Oh I get it," Kris said. "The pathologists listen to 'Autopsy' when they do a post-mortem and to 'Grateful Dead' when they don't."

Schmidt laughed long and hard at the trumping of his joke. "Thanks, Kris. I needed that, after the session with the Millers. Ready to go in?"

She nodded.

Schmidt knocked on the door to the autopsy room and they entered. It was chilly inside, and the smell of a chemical preservative permeated the air. Renk's mottled, swollen body was laid out on a shiny metal table. The striking similarity in appearance to Junior Murphee's corpse unsettled Kris. She closed her eyes briefly and vowed to not think about herself ending up like that. As she stepped closer, she could see the incision that had opened the abdomen from the sternum to the pubis. The liver had just been removed and was being weighed by the pathology resident.

The Chief of Pathology, Dr. Simon Wu, was peering into the abdominal cavity. He looked up and recognized Schmidt's blond hair. "Hey, George. You're just in time to help me decide what else to carve out of your man here. Who's your friend?"

Schmidt introduced Kris to Wu and the pathology resident.

Kris leaned over to look at Renk's exposed abdominal contents. "What have you found so far?" she asked.

Wu shook his head and pointed a gloved finger at the dark yellow blob of tissue in a metal dish. "I've never seen a liver that necrotic. Not even from a massive Tylenol overdose."

"Anything else notable?"

"The spleen's big but that could just be from HIV. Then there're the usual visceral and skin hemorrhages from coagulopathy and lots of tissue edema secondary to capillary leak from his sepsis syndrome. See that all the time. Main abnormality is the liver, or what's left of it – just capsule enclosing yellow mush, bile ducts and blood vessels, at least on gross inspection. This must be some nasty bug. You sure there's no airborne transmission?"

"Yeah, blood and sex mainly. Maybe tattoo needles. Not sure yet, but this guy may have gotten infected from self-injecting a virus-contaminated drug. We're working with the DEA to investigate that possibility."

"So it wasn't from sex or his tattoo?" Wu swept his right arm through the air as he snapped his gloved right thumb and middle finger. "Darn. I was kinda hoping to include 'died by the sword' in my summary. Wait a minute. Contaminated drug? Do we need to get the Medical Examiner involved?"

"Not just yet. We'll know more in a couple of days. By the way, be sure to freeze fresh liver at –70 and to save extra serum. Did you biopsy his arm ulcers?"

"Got a piece of both. Strange feel to them. Rubbery, kinda like a syphilitic chancre. We'll see what the histopathology shows. Oh, that reminds me. Norm Kaelin, my counterpart at Tulane, told me this morning that they'd autopsied a kid with fulminant hepatitis on Monday."

"We heard. Dr. Ed Beaufain of the Health Department is over there looking into that case as we speak."

"What's interesting is that kid not only had the same massive liver necrosis but also a rubbery skin ulcer on his chest. Did these two know each other?"

Kris felt a chill. "I don't know, but from what you're telling me, that kid will likely be the sixth outbreak-related case and the fourth death."

Wu whistled underneath his mask. "I'm going to be the first to line up for the vaccine."

Kris wagged her index finger at him and said, "Oh no. There're several of us already lined up ahead of you. So, was the Tulane case a drug user with hep C? Any tattoos?"

Wu shrugged. "Norm should know."

Kris nodded. "I'll find out." Her stomach started to feel queasy and rumbly again and she suspected the Imodium was beginning to wear off. She sat down on a stool and turned to Schmidt. "Listen, George, I'm not feeling great. I've got a bunch of phone calls to make, so I'm going to head back to my hotel. I'll get back with you later today or tomorrow about the NIH. Call me anytime if you need to. I'm at the Clarion Hotel on Canal Street."

"So do you need any other tissue samples?" Wu asked. "I'm happy to quit now."

"You can close him up. George has my card to fax your report. Hold onto the frozen liver specimens and extra serum until you hear from us."

Kris excused herself and left the autopsy suite. She decided to walk the few blocks back to her hotel unaware that there were people outside waiting for her.

Chapter 11

In the front lobby of Parish General hospital, Kris saw a sign to the cafeteria. It occurred to her that she should probably eat something, but she was feeling too queasy, crampy, and tired. A rest – maybe even a nap – some drugs to calm her GI tract, and a clean private bathroom close by, appealed to her much more than food.

It was muggy outside, with hazy sunshine. She stopped to put on her sunglasses. As she left the hospital grounds, she didn't notice Gareth Miller who was on the sidewalk a half block away. He had spotted her and started after her at a fast trot. He was catching up quickly as she crossed Tulane Avenue to go down LaSalle Street to her hotel. Preoccupied with possible connections between the Girardeau case and King Dewey, she was almost across LaSalle Street before she happened to turn and recognize Miller running toward her.

Kris stopped, frozen by uncertainty. She couldn't outrun or outfight him. She would have to stand her ground and try to defuse him with kindness or humor.

A half block up LaSalle Street, a black sedan lurched forward with a slight squeal of the tires. It accelerated toward Kris Jensen, who was standing near the curb. Her attention remained fixed on the fast-approaching Gareth Miller.

Miller saw the sedan heading for her, and started to yell and point as he ran toward her. Kris didn't comprehend his shouts and gestures, and her apprehension was intensified by his seeming craziness. Her instinct was to run, but she didn't.

It was then that she heard the car behind her. She turned to see it headed straight for her. The driver's face was obscured by the tinted windshield but the intent to hit her was obvious. She moved to save herself.

As she started a headlong dive to the safety of the sidewalk, the impact of Miller's body against her accelerated her lateral movement. The sedan roared past and missed Kris, but the right front wheel ran over Miller's trailing right foot. He screamed in pain just as Kris landed hard on the sidewalk. She was momentarily dazed, but scrambled out from under Miller, whose upper body had ended up on top of her legs. She looked around for the black sedan, but it was gone. Her right hand was numb and her right forearm was stinging, but she didn't seem to be hurting anywhere else.

Miller lay on the curb groaning in agony over his right ankle, which was flopped sideways at a grotesque angle. Kris stood over him, angry and shaking, but also relieved that he was too incapacitated to get up after her. She leaned over and shouted at him. "What the hell do you want from me? I'm trying to help B.J.!"

Sudden onset of weakness and nausea then forced her to sit down on the curb next to Miller. A businessman who had witnessed the entire incident approached them to offer help. He had called 911 on his cellular phone, and the siren of an ambulance a block or two away could already be heard.

Miller spoke to Kris through gritted teeth. "I was coming after you to apologize when I saw the car coming. I think they were trying to kill you."

"Kill me? Why didn't they just shoot me?" She knew he was right, and she felt even angrier. She had less than a week of life left, and someone was trying to shorten it. For no obvious reason.

A Parish General-based ambulance arrived. The two paramedics checked vital signs and then one splinted Miller's ankle while the other examined Kris'right forearm. Her wrist and hand were still numb and stinging, but seemed to be functional. The paramedic applied an elastic wrap and recommended an x-ray at the Parish General ER.

"Sit around for four hours in the ER waiting room? Forget it. Besides, I'm a doctor. I'll be okay."

The paramedic who had wrapped her arm shrugged and rolled his eyes at his partner.

Kris put a hand on Miller's shoulder. "Listen, I'll do everything I can for B.J. And thanks for helping me. I'm really sorry you got hurt. You can report this to the police if you want, but I've got to go. I'll try to stop by the hospital later to check on you."

Miller looked up at her. "Think they'll let me back in now?"

She smiled and nodded.

"Watch your back," he said as she turned to go.

When she stooped to pick up her briefcase, she felt an aching stiffness in her right hip. She looked down and noticed her pants were torn at the knee. She tried to brush the dirt off her jacket, and to fix her hair a bit with her hand. She sighed and forced a smile for the businessman who was still hanging around. "I must look like the wrath of God," she said, quoting one of her mother's favorite expressions. She didn't wait for his response, but limped off in the direction of her hotel while keeping an eye out for the black sedan.

At the next intersection, she saw a drug store and entered it just as an NOPD cruiser screeched to a halt at the accident scene. She didn't look back.

Fifteen minutes later she was back in her hotel room. She considered requesting a room change for security, but she was too tired and bolted the door instead. After a shower, she gulped down a Gatorade-equivalent sport drink along with Benadryl for jitteriness and nausea, ibuprofen for her aching hip, and Imodium for prevention of Canal Street Waters. After re-examining her forearm and wrist, she put on clean clothes and lay down on the bed with the intention of closing her eyes for just a few minutes.

Two hours later, at 3:00 p.m., the ringing of the telephone woke her up. She picked up the receiver still groggy from sleep and the Benadryl. It was Ed.

"Sorry. I've been sleeping on the job," she mumbled. "I've got a lot to talk to you about."

"Don't apologize. You must have needed sleep. And I need to tell you about the Girardeau kid. Also, I've arranged a 4:30 meeting with Benjamin Cline. He's a tropical disease pathologist and one of my former mentors in public health school. I'll explain on the way over there."

"Can you come by in a half hour? Come on up to my room – number 350."

"Sure. See you in a bit."

She hung up the phone and was tempted to roll over back to sleep. A can of cold tea from the minibar chased away her sleepiness and counteracted the lingering effects of the Benadryl.

Fully awake, she called Dan Stevens. She updated him on King Dewey, the two New Orleans deaths, and the vial of sparkly drug. "So what's going on up in Corham?"

"LaDonna's going downhill fast. Earlier today she was talking out of her head. Liver numbers are a lot worse. The first two cases died so quickly they want to get her on up to UT–Memphis and are trying to arrange a helicopter transfer."

"Poor thing. Ever get any more information from her?"

"She's been too out of it to answer questions. Got so combative, they had to restrain and sedate her. She's been hallucinating about a 'Billy.' Keeps telling him to get away."

"Billy Herman? I thought she'd 'run them boys off with the dogs.' Didn't she say that?"

"She did say that," Stevens replied. "But a handful of wieners will get you past most trailer hounds. LaDonna looked so scared, I'm wondering if Billy Herman sexually assaulted her."

Kris winced at the thought and said, "That might have been how she got the hepatitis. She said she hadn't had sex with Junior for a couple of weeks, but maybe she was too ashamed to mention Billy. It could've happened that weekend Junior went to New Orleans, about ten days ago."

"We may never know for sure. I expect that the UT-Memphis docs will want to talk to you about her hepatitis."

"I'll be glad to. I'm not sure what they'll be able to do except support her. A liver transplant might buy her a week before this virus would eat it up."

"By the way, how's your finger?"

"It's still sore."

"Are you still feeling okay?"

"I've got some GI bug."

"Take care of yourself. I've got to go. UT-Memphis is on the other line."

Kris said good bye and hung up the phone. The news about LaDonna saddened her. She sat in silence, wondering why bad things happen to innocent people – women in particular. She whispered a short prayer for LaDonna, then one for B.J., and then another for herself for guidance.

Kris had had a strict Lutheran upbringing, but attended church only rarely since she'd moved to Atlanta. She smiled at the thought of the old saying about the absence of atheists in foxholes. Raising her eyes upwards, she whispered, "The face of death makes for a heckuva wake-up call." She closed her eyes. "And God help me to not lose my sense of humor in the coming days."

She would have to tell someone about her hepatitis as she became sicker and weaker. She had no fear that she would die alone. Her mother and brother would no doubt rush to her side once they found out that she had a terminal illness, but right now they would probably also get in the way of any investigation she might still be able to conduct.

It only made sense that whoever had tried to hurt her had done so to interfere with her investigation. "Hell, if they want to stop me, all they need to do is tell my mother I have hepatitis, or tell Mike Bauman that my life is in danger," she said to herself. Her chief would immediately pull her back to Atlanta.

In recalling the two attempts on her life, her anger flared, fueling the determination to find answers. It was 3:15. She pulled out Dennis Foster's business card and called him.

He was as friendly as ever over the phone. "Hi. How's your investigation going?"

She wasn't exactly sure why, but she had decided to not tell the DEA about Charlie working independently on Renk's drug. "Slow. Nothing new on the drug connection."

"That vial of white powder you found was heroin all right. Almost pure stuff. Gas chromatography indicated Colombian origin. I showed the little sparkly bits around the office, and no one had seen them before. We'll see what our people on the street can tell us. The X-Ops report on the sparklies may take a little longer."

"Let me know as soon as you get a report. Did you get a chance to check your files on Dewey Duarte?"

"Yeah. His name and tattoo parlor came up a few times, but we've never pinned anything major on him. Just one marijuana bust. There was a note that he was dishonorably discharged from the Army for drug use in Vietnam. Had to do with the Trang Son incident."

Kris perked up. "What was that?"

"At the start of the Tet offensive, some of our troops were high on drugs at a base camp near the village of Trang Son. That allowed the Viet Cong to sneak through, then ambush and kill three of our guys. Duarte was mixed up in that, although I'm not sure of his exact role. That's all I have. Anything else?"

"Not right now, thanks. But keep me posted." She hung up the phone and lay back down on the bed to think.

"Colombian heroin," she whispered. It didn't make any sense that the drug cartel would want to kill or scare off their best customers with drug laced with a deadly virus. If Charlie could confirm virus in the sparkly drug, that would be big deal bioterrorism that would bring in the DEA, FBI, Homeland Security and bigwigs at PHS. She was hoping that she would still be around to be involved when there was a knock on the door.

Adrenalin surged into her bloodstream from the thought of her attackers having tracked her down. Another softer knock. She took a deep breath and shook her head slightly. "Nah," she muttered. "The bad guys aren't that polite. But it better be Ed and not a pizza man." She hobbled to the door to check the peephole. It was Ed.

"What happened to you?" Her Ace-bandaged arm and limp were obvious as she went to sit on the couch.

"Someone in a black car tried to turn me into roadkill on LaSalle Street this afternoon. They missed."

"What? Tried to run you over?"

"Yes."

"You're kidding. Intentionally?"

"I guess so."

"Who?"

"Couldn't see through the tinted windshield. Probably the same people who ran me off I-10 on my way into New Orleans last night. I thought that was accidental, but maybe not."

"Have you been to the police?"

"What can they do? They probably wouldn't believe me anyway."

"Why would anyone want to hurt you?"

Kris shrugged. "I didn't know I had enemies. No gambling debts, no jealous ex'es, no deranged fans." She set her jaw and looked him in the eye. "Let's just forget about it for now."

Ed frowned. "Okay – for now."

"All right. Let me bring you up to date. B.J.'s got the hepatitis, LaDonna Fry's dying of it up in Corham, Renk's autopsy just showed liver rot, and the DEA said the sparkly drug is high-grade heroin out of Colombia. By the way, the Parish General pathologist told me that the Girardeau kid had a skin ulcer on his chest."

"That's right. Smack in the middle of a medieval mace tattoo."

"You're kidding. Was he an IV drug user?"

"Not according to his medical record. Kaelin, the pathologist, didn't know either. Does it matter?"

"It would make for a cleaner tattoo-only-related case. I wonder if Hugo did his mace."

"Have you looked at Hugo's work log?"

She shook her head. "Haven't had time. Let me get it." She found the worksheets in her briefcase and spread them out on a table. "Okay. We're looking at the weekend of March 13th. We've got times, types of tattoos, and a bunch of weird names and initials. A large dragon tattoo was done on 'Skunk' on Saturday and one on 'Rebel Rouser' on Sunday. Three mace tattoos: 'J-Bird' and 'Gumpy' on Saturday, and 'Jacko' on Sunday. After Monday, Hugo was a no-show at work."

"Did anyone else do mace tattoos?"

"I don't know. We could probably find out. 'J-Bird' could be Johnny Girardeau. Think we could ask his family about nicknames and maybe about drug use?"

"Before I approach that family, I'd need to run it by John Palmer, our Director."

"Do it. It could help us nail King Dewey. So – is Junior the 'Rebel Rouser' or the 'Skunk'?"

Ed shrugged. He was looking at an earlier work schedule. "I don't know, but on March 7th there's another 'Rebel Rouser' entry for a dragon tattoo that's written in but then crossed out."

She studied the entry and looked up. "Maybe Junior just changed his appointment date." She paused and drummed her fingers on the tabletop. "Or maybe Junior made two trips to New Orleans a week apart. I don't think we ever asked LaDonna about that. He could've gotten the sparkly drug that first weekend and given it to Billy the week of Monday the 8th. Billy died the 17th – so that would fit."

Ed countered, "So who gave the drug to Junior, and why?"

"And who gave it to Renk? Obviously someone at the tattoo parlor."

"King Dewey? Hugo? Ramon? Speaking of Ramon –" He glanced at his watch. "It's five after four. Do you have his number?"

"Here it is."

Ed winked and said, "I'll call. He just might respond better to a man."

She handed him the telephone.

"Hello. This is Dr. Ed Beaufain with the Orleans Parish Health Department. Could I speak to Ramon, please?"

Kris was thinking about questions to ask Ramon when she heard Ed say, "Oh, it's you, Micah. This is *your* number."

Chapter 12

Ed raised his eyebrows at Kris, who nodded understanding. "Micah, I'm here with Dr. Jensen. No one else. I'm going to put you on a speaker phone so that we can both talk to you. Or do you want us to meet with you in person?"

"No. This is okay."

"Hi, Micah. This is Kris Jensen. You seemed nervous this morning. Are you worried about something?"

"Getting hepatitis, mainly."

"That's all? Nothing else?"

Micah hesitated. "Umm – that's it."

"Have you been feeling sick?"

"Not really."

"Then, if you haven't shot up drugs or had a tattoo lately, you should be all right."

"You sure?"

"Yes. I'm sure. Listen, Micah, Dr. Beaufain and I want to ask you about some people at King Dewey's."

"Okay."

"Who all does the mace tattoos?"

"Pretty much everyone."

"Including Hugo?"

"Yes."

Ed was doodling a mace. "Did Hugo do a mace differently than the other tattooists?"

"He put 7 or 8 spikes on the club end. A lot more than the others."

"I'll check with Kaelin," Ed whispered.

Kris nodded. "Did Hugo look sick when you last saw him?"

"He was real tired. 'Gettin old,' he said."

"Hepatitis can make you tired. Did he have skin bruises, yellow eyes or skin, or maybe dark urine?"

"You know, Jimmy did say Hugo's eyes looked a little yellow. He wore tinted glasses, so I couldn't tell. Do you think he had hep?"

"Maybe. Did Hugo smoke?"

"Heavy. That's another thing. He said cigarettes didn't taste right no more."

"Micah, one more question about Hugo," Ed said. "Did he do drugs?"

"I guess so. Most of them did."

"What kind of drugs?"

"Heroin and coke."

"Micah, do you remember a big white Mississippi kid named Junior Murphee?" Kris asked. "Had three large dragons on his upper body. Hugo did the last one about ten days ago – on Sunday the 14th."

"Hmm. Maybe – "

"He was a drug user. Only used clean needles."

"Oh yeah. The clean needle freak. But he used a different name."

"Rebel Rouser?"

"That was it."

"Did he come in to see Hugo the week before also?"

"Yeah. I remember because he argued with Hugo about the price of the dragon he wanted. King Dewey worked out a deal for him to come back a week later to have it done."

"What kind of deal?"

"All I know is the dragon was a freebie when he came back for it."

"Do you remember a street person named Homer Renk?" Kris asked. "Ramon did a penile sword tattoo on him."

"A pork sword? What'd the guy look like?"

She had to guess at Renk's normal appearance. "White. Five foot six or so. 30 something. Black, greasy hair. Dark, beady eyes. IV drug user."

"Sounds like that guy who paid with funny money a month ago. King Dewey got mad at me for accepting it, but then he said he'd take care of it. One of King Dewey's biker pals – ah – escorted the guy back in about ten days ago, but I swear he left smiling. That's all I know. Listen, I gotta go. There's someone at the door."

"Okay, Micah," Kris said. "Thanks for your help. We'll probably want to talk to you again soon."

Micah hung up. They both heard a faint but distinct second click, amplified by the speaker phone.

"What was that?" Kris asked. "I heard something like it earlier this morning."

Ed switched off the speaker phone and turned to her. "Could be a phone tap."

"Someone listening in? C'mon. Aren't we getting a little paranoid? That's illegal isn't it?"

"I'm not so sure. Better use your cellphone from now on, though it's probably not completely secure either."

She looked at him incredulously. "This is starting to sound like the script of a bad spy movie."

Ed checked his watch. "We can talk about it more later. In ten minutes we're supposed to be at the School of Public Health to meet with Ben Cline. It's only a few blocks, but we'll take the van. I'll explain who he is and why we're meeting him on the way over."

"All right. Let me pop a few pills, and I'll be ready in a minute."

As Ed drove the van out into the traffic on Canal Street, Kris looked behind them. "Watch out for black cars trying to ram us."

He smiled. He had already been doing so.

Her eyes flashed. "I'm serious. Your life might be in danger, too."

He kept his attention on the traffic around them. "Don't take this the wrong way, Kris, but right now I'm more worried about protecting you." He turned to look at her and their eyes met briefly. "I'm not going to let anything more happen to you."

She looked to his face and put her hand on his shoulder. "Thanks, Ed. That's sweet of you. Let's hope I won't need any more protection." There was a brief awkward silence that she broke in a low, growly voice. "Okay, Mr. Bodyguard. Keep them eyes on the road."

"Yes, ma'am," Ed said. "So what do you think we got from Micah?"

"Not everything that he knows, but still a good bit. We found out Hugo was sick with fatigue and yellow eyes and had a loss of taste for cigarettes, which are all classic symptoms of viral hepatitis. Junior made two trips and maybe a deal with King Dewey. Renk tried to cheat the parlor and might have paid for it with his life. Everything leads back to the tattoo parlor and King Dewey. No dripping needle just yet, so I don't think we have enough to go to the police. If we find virus in the drug, we'll get plenty of help from the FBI."

"Should we be looking for Hugo?"

"If Hugo was yellow from this hepatitis ten days ago, he's a dead man." She looked out the side window and sighed. "And I'm dead tired still, even after that nap. So who are we going to see?"

"Benjamin Cline at the School of Public Health. He's the top tropical disease pathologist this side of the Hospital for Tropical Diseases in London, and he has an interest in liver disease. Kaelin, the pathologist at Tulane, suggested we have him review Girardeau's liver histopathology. The cells were mostly necrotic and empty, but Kaelin found a few liver cells with unusual inclusions he thought might be evidence of a virus. I called Ben earlier and described our hepatitis cases and the inclusions. He was quite interested in having a look at the slides."

Benjamin Cline's office was on the third floor of the Public Health School building on Canal Street. Cline was 60-ish, tall and thin with a trim gray beard. He had a long nose, and his eyes had an intensity that made Kris slightly uncomfortable. As she was being introduced, a fist-sized ball of large white worms in a jar on a shelf attracted her attention.

"That Ascaris worm ball caused intestinal obstruction in a five year-old Nicaraguan boy," Cline said.

"I was pretty sure it wasn't pasta," she said. "And what's this?" she asked, pointing to a larger jar that contained a human brain, riddled Swiss cheese-like with pea-sized cysts.

"That man had cerebral cysticercosis. That's brain involvement with larval forms of the pork tapeworm. Life can be a living helminth."

The surprise witticism made Kris smile. Clever people who didn't take themselves and their work *too* seriously appealed to her. With her best look of disgust, she said, "Ugh, I never did like the worms in parasitology class. Especially that squiggly larval hookworm rash called 'creeping eruption.' It made my skin crawl."

"Yeah, I felt the same way," Ed said. "In my MPH parasitology course, even the lowly pinworm made me squirm in my seat."

Cline laughed. "Good lines. I might steal them to liven up my next lecture to the MPH students."

"As I remember, your presentations were already pretty lively," Ed said.

Cline acknowledged the compliment with a smile as he switched on the microscope that sat on his desk. "Let's see what you've got."

Ed handed him a tray of glass microscope slides each of which had a thin section of Johnny Girardeau's liver stained shades of red, blue, and green by the various chemicals and dyes used to highlight specific histopathologic features of human tissue.

Cline picked out several slides and examined them in silence, first under low power and then using the 100x oil immersion lens. Finally, he looked up and said, "Nasty looking liver necrosis. There are a few intracellular inclusions. I've got the arrow pointing on one. Have a look." He switched on the side-arm microscope viewer and swung it in Kris's direction.

She squinted through the eyepiece of the side-arm. "That little dark dot?"

"Yup. Looks viral but it's not yellow fever, and I've never seen inclusions in hep A, B, C, E or delta."

"Then do you have any idea about what it might be?"

Cline picked up a manila folder thick with medical journal articles and began to page through them. "I looked through my file on fulminant hepatitis earlier, and I came across – here it is. A one-page case report recently published in the Bulletin of the Pan American Health Organization. A Dr. Jorge Cruz in Caracas described a case of fulminant hepatitis in a Yachabo Indian just arrived in the city from his tribal homeland in western Venezuela. The liver pathology showed viral inclusions. Cruz called it a yellow fever variant. The image in this report is not the best quality, but I would say the inclusions resemble the ones in your case."

"That is provocative," said Kris, "but maybe not quite enough. Now if you told me the Indian was an IV drug user –"

Cline shook his head. "Nothing about drug use. Cruz only reported that the Indian had been in excellent health. He was sick for a week and then died with generalized swelling, yellow-green skin mottled with hemorrhages, and multi-organ failure. And get this, on his leg, he had a rubbery ulcer that tested negative for syphilis, leishmania, TB, and fungus. Didn't your cases have skin ulcers?"

Kris jumped up and reached for the case report. "Yes, all of them. How can I get in touch with Dr. Cruz?"

"You'd need a spiritualist to do a seance. Cruz died in a car accident a few months ago. The reason I know is that his brother is currently a visiting professor here."

Her face fell. "Did anyone ever investigate the hepatitis further?"

"Not that I know of. I was interested when I read the report, but I wouldn't get funding for a study based on a single patient. Not only that, the Yachabo homeland is in a remote area that's considered highly dangerous due to Colombian guerilla activity. I never pursued it."

Kris was studying the case report. "Do you know any more about the Yachabo?"

"I have this reference." Cline retrieved and opened a book titled *Native Indians of South America.* "Yachabo – small tribe, relatively primitive, numbering less than a thousand, living in and around an Andes mountain valley, *El Valle Amarillo*, in western Venezuela near the Colombian border. A Catholic mission and hospital is there. Homeland remote and accessible by small aircraft, by horse or burro, or on foot. Roads poorly maintained and often impassable." Cline looked up. "That's it. You might try an Internet search for more info on the tribe. "

"Good idea," said Kris. She held up Cruz' report. "I'd like a copy of this article as well as that book section on this tribe. As far as I'm concerned, the Indian case matches ours. I'm almost ready to jump on a plane to Venezuela, but I'll need Mike Bauman's support and he'll want corroboration of ongoing cases among these Indians."

"That would seem reasonable," said Ed

Kris nodded agreement and turned to Cline. "Do you have a copy machine and an Internet access I can use?"

Cline pointed to a side door. "Both are in the conference room next door."

"Great. – Thanks. I also need to make a couple of phone calls so it'll be a few minutes."

After Kris left the room, Cline turned to Ed. "Exciting stuff, this hepatitis"

"It's been tremendous working with Kris. It's tempted me to apply to the EIS Program."

"You should. You're bright and committed to public health. I'll be glad to write you a letter."

"I appreciate your offer and I just might take you up on it after this hepatitis outbreak is over."

Twenty minutes later Kris rejoined them, her eyes bright with excitement. "I lucked out. First I got on the World Catholic Health Missions website and found out there is a small mission hospital that serves the Yachabo. And get this: in the medical director's last annual report, he mentions fulminant hepatitis that may be non-preventable by hep B and yellow fever vaccines. That's at least some corroboration."

Ed looked skeptical. "You might want to get in touch with that medical director."

"I agree," said Cline. "Could have been fulminant cases of delta virus. That's been reported in the region and vaccination of a hep B carrier wouldn't prevent it."

"You're right. But the director, a Dr. Paterson, also referred to communication issues. Telephone service is almost non-existent and mail is twice a month by small plane depending on the weather. Dr. Paterson uses a ham radio to call back to the U.S."

"No satellite uplink or other high tech communication?"

Kris shrugged. "Must not be in their budget. Then I was able to catch Mike Bauman at CDC. He wanted a copy of Cruz's report and more information about the Yachabo. He okayed for me to start looking into a trip to Venezuela and suggested working through the DEA in Caracas. He and Essex will decide after the planning meeting tomorrow. With the WAR protest on our doorstep, it won't be a dull morning."

"I'd love to be there, but I've got too much to do here," Ed said. "Think the DEA would co-operate?"

"That was my third call. Dennis Foster told me that the Venezuelan government expelled all DEA personnel a few years ago for supposedly spying, so all DEA operations there have ceased. But he suggested I contact a Cory Flint, who was their associate chief in Caracas and who still lives there. I have his e-mail address."

"You can use my computer if you want to send a message out tonight," said Cline.

"Thanks, but I'll use my smartphone," she said with a slight frown.

"What's the matter?" Ed asked.

"Something else Foster told me. The X-Operations report came back to say the little sparklies were just bits of plastic. That's not what Charlie in our lab found, and I trust Charlie – completely."

Chapter 13

"We need to talk," Ed said as they exited the Public Health School building fifteen minutes later. "How about over dinner? I know some great places." He turned to Kris when she didn't answer. "GI tract not ready yet?"

She shook her head. "I'd be a cheap date. Breadsticks and water. A little broth maybe. I'd like to go but I want to stop at the Parish General ER first to check on Gareth Miller."

"That's B.J.'s father?"

Kris nodded. "His ankle was run over as he pushed me out of the way of that black sedan." On the short ride to the hospital, she summarized the interview with B.J. Miller and recounted the incident on LaSalle Street.

The Parish General ER was jammed with patients, some on gurneys parked in the hallway. As they made their way through the ER to find Gareth Miller, a baby was wailing. In response to its cries, a Hispanic woman patient in a distant room repeatedly shrieked, "*El niño es mio!*"

Kris turned to Ed. "What's she saying?"

"She's saying 'the child is mine,' but I doubt it."

They passed a twirly-eyed, bushy blond-haired man with arms and legs in hard leather restraints. He tried to lunge at them while he roared like a lion. Across from him, a drawn curtain hid the sight but not the sound of a patient retching.

Kris whispered to Ed, "This place reminds me why I didn't go into emergency medicine."

A few steps farther on, they found Miller on a stretcher in a holding area. His ankle had been re-located and splinted, and he was waiting to be taken for another x-ray. He looked depressed, but his expression brightened when he saw Kris.

She introduced Ed and put her hand on Miller's shoulder. "Thanks again for your help." She nodded at his injured leg. "At least your foot points in the right direction again."

"Yeah, but they need to operate yet tonight to stabilize it. At least that'll get me out of here. I've been here almost five hours. What a zoo." He was interrupted by another lion roar from the man in restraints. With a look of irritation, Miller turned in his direction. "Case in point. They need to find Leo a cage or throw him a hunk of raw meat or something." Miller shifted his weight and winced at the wave of pain from his ankle. He sighed and shook his head. "Two tours in Vietnam and never got a scratch."

Kris looked up from her inspection of his splinted ankle. "You were in 'Nam? What branch?"

`"Army – Captain."

"Many Louisiana boys in your unit?"

"Quite a few."

"Ever heard of the Trang Son incident and a soldier named Dewey Duarte?"

Miller's facial expression hardened. His eyes hinted at the anger she had witnessed in Schmidt's office. He was silent as he looked away from her. "He's one reason I hate drugs and drug users. He and four of his drug buddies were high on heroin that night the Cong slipped through and killed three of our guys. Duarte got off with just a dishonorable discharge."

"Why not prison?"

"He was the only one of the druggies who was not on duty, and he testified against the others. A lot of people thought he was the ringleader, and blamed him. Especially the Madmen."

"Madmen?"

"M-A-D stands for Military Against Drugs. It's a group that got started back then. So what's your interest in Trang Son and Duarte?"

Kris hesitated. She didn't want to say that King Dewey might be responsible for Renk's hepatitis without stronger evidence, and she was concerned that Miller's response might interfere with her investigation. "Duarte runs a local tattoo parlor where three of our hepatitis cases had tattoos done. So we're looking into his background."

Miller didn't react much to the news that Duarte was in the neighborhood, so Kris asked, "Did you know he was around?"

"I guess I heard it a while back."

"You really think the driver of that car was trying to hurt me?"

"Yes."

"Then why didn't they just drive by and shoot me?"

"Too obvious. Maybe you were being set up for a KO."

Kris raised her eyebrows. "A knock-out?"

Miller shook his head. "K stands for potassium, O for overdose. They'd try to finish you off later in the hospital with a potassium injection. I'm sure you know a slug of IV potassium can stop a heart quicker than a slug from a gun – without all the mess. And the murder weapon is damn hard to trace. Let's face it. Hospital patient security sucks."

"But who? I don't have any enemies."

"Someone must not want you to investigate this hepatitis."

Kris knew that already. "So what did you tell the NOPD out on LaSalle Street?"

"They handled it as a hit-and-run. They're looking for the car. I kept your name out of it."

An anesthesia resident physician wearing green scrubs and a puffy blue OR cap appeared, carrying Miller's chart. The resident introduced himself and said to Miller, "You'll be going to x-ray and then straight to the OR. I've got a few questions I need to ask you on the way." He turned to Kris and Ed. "If you'll excuse us?"

Miller looked up at them. "Watch your backs, – both of you. And please do everything you can for B.J." He then turned to the resident and pointed a finger at his injured leg. "Remember – the *right* ankle. Let's roll."

Moments later, Corrine Miller appeared and intercepted the stretcher. She spoke to her husband briefly and gave him a kiss. Recognizing Kris, she came over to them.

Kris gave her a hug and introduced Ed. "I'm sorry about your husband's leg. Now you've got two in the hospital."

Corrine Miller wrung her hands and forced a weak smile. "Yes, but Gary expects to be released tomorrow. I'll stay overnight and divide my time between the two of them. Any more information on treatment at NIH for B.J.?"

Kris shook her head. "But there's a big meeting on this outbreak tomorrow morning at the CDC in Atlanta. I promise I'll ask around about treatment, and I'll call Dr. Schmidt right afterward." She had forgotten to ask Bauman about the NIH.

Mrs. Miller nodded. "We'll wait to hear from Dr. Schmidt."

"We were chatting with your husband about Vietnam. When did he leave the Army?"

"I think it was July of 1985."

"What does he do now?"

"He's a private security consultant."

"Did he ever talk about a group organized in Viet Nam called the 'Madmen'? M-a-d is military against drugs."

"A couple of years ago I heard him yell at a person on the telephone about 'madmen.' I only remember because it's such a strange name. When I asked him who they were, he got angry and refused to explain."

"Did he ever mention a drug user named Dewey Duarte?" Kris asked.

Corrine Miller pursed her lips and shook her head.

"Also known as King Dewey," added Ed.

She turned to him. "A couple of times he's mentioned a King Doughy. Is that who you mean?"

A wisp of a smile showed on Kris' face. "Maybe so. Who's King Doughy?"

"I don't know. A man he talked to on his cellphone. I assumed it was one of his security clients. Gary sometimes works with strange people."

"Anything else you remember about this King Doughy?"

"It sounded like they were going to meet, but the way Gary talked, I don't think he liked that person. Why are you asking me all this instead of Gary?"

"I was just getting around to it when they whisked him off to surgery."

Corrine Miller shrugged. "That's all I know. Anything else?"

Kris shook her head.

"Then I'll be in room 698 with B.J. if you need me."

They watched her leave. "I believe that's all she does know," Ed said. "She seems like a straight shooter. King Doughy has to be Duarte."

Kris nodded. "Let's go talk about it over breadsticks and water."

They found a quiet side table with a green-checkered tablecloth and a candle at Gambino's, the Italian restaurant that Jeff Wilson had recommended. It was also one of Ed's favorites. It was 5:45 and the restaurant was filling up fast. "There'll be a long line outside in a half-hour," Ed said as he studied the menu.

The waiter brought warm bread that looked and smelled freshly baked. "I think I'll take a chance and have a roll with my water," said Kris.

Ed sighed. "Too bad for you. The crawfish etouffee here is excellent as are all the Italian-Creole shrimp dishes." He scanned the other diners around them and whispered, "It should be safe to talk here."

"Don't be so paranoid. You're making me crazy."

"Just because I'm paranoid, doesn't mean someone isn't trying to listen in on us."

Kris giggled. "You're right. So what's your take on Gareth Miller?"

"Seems genuinely concerned about us. I guess because we're the key people to help his daughter. Don't know why he didn't tell us more about Duarte. I doubt he was one of Miller's security clients."

"I agree. So why *would* Miller have anything to do with a drug user he said he hated? I can't see Miller interested in the tattoo business or involved with dealing drugs. If he's warning us about people he knows but doesn't name, that means he's mixed up with them. And if those people are distributing virus-contaminated drug, Miller must be a tormented man because that virus is probably going to kill his daughter."

Ed raised his hands in frustration. "We need to get him – and King Dewey – to talk –somehow. Doesn't CDC include thumbscrews in your travel pack?"

Kris shook her head. She was appreciating Ed's sense of humor more and more, and it was hard not to like someone who made her laugh. "Maybe if I told Miller that it's critical information to help B.J., he'd come clean on King Dewey."

"I'm not sure he'd buy that. Are you going back to the hospital tonight?"

"No, it'll be hours before he's fully awake after surgery. I'll have to get up at 3:30 to catch the 6:00 a.m.Delta flight to Atlanta, and I'm pretty tired already. You get to interview him in the morning."

"No problemo. So who do you think is threatening us?"

"Whoever brought the virus and presumably mixed it in with heroin. Someone who wants drug users to go on dying and doesn't care if others get infected in the process." She glanced at her finger as she said it.

"Makes sense, but *who* are they? Not the Colombian drug lords. Bad for business."

Kris nodded. "I agree."

"Then I suppose there're always foreign bio-terrorists like Islamic extremists. But let's face it. There's not much terrorism bang for the buck in killing off drug users. They're pretty low on our societal totem pole. America didn't worry much about AIDS until non-drug-using heterosexuals started to get it."

Kris raised one finger. "Unless – this is just a trial run. We know this virus is not a slate-wiper. By that, I mean it's not an Andromeda strain that's transmitted by casual contact. But what we don't know is whether bio-terrorists could infect large groups of people with a concentrated virus aerosol or by virus contamination of food."

"Scary thought," said Ed.

"On the other hand, a food contamination trial run would've been easy to do. I'd expect the method used in a test exposure to match that of the big exposure that would follow."

"Any other potential perpetrators?" he asked.

"How about a mad virologist with a vendetta? Maybe he or she got hep C or AIDS, or maybe they lost someone close to them because of infection that came from a drug user." She shrugged. "Or maybe drugs or drug users were somehow otherwise responsible for a loss of life."

"That could describe Miller's Madmen."

Kris considered the suggestion. "Maybe. But Vietnam was over thirty years ago. Seems unlikely anyone would hold a murderous grudge against drug users for that long. Why wait so many years? Is the group even still active? Who are they, anyway?"

"Mrs. Miller said her husband mentioned Madmen a couple of years ago, so they could still be active. I'll try to pin Miller down about them tomorrow." Ed put his hand to his forehead. "Listen, Kris. At what point do we call in the police, or even the FBI? Seems to me we already have plenty of evidence of danger to you and enough suspected criminal activity to ask for their help."

"Once we find virus in the drug, especially if it's in the little plastic beads, that'll be the hard evidence to bring in the FBI. Charlie was going to start testing for hepatitis enzyme elevation in the inoculated animals this afternoon. And to be honest, Ed, if Mike Bauman found out that my life had been threatened, he'd yank me back to Atlanta. I don't want to take that chance. I think we're on the verge of a breakthrough."

"But maybe you really do need police protection. I'd hate to see anything happen to you."

"Okay, here's the deal. One, I didn't stick around to report either incident so they may not even believe me. Two, we don't yet have hard evidence of criminal wrongdoing. I don't want to waste days trying to convince the police without more evidence. Three, it's not about me – someone is trying to interfere with the investigation and anyone who replaces me would be threatened. I am willing to bear the risk so for now you'll just have to be my bodyguard. "

"All right," Ed sighed. "For now. What plastic beads?"

"Charlie discovered the little sparklies were tiny hollow plastic beads. The shells melted down easily and released a bit of brownish material that he was going to try to ID and also inject into animals."

"Didn't the DEA report say they were only bits of plastic?"

"According to Foster."

"The two drug samples looked the same to me," Ed said. "So – does that mean the DEA report is just sloppy lab work, or what? Do they know you sent a separate sample to CDC?"

"I never told them."

"So what do you think?"

"I'm not sure what to think. I know the DEA is not doing well in the war against drugs, at least around here. The Mississippi state epidemiologist, told me there's a record amount of heroin coming into that state. Maybe the DEA lab didn't have the personnel or funding to properly evaluate the sample."

Ed shook his head. "I don't buy that. X-Operations is a new program within DEA headed by that ex-Marine Colonel – Arnett, I think. They should have plenty of funding and qualified staff for their lab."

"You're probably right, but I don't see any reason to question them about their report right now. They ID'd the drug and source for us. We'll use CDC for the microbiologic analysis. Let the FBI sort it all out later."

Their waiter approached to take their order and Ed rescanned the menu. Kris ordered a glass of water and he interjected, "She'll have the Arkansas spring water."

"What's the matter, Ed?" she asked after he had ordered. "Can't we drink the local water?"

"A number of years ago, there was a study done that exposed bacteria to city water and it showed an incredible mutation rate in the bacteria. The Arkansas water caused only a low mutation rate, and the local bottled water was somewhere in between. I *have* wondered whether the population here is slowly being poisoned by all the chemical plants between Baton Rouge and New Orleans. But I love the area and its food. I may be doomed, but what a way to go."

"Are you from here?"

"I grew up in Grand Isle. My father was a Cajun shrimper and my mother is Costa Rican. Mama lives in Thibodaux now."

"Now I understand how you got named Eduardo. Are you fluent in Spanish?"

Ed nodded. "And Cajun."

"I had a little Spanish in high school. About all I remember is 'Spanish is the language where *sopa* isn't soap, *ropa* isn't rope, and butter is meant-ta-kill-ya.'"

He pretended to look shocked and reached to pull the butter dish away from her. "Hey, that's right. *Mantequilla* – can't have any with your bread."

Kris laughed. "You should come with me to Venezuela as a combination bodyguard-translator-investigator. Not necessarily in that order."

"Do you think you'll get to go?"

"I think Bauman will let me. I told Cory Flint in my e-mail to expect me in Caracas by Friday. I'd lobby hard for CDC to cover your trip. You'd be a big help."

"I'll ask my Director. Someone would have to pick up the investigations here in New Orleans."

"I expect CDC will soon mobilize a lot of people for this outbreak," Kris said. "Including your state EIS guy."

"Would I need a visa?"

"Nope. Checked that out already."

The waiter brought their drinks and Ed took a sip of iced tea. "Are you ready for the big meeting tomorrow?"

"I think so. Bauman told me earlier that a WAR leader named Rex Aburcorn showed up this morning at the Hepatitis Division and asked our chief, Carl Essex, if he could sit in and observe the meeting. Essex wasn't going for it, but the Director's office leaned on him to include Aburcorn."

"I've heard of that guy. Watch out for him. He's a radical, end-justifies-the-means type."

"I know. Bauman expects he won't be able to keep his mouth shut, and will have to be escorted out."

"How are you getting to the airport tomorrow morning?"

"I was going to leave my rental at the hotel and call a cab."

"I'll take you."

"You sure? I should be there by five in the morning to check in and clear security."

"Can't you tell?" He patted the top of his head. "I'm wearing my driver-bodyguard hat."

The wave of nausea came suddenly. She was afraid the bread she'd just eaten was about to reappear, but it didn't. A weak feeling and a cold sweat followed. She got up to go to the ladies' room. "Excuse me. I need to go take more pills."

Ed nodded with a look of concern on his face. He watched her limp and wobble a bit on her way to the restroom, and kept an eye out for anyone suspicious following her.

When she returned, he said, "I'm worried about you. You don't look good. Maybe we should have gotten you some IV fluids back at Parish General."

"Ed. Quit worrying. I'll keep up with my fluids. It's just a little relapse of that Big Queasy thing – a 24-hour GI bug."

"But it's been over 24 hours already."

"I don't want to talk about it anymore," she said. "Now where were we?"

Ed looked away and spoke softly. "I was going to pick you up at 4:30 in the morning."

"I'm sorry I barked at you. When I'm not feeling so hot and especially when I'm tired, I can get snappish. Don't take it personally. Let's just talk about something else."

The waiter brought Ed's order of crawfish etouffee over rice.

"Mind if I start eating?"

Kris pointed to his dinner. "Normally I would love to have that, washed down with a few Dixie beers. But not tonight." She took a sip of her spring water. "Hmm. Tastes great – and less filling."

He grinned. "Aha, a beer drinker. Didn't you say you're from Wisconsin?"

"Born and raised in Oshkosh. My mom still lives there. I've always liked the taste of beer. Must be my Swedish-German heritage. My uncle Hans has a Milwaukee goiter."

Ed looked concerned. "Is it serious?"

"Oh yes." Kris kept a straight face. "A very serious beer belly."

The antihistamine she had taken seemed to resolve the nausea, and Kris felt much better. For the next 30 minutes they talked about their families and shared laughs over the exploits of their quirky relatives. It was the most relaxed and happy she'd felt since she had left Atlanta. After their waiter had come back a third time to ask if there was anything else, they got up to go.

As they walked back to the van through the French Quarter, a group of LSU students whooping it up on their way to Bourbon Street came between them. She glanced across at Ed. "Ed, it's been fun," she whispered, "but it's about this deadly disease I have."

After the students had passed, Ed smiled at her and asked, "What were you muttering?"

"Nothing important," she said with a slight shake of her head.

Chapter 14

The hotel wake-up call came at 3:45 a.m. Still half-asleep, Kris stumbled to the bathroom. A glance at the flushing toilet caused her to stop brushing her teeth and lean over to take a closer look. She spit the toothpaste into the sink, turned and said, "Damn it" at the tea color and yellow foam of the swirling toilet water. Her blood level of bilirubin, a bile pigment being released from her sick liver, had risen high enough to show up in the urine. Yellow jaundice of her eyes and skin would follow when the level of bilirubin rose further.

She examined herself in the mirror. Her face was already thinner. She had always kept herself trim, so her co-workers at CDC might not notice her weight loss, and she could finesse an explanation for that anyway. Jaundice was something else. Make-up might hide yellow skin color but not yellowing of the normally white sclera of her eyes. She took a closer look but her conjunctivae were bloodshot from the interrupted sleep. In the artificial bathroom light, she couldn't tell if there was any yellow tinge to the underlying sclera.

Bilirubin in her urine was a sign of progression of her hepatitis. It was disconcerting, and pierced the armor of her denial. She stared at her mirror image, took a deep breath, and reaffirmed to herself: – *As long as I can function and not endanger anyone, I'll keep going.* Her malaise and fatigue were probably from the hepatitis, but those symptoms were still tolerable. She was thankful that the diarrhea seemed to have resolved and that the nausea was at least temporarily in remission.

By 4:30, she was ready to leave. When she opened her door to check out, she heard Ed down the hall shouting her name and pounding on the door to room 350. She stepped out of her doorway and called out, "Hey, Ed – hush. I'm okay. I changed rooms."

His expression was a mixture of exasperation and relief. "I was just about to kick the door in. I called up to room 350 and when no one answered, I –"

"I understand," she said. "Let's get going."

The early morning traffic on I-10 westbound to the airport was light. Ed had calmed down considerably. "That was smart to change rooms."

"I'm so glad to have your blessing after the fact."

"What'd you use for an excuse?"

"It's probably not in your repertoire," she said. "I told them I thought I'd seen a mouse in the room."

"Ah, yes – The eek technique. You're right. Wouldn't work for me."

"I don't like using a woman's weakness as a means to an end."

Ed shrugged. "Nothing new in that. Neanderthal women probably used it to get a new cave. You're not afraid of mice, are you?"

"No. My only real phobia is big bugs. Insects should all be tiny, like ants or gnats. Don't care much for snakes, either."

"Duly noted by your bodyguard. I'll be a one-man swat team at the ready."

"Thanks." She yawned.

"So how do you feel this morning?"

"Better. Just tired. I didn't sleep too well."

The New Orleans airport was surprisingly busy with people arriving for the early flight departures. She got her boarding pass at the ticket counter and they walked to the security checkpoint.

"So did you get a one-way or round trip ticket?"

"Is that your way of asking when I'll be back?"

"I guess so."

"Not sure yet. It'll depend on the outcome of the meeting later this morning. I still intend to go to Venezuela and I'll request that you come along, though there's a lot to do yet here in New Orleans."

"True." Ed nodded as he scribbled on a note pad. "Here's my cell number. Better give me yours so I can tell you what Miller has to say later on this morning."

They exchanged phone numbers. She glanced at her watch.

"Time to go?" he asked.

She nodded as their eyes met. She pointed a finger at him. "Listen, Ed. I'm worried about *you*. Take Miller's advice and watch your back."

He was going to joke about not having eyes in the back of his head, but he could see that she was serious. "I'll be careful. If it's okay with you, later today I'm going to get my friend Pete at NOPD involved with our investigation."

"That's fine. Have them assign *you* a bodyguard."

They shook hands. After passing through the metal detector, she turned to look back. He was still standing there, watching her. She gave a wistful smile and waved good-bye. She wasn't sure if she would see him again.

Once settled into her seat, Kris searched the seat pocket in front of her for the airsickness bag. *The airlines probably phased out the barf bag when they cut out meal service.* Never in hundreds of previous flights had she needed one, but she had no doubt that the nausea was going to return. It had been only partially controlled by the over-the-counter Benadryl; she would need a stronger drug. Janie had had the stomach flu with vomiting a few weeks earlier. Kris was sure Janie would let her have the leftover Phenergan tablets that were in the medicine cabinet in their apartment.

She decided to take a prophylactic dose of Benadryl, and try a candy bar right after take-off. Drowsiness from the anti-histamine started to set in just as she finished the Baby Ruth. Sleep followed quickly and lasted until she was jolted awake 90 minutes later by the touchdown of the 757 on the runway at Hartsfield airport.

Her dark green Volvo 240 sedan was in the parking garage where she'd left it four days earlier in her rush to catch the flight to Memphis. The Volvo started right up with the usual shudder, followed by a rumble and a puff of blue exhaust smoke. Her mother had given her the car, convinced that the sturdy Volvo was the safest car on the road. Kris was happy with it. She had never sought out fast or flashy wheels. Safe, basic transportation was all she had ever wanted.

It was 9 a.m. when she left the airport and turned north on I-85 toward the city. Rush hour traffic had thinned out. She was thinking of how best to present the information gathered over the previous four days when her cellphone rang. It was Ed.

"Got there all right?"

"I slept all the way."

"Bad news. Gareth Miller's dead."

"What happened?"

"Apparent cardiac arrest about 3 a.m. His wife found him unresponsive. They called a code blue, but couldn't resuscitate him."

"Autopsy?"

"Most likely. They're discussing with the Medical Examiner's office whether his death was an indirect result of getting hit by the car."

"I'd say so. They need to do a post. Could have been a massive pulmonary embolism, heart attack, or a – " she hesitated.

"KO?"

"Yes. Was his wife with him all night?"

"I asked her. He insisted that she stay and she did, but thinks she may have dozed off."

"Poor thing. I hope she's not blaming herself. I'll call her after I find out about the possibility of B.J. being treated at NIH."

"Right now she's an emotional basket case. She may end up in the hospital herself. I'll keep you posted."

"Please do." Kris was worried about her.

"With Miller gone, that leaves King Dewey as our biggest untapped source of information. Pete may want to interrogate him."

"Try to establish that Johnny Girardeau was not a drug user first. That will incriminate the parlor and help legitimize a shutdown."

"I have a meeting at noon with my Director and a couple of the nurse epidemiologists. We're going to start active hepatitis case finding and set up a surveillance system. I'll add Girardeau to the agenda."

"You should follow up with Micah, too. Maybe your detective friend can spook him into telling us more about King Dewey's."

"Got it. Listen, Kris, someone from the Medical Examiner's office is here for me. I'll call you later today."

She set the phone down and drove on in silence. She felt terrible about Miller's death, but couldn't see how she could have prevented it.

It was 9:35 when she arrived at the Peachblossom apartment complex where she and Janie lived, about two miles from the CDC. Parked in her usual spot was a red Corvette stingray that she recognized as belonging to Janie's brother Ryan. With a slight shudder, she whispered, "Wouldn't be caught dead in that macho muscle-mobile."

Inside their apartment, Kris saw the keys to the Corvette next to a welcome home note from Janie that explained that she had refused to take her brother's car in to be serviced. The keys were there in case Kris wanted to reclaim her parking spot.

She washed up and checked her eyes in the mirror again for any yellow tinge. Seeing none, she looked in the medicine cabinet and found Janie's bottle of leftover Phenergan pills. Leaving her travel bag unpacked, she quickly changed clothes, grabbed her briefcase, and was out the door by 9:55. She still had more than an hour before the meeting, but she wanted to get to the Hepatitis Division early to talk to Mike Bauman and to get the latest lab results from Charlie.

Local traffic seemed unusually heavy for mid-morning. It slowed to a standstill a half-mile from the CDC's main complex on Clifton Road. She first assumed there had been an accident, but then remembered that the WAR protest had been scheduled to start at 8:00 a.m. By driving on side streets, she managed to bypass most of the back-up, but encountered a police roadblock when she turned back toward Clifton Road.

Despite the CDC parking sticker on the windshield of her Volvo, a Dekalb policeman signaled her to a halt. With the window down, she could hear the noise from the WAR protest two blocks away.

The officer leaned over and said, "Your lot 20 is blocked off. You'll have to park in lot 52 across the street. And could I see your identification card, please?"

"Sure." Kris handed him her CDC - Hepatitis Division picture ID.

After a brief inspection, the officer returned it. "One more thing. If these WAR crazies know you work in Hepatitis, I suggest you get one of our guys to escort you across the street."

"I doubt they'll recognize me. Are they that dangerous?"

"Yes, ma'am. They call it a WARpath. We've arrested five of 'em already."

Chapter 15

As Kris arrived at the CDC complex, several hundred WAR demonstrators were angrily gesturing and shouting from behind a police barrier on Clifton Road, across from the main entrance. Most were white and looked to be in their 20s and 30s. As she drove past the crowd of protesters and entered lot 52, Kris was glad her Volvo bore no indication that she worked in Hepatitis.

The sound and fury of the demonstration became more evident as she stepped out of her parked car, forty yards behind the main group of protesters. They had started to chant "Hep-a-ti-tis – it-don't-fright'n-us" followed each time by a bullhorn-amplified "C-D-C – Butch-er-y."

Kris watched from the parking lot, taken aback at the vehemence of the protest that targeted her Division and investigation. When she saw a large sign that read *Stop Essex and his Pet Projects* under a picture of her Division Chief and another sign with Charlie's picture and the caption *Death Angel*, she wondered if the protesters would recognize her. She reconsidered the suggestion of a police escort. She put on sunglasses and started toward one of the Dekalb officers stationed in lot 52, but decided that a police escort might draw too much attention.

No one seemed to notice her as she made her way through the demonstrators, or when she flashed her CDC badge to pass through the police barrier. Halfway across Clifton Road, she slipped on a patch of green mush and almost fell, which prompted a cheer from the crowd behind her. She waved in response, but never looked back.

Kris normally went up the stairs for the health benefit, but to conserve energy she took the elevator to the fifth floor of Building 2, where the Hepatitis Division occupied all of the top floor offices and lab space. Just outside the elevator, Kris encountered Gina Poluzzi, the Division's buxom, raven-haired head secretary.

Gina greeted her with a big hug.

"Am I glad to see you. Bauman's asked me about you three times already this morning. Did the maniacs out front give you any trouble?" Before Kris had a chance to respond, Gina stepped back to scrutinize her. "Have you lost weight? Either that or I've gained again. And your color doesn't look good." Gina was a mother hen to the EIS officers assigned to Hepatitis, and nothing much got past her watchful eyes.

Kris gave a weak smile. "I've lost a few pounds from a GI bug I picked up in New Orleans. Didn't get much sleep last night, either."

Gina seemed to accept Kris's explanation. "I knew something was wrong when I saw you'd taken the elevator. Just in case you're still sick, I better tell you now that engineering still hasn't fixed our ladies' room. It's either the fourth floor or the men's." Gina leaned close and whispered, "Betty and I are using the men's, as our little protest to get their attention."

Kris shook her head slightly. "Sorry. If I need to, I'll go downstairs." She changed the subject. "So, did you get past the WAR crowd okay?"

Gina's eyes flashed. "Yes, but I can't believe security made us park across the street so that we had to pass by those WAR crazies. They recognized Charlie, Dr. Bauman, and Dr. Essex and threw veggies at them. They screamed *Death Angel* at poor Charlie and hit him with a couple of tomatoes. They're dangerous!"

Kris nodded. "Veggies *are* dangerous. I slipped on a zucchini road pizza crossing Clifton Road. I almost landed on my butt." She leaned back and wildly windmilled her arms in a re-enactment of the near-fall.

When Gina started to giggle, Kris put her arm around Gina's shoulder and whispered, "God help us if we ever lose our sense of humor in times of trouble."

Gina turned to her. "Amen to that."

"Let's go find Mike."

They walked together down the main corridor toward the large conference room where the 11 o'clock meeting would be held. The door was open. Kris stopped when she noticed a gaunt, woolly-haired middle-aged man whom she didn't recognize, setting up AV equipment.

Gina saw who she was looking at and frowned. "That's that Aburcorn character," she whispered. "It boggles my mind that they're letting that twirly-eyed leader of the WAR pack attend – and videotape the meeting. They even let him bring in equipment last night."

Kris glanced at her and shrugged as they walked on. "I was going to ask Mike about him. I heard it was a political concession that came down from the Director's office."

Gina nodded.

Kris stopped at the door to her office. She looked back toward the conference room. "I would have preferred a more private strategic planning meeting, but there should be time for that later today." Kris stepped inside the door and left her briefcase on her desk. "Is Mike in his office?"

Gina hand-signaled her on down the hallway. "Yes, and impatiently waiting for you." As Kris turned to leave, Gina said, "I'm going to bring my special pasta for your lunch tomorrow to fatten you up a bit."

Kris looked back with a smile as she headed toward Mike Bauman's office at the end of the hallway.

As she passed the entrance to the Division lab, she hesitated. She considered going in to get the latest lab results, but it occurred to her that Bauman would already have them. Bauman's door was open, so she knocked briefly to announce her arrival and went on in.

Mike Bauman was at his desk listening on the telephone. He waved to her and beckoned her in. Charlie Sable, the Lab Branch Chief, sat next to him studying a sheaf of data printouts. He barely looked up.

"Okay with me," Bauman said. "We'll see them in about 20 minutes in our Division conference room. Bye."

As Kris sat down, Bauman said, "Welcome back." He studied her physical appearance. "You don't look well. Have you been sick?"

The question prompted Charlie to take another look at her but he only shrugged. "She looks the same to me," he said, and returned his full attention to the lab results.

Bauman had trained in Internal Medicine and wouldn't let her off so easily. He continued to scrutinize her appearance.

"I caught an intestinal bug in New Orleans and I *am* behind on sleep. I'm still having GI symptoms, so if I happen to duck out of the meeting for a few minutes, that would be the reason."

"You do look tired," Bauman said. "But your skin color is different – Sallower, maybe."

Kris shook her head. "Mike, I am fully able to present and participate in this meeting. So can we get on to specifics? Plus I want to hear the latest results from Charlie."

Bauman glanced at his watch, nodded, and handed her a list of guest attendees as well as an agenda. "I'll start off with five minutes of intros and a little background to your investigation, and then you're on. How much time will you need?"

"I can summarize my part in about 10 minutes, but I imagine there'll be a lot of questions. More questions than answers, for sure."

Bauman waved her off. "I want Charlie's results to follow right after you, and then Essex wants to give his overview and ideas for further investigation and control measures."

"Just leave some time for questions," Kris said. She turned to the Lab Branch Chief. "So Charlie, don't keep me in suspense. What have you found so far?"

"I've got serology and liver function test results as of this morning's run. We'll have another batch out by two p.m. Anyway, Renk and Murphee's hep A to G serology panels were only positive for immunity to hep B and for active hep C, and both were hep C

IgM negative, so C was not a new infection for either of them. The girl LaDonna Fry was seronegative for the whole panel."

Kris nodded. "No surprises so far. What about the animals you injected?"

"Now it gets interesting." Charlie smiled. "At 36 to 48 hours after inoculation with serum from any of the three human hep cases, 100% of the mice, rats and rhesus monkeys had elevated liver enzymes. Those that we double-dosed had even higher numbers, and some of them already show sick behaviors consistent with hepatitis and liver failure. We could even have a few animal deaths by tomorrow. I've never seen anything like it. This virus feasts on liver tissue like – like the feeding frenzy of a school of piranhas!"

Kris had never seen Charlie so animated or wax so descriptive. "What about the liver pathology?"

"We'll have liver sections stained for review early tomorrow. Those will give us a picture of the early hepatic cytotoxicity, and we'll look for the intra-cellular viral inclusions that the pathologist saw in the New Orleans case."

"Electron microscopy of liver for viral particles should also be ready tomorrow," Bauman added.

"What about the drug sample I sent?" asked Kris.

"Remember we only got it yesterday," Charlie said. "It's been harder to work with. We first separated off the sparkly beads. Then we injected the heroin component alone but lethally overdosed two rats and a rhesus monkey. The rest of the heroin recipients are fine and asking for another fix today. More importantly their livers are fine – so far, anyway."

"We will of course neglect to mention the OD deaths in this morning's meeting with Aburcorn," Bauman said.

Kris nodded understanding. "And the sparklies?"

"The beads? Charlie said. "They definitively contain human DNA. Once heated, the meltdown product consisted of the human-origin content plus gooey plastic material that I couldn't separate off, so we had to inject the meltdown mixture. The recipient animals all have elevated liver enzymes at 24 hours but I can't be sure it's not a hepatoxic effect of the injected plastic component. So we'll have to draw serum from those animals and inject it into a second set of animals to document the same viral pathology caused by the three human case sera."

Kris sighed. "So it'll be at least another couple of days before we know for sure that the sparkly beads contain the hepatitis virus?"

"That's right," Bauman said. "But once that's established, this outbreak investigation of yours will immediately morph into a mega-deal bioterrorism investigation involving the FBI, Homeland Security, the DEA, and our bosses in PHS. Not only that, it will spark a media frenzy once it gets out. So let's try not to get into it at today's meeting, other than to say that virus-contaminated drug is a strong possibility, but still unproven. As it is, we'll be busy enough moving all lab work with this virus into a higher level of biocontainment. It's now obvious to me that the hepatitis it causes is not only of short incubation, but is also extremely lethal and untreatable at this point in time."

"That reminds me," Kris said. "I need to talk to you today about who at NIH might be willing or able to treat the Parish General hospital nurse with the needlestick-related infection."

Bauman closed his briefcase and stood up to leave. "Got to catch Essex for a few minutes before the meeting. I do have suggestions regarding NIH. See me afterwards."

After Bauman left, Kris turned to Charlie. "In the sick animals, did you look for a blister or ulcer developing at the inoculation site?"

"Yes, we did. Found a reddish bump at the injection site, mainly in the animals that were skin popped. A couple of the bumps have started to look a little blistery. No actual ulcers yet." Charlie shook his head slightly. "Injection site skin lesions – that's another unique aspect of this. I'd love to see what the human inoculation site ulcers look like."

Kris easily resisted the urge to show him. "I'll try to get you pics." She pointed her healthy right index finger at him. "Listen, Charlie, you or someone needs to point out in this morning's meeting the crucial role that animal studies play in answering questions about a new disease and its pathogenesis. What you've already accomplished in the animal lab with the serum and drug samples from this outbreak is a perfect example."

"I understand Essex will say something along those lines in his summary."

"I hope that he does and that he gives it a proper presidential finger-wagging, make-no-mistake emphasis aimed directly at Aburcorn. I may be tempted to speak up if Essex doesn't come through."

"Kris, be careful. This animal rights issue is a political hot potato right now."

"Okay. One last question. Why let Aburcorn videotape the meeting?"

"The plan is to allow him to do it, but then confiscate the videotape and embargo it until it's reviewed and cleared for release by Public Relations."

"Does he know he can't leave with it after the meeting?"

"I don't think so. But our security people have been made aware, and will pry it from his fingers if need be."

Kris took a deep breath and let it out slowly. "This is not going to be a dull meeting. I'm expecting fireworks."

Chapter 16

Five minutes before the 11 a.m. meeting, Kris was sitting at her desk for a final review of her outbreak investigation notes when the weakness and nausea returned. To her, the room seemed warm yet her forehead and the back of her neck were clammy. Just as suddenly as the wave of nausea came on, it went away. She was glad of that, but upset over the unpredictability of her symptoms. *What if I'm in the middle of my presentation and I suddenly get urpy followed by the classic Technicolor yawn?* There was really nothing to do except carry on, but when she stood up to put her notes in her briefcase, the queasiness returned. She sat back down in hopes that the symptoms would again resolve. After a minute and a few sips of bottled water, she felt better. She left her office for the conference room down the hall.

As Kris entered, she waved to Jenny Billings, the EIS officer in her class who had landed the coveted assignment to the Special Viral Pathogens Branch. Kris was on her way over to chat with Jenny when Mike Bauman intercepted her.

"Go introduce yourself to our special guest," he whispered. "Try to soften him up a bit. We start in about five minutes." He gave her a not-so-subtle nudge in the back that directed her toward the corner of the room, where Rex Aburcorn stood alone as he adjusted the set-up of his video camera.

As Kris approached him, she was struck by how thin and unwell he appeared. The taut skin over his cheekbones reminded her of the terminal-stage AIDS and cancer patients whom she had cared for during her medical training.

He turned toward her. His face was as expressionless as Dewey Duarte's had been, but Aburcorn's look was intense and penetrating, vastly different from the glazed-over gaze of the drugged-out tattoo king. Her immediate impression was of a grim, humorless man with a passion for his mission.

He nodded slightly to acknowledge her approach. "Yes?"

Kris smiled as she held out her hand. "Hi. I'm Kris Jensen, the lead field investigator of this hepatitis outbreak. I was –"

"I know who you are," he interrupted, "and I know about this outbreak." He declined to shake her hand.

Kris ignored his rudeness. "You'll hear a lot more about it shortly. Please keep an open mind about the research methods that medical scientists sometimes need to use to learn as much as they can as quickly as possible about a new lethal viral disease. I assure you that innocent people are dying from this hepatitis."

"And I assure you also that innocent animals are dying of it. Right here in this building, on this floor, as we speak."

Kris knew that to be true. "Look at it this way. This hepatitis virus is new to us, but probably exists in nature in animals somewhere on this planet. I guarantee you it's killing animals in the wild."

Aburcorn remained impassive. "But the killing here can and will be stopped."

"Let me give you an example," Kris said. "When medical scientists first researched rabies virus trying to develop a vaccine, animal studies were done and I imagine a few died. But the vaccine that resulted from that research has since then *saved* the lives of millions of animals, both domestic and wild."

Aburcorn's demeanor softened slightly. "I'm sure you mean well, but you are involved and will suffer the consequences along with the others. I guess we all do what we believe we have to do."

Kris met his eyes and nodded slowly. "Yes, we do."

Bauman asked everyone to get seated. "Maybe we can talk more after the meeting."

Aburcorn shook his head and walked away to take his place at the conference table.

Kris sat and looked over at Aburcorn. She was disturbed by his threats and seeming cold-hearted determination. *Suffer the consequences? Will be stopped? What could he or would he do? I sure hope Security searched him for weapons.*

Mike Bauman stood up to get the meeting started. "Everyone – please take your seats," he said. "Let's go ahead and begin. All of you should have an agenda. I would first like to welcome and introduce the guests we've invited to this meeting. Starting over to my left is Don Stennet, Epidemiology Branch Chief of Special Viral Pathogens, and next to him is his EIS officer, Jenny Billings. Across from me is Arthur Martino, who is with the Atlanta Field Division office of the DEA."

"Finally, over to my right is Rex Aburcorn, who is the Eastern Region President of the Watchdogs for Animal Rights, or WAR, as the group has been called. As you all surely noticed on your way in this morning, WAR is staging a protest demonstration at the main CDC entrance that targets our Division's use of animals in research."

Bauman looked over at Aburcorn to give him an opportunity to say something, but the WAR leader remained silent. "Mr. Aburcorn had asked to sit in on this meeting. I hope that the presentations he will hear shortly will help him understand the crucial role of animal studies in the investigation of lethal new micro-organisms such as this fulminant hepatitis virus." Aburcorn made no attempt to comment, so Bauman continued. "Speaking of fulminant hepatitis, let me next briefly summarize our past experience with clusters of fulminant hepatitis in injection drug users."

While Bauman was describing the New Bern outbreak and the subsequent large outbreak of hepatitis B – Delta virus in Massachusetts in the 1980s, Kris looked around the room. The DEA representative looked like a baby-faced kid fresh out of training, but Kris smiled as she recalled the Corham coroner's remark about "expectin' someone a little more senior." Twenty CDC people were present in the room, all from the Hepatitis Division except for Jenny and her Branch Chief.

Kris glanced over at Aburcorn, who sat motionless and whose face remained expressionless, almost as if in a trance. His video camera was across the conference room table from where he was sitting. On the table in front of him was a remote control device, which Kris assumed activated and moved the camera.

Aburcorn's odd behavior made Kris uneasy. It also unsettled her gastrointestinal tract, as she began to feel queasy and clammy again. She took a sip of bottled water and tried to concentrate on her presentation notes on the table in front of her.

Bauman said, "And next we'll hear from Kristen Jensen, our lead field investigator on what she found in Mississippi and New Orleans. Kris?"

Kris felt awful, but smiled as she looked around the room. "I'm not feeling quite myself this morning, so I'm going to do this sitting down." She fought back the waves of nausea and managed to finish her presentation in eight of the allotted ten minutes.

Bauman stood up again when she had finished and gave her a thumbs-up sign. "I'm sure there are questions, but we're going to defer them to the discussion time at the end. Next, we'll hear from our Lab Branch Chief, Charles Sable, on the serologic results and what we've found in animal studies so far."

Kris felt that it was inevitable that she was going to vomit. As Charlie started his presentation, she picked up her purse and took a deep breath. She got up, tottered a bit going over to Bauman and whispered, "I'll be right back."

As Kris made her way to the door, she noticed Aburcorn appeared to be meditating. He was oblivious to her departure.

Because the fifth floor women's restroom was still non-functional, rather than barge into the men's, she headed for the back stairwell to use the fourth floor ladies' room in the Influenza Branch offices. She hoped she wouldn't throw up along the way. She did not, but began to retch immediately after closing the stall door behind her.

At 11:22 a.m., four minutes into Charlie Sable's presentation in the Hepatitis Division conference room, Rex Aburcorn looked up at the Lab Branch Chief and shouted, "DEATH TO THE DEATH ANGEL!" He slammed his hand onto the remote control device in front of him. The electronic signal generated activated a detonator embedded in ten pounds of C-4 plastic explosive that had been hidden in an AV equipment bag under the conference room table, as well as the detonator of another ten pounds of C-4 hidden in the Hepatitis laboratory wing. The massive blast shock wave of the twin explosions destroyed internal walls of offices and laboratories, blew out all windows, and caused a partial collapse of the roof. The force of the blasts and the fires they caused left no human or animal survivors on the fifth floor.

The shock wave of the explosions stunned Kris and threw her to the floor of the bathroom stall. The restroom went dark. Pieces of ceiling tile rained down onto her. When she heard the roar and felt the shake of the building collapsing above, she instinctively curled in a ball and covered her head with her arms, unsure of whether she was about to be crushed. When it stopped, all she heard was distant shouting and screaming. She realized where she was and that she was alive and physically intact.

What the hell was that? 9-11 again? She started to cough from the dust and particulate matter in the air. *I need to get out of here and help my friends upstairs.* She groped around the floor in the dark for her purse and found the penlight in it. Stiff and sore all over from being slammed to the floor, she managed to stand up. She was only a little dizzy. The nausea had been overpowered by the adrenalin rush of surviving whatever happened to the building. The penlight helped her get oriented and find the door to the hallway, which was jammed. It opened enough to let her out when she pushed hard.

The air in the hallway was even dustier and harder to breathe. She started to cough again. The penlight was useless in the dusty murk. She was feeling her way toward the back stairwell when she heard, "Help me! Please – somebody!"

"I'm here," Kris answered. "I'll help you." She inched her way toward the voice in the dark and found the woman on the floor. "Are you hurt?"

"I hit my head and something fell on me. I think my right leg is broken."

"Don't worry. I'll help you, but we've got to get out of the building. Can't wait for EMS. We're going to try to go down the back stairwell."

"But my leg hurts so much." The woman started to cry. "I'm scared."

As Kris knelt down beside the woman, she remembered to use the penlight to check her own arms and hands for bleeding. Seeing none, she held the woman's hand and said, "I'm Kris Jensen from Hepatitis. I was using your restroom when this thing hit. What's your name?"

"It's Jessie – Jessie Clark. I'm Dr. Mikel's secretary."

"Okay, Jessie. We're going to get you up on your good leg and I'll support you. I think I see the emergency exit light for the back stairwell. C'mon, we can do it."

Kris helped her up and they hobbled together to the stairwell, but the door would only open a few inches. Acrid smoke came through the partially opened door.

Jessie said, "I smell smoke!"

"Me too. Something's blocking the door. Lean on the wall while I see what it is." Kris pushed hard on the door which only opened another inch. She got down close to the floor. Using the penlight, she saw that it was rock and a big piece of metal. "It's building rubble. I'll try to move it." She pushed at it with her foot and was able to open the door enough to go through and clear the rubble from the other side.

To her relief, the air in the stairwell was clearer and fresher. She thought about trying to get up to the fifth floor but the up staircase looked completely blocked off by rubble that had cascaded down the stairwell from the fifth floor.

A loud crash reverberated overhead and the building shook slightly. Kris smelled smoke again, but she was pretty sure the smoke was being blown down the stairwell which meant that the fire was only above them. Looking up in desperation, the realization hit her hard that it would be hopeless for her to try get up to the fifth floor to help anyone who might still be alive up there. It was probably dangerous even to remain where they were.

"Kris – get me out of here!" Jessie's plea helped clear thoughts of the fifth floor out of Kris' mind and refocus it on getting them out of the building.

"Okay, I'm coming." Together, they made it down a flight of stairs to the first landing. Kris heard people below them. She shouted down the stairwell toward the voices. "Hey, we need help up here!"

Two men came up from the third floor landing. Kris said, "I'm okay, but she might have a broken leg and needs your help to get down to the ground floor."

One of the men said, "No problem, we got her."

The two men took over helping Jessie. Kris said to her, "You'll be fine. I've got to go check on my friends."

Jessie called after her, "Thank you so much, Kris. Bless you."

Kris turned to wave and headed down the stairs. She felt more stiff and sore than ever as she hobbled down the rest of the way, holding onto her purse and the railing as she went.

CDC staff were exiting calmly without pushing or shoving. At the ground floor landing, Dekalb County firemen and paramedics were coming in to help. Kris stopped one of them, pointed up and asked, "What happened up there?"

He looked at her. "Explosion and fire on the top floor. You need to get out."

Aburcorn, she thought and went out the door.

Chapter 17

Outside Building 2 was chaos. Pieces of plaster, tiles, glass and paper littered the ground. CDC staff were streaming out the ground floor exits and moving quickly away from the building. Most appeared to Kris to be uninjured, but many looked scared and a few were crying. EMS workers were assisting the injured. Police officers shouted orders while multiple sirens wailed in the distance. A dozen fire trucks and ambulances had already clogged Clifton Road, and a helicopter circled overhead.

Kris limped away from Building 2, then turned to look back. Parts of the fifth floor outer wall were missing. She could see an area where the roof had collapsed. Thick black smoke billowed from the top of the building and flames licked out from several blown-out windows. The visual impact of the damage to the fifth floor caused Kris to put her hands to her face and sink to her knees.

Oh my God! No one got out alive. How could they have?

A paramedic knelt down next to her. "Ma'am, are you hurt? Do you need help?"

Kris looked at him with tears in her eyes. "I'm all right – b-but those were my friends up there."

The paramedic said, "I'm sorry. Maybe some of them made it out. We need you to move farther away from the building."

Kris nodded. "Okay."

As he helped her up, she noticed for the first time that her arms and clothes were covered with building dust and bits of plaster. She reached up to check her hair. It was caked thick with dust and debris. She wiped a tear from her face and sighed. "I must look like a mess."

The paramedic grinned. "If you're really physically okay, just go home and get cleaned up. Stay with your family. You'll need help with the emotional shock. I need to go in."

"Okay. Thanks." Kris watched him leave. She looked up again at the destruction on the fifth floor. *There's nothing I can do here. Once I'm caught up in the investigation, they won't let me go anywhere and I'll be dead in two or three days. I can do more on my own, maybe with Ed's help.* She looked over at the traffic congestion on Clifton Road. She'd never get her car out. She made her way to a nearby bike rack and commandeered the first one she found unlocked. *I'll return it later.*

Kris walked the bike to Clifton Road. With her purse over her shoulder, she climbed on and wove her way through the cars. It was easy; traffic was at a standstill. On the way to her apartment, she received a number of curious stares from pedestrians and from people in their cars, but Kris didn't notice. The breeze from the ride felt good, and she was preoccupied with the dilemma of being car-less. She pondered her transportation options and possible ways she might get back to New Orleans.

The solution came to her 15 minutes later when she saw Ryan Jaskwich's red Corvette in her parking spot. *I'll have to borrow the 'vette.*

In 20 minutes Kris had showered, changed clothes, and packed the Corvette with her unopened travel bag, snacks and drinks. Her briefcase and computer had been presumably destroyed in the explosion and fire, but she still had her smartphone, credit cards and ID's in her purse. Her narrow escape from the explosion had hypercharged her body's adrenaline output. Her apprehension that enemies might show up on her apartment doorstep at any moment, kept it flowing. The adrenaline kept her moving and seemed to keep the nausea and fatigue away. She considered leaving a note for Janie, but decided to text message her later instead.

The Corvette started right up with a varrrroom sound. It left a patch of rubber as it roared out of the parking lot. Kris was impressed with the pick-up and power of the Corvette as she drove it in the direction of I-85 southbound. *I can't believe I'm driving this muscle car. Better be careful and not get pulled over.* She wanted to get on the Interstate and formulate a plan to get to Venezuela. She would pass right by Hartsfield Airport, but a terrorism alert might shut it down. She didn't want to take the chance of being detained or delayed.

The corvette was approaching the on-ramp for I-85 southbound when it occurred to Kris that it might take seven or eight hours to drive to New Orleans. *Do I really need to return there?* She doubted she had the stamina regardless. She pulled over into a gas station lot and used her phone to search the internet for airline connections to Caracas. She found flights leaving from Miami, Atlanta, and Houston. The overnight flight from Houston International seemed the best bet. Non-stop flights left Birmingham for Houston at 4:00 p.m. and 6:30 p.m. both connecting to the Caracas flight. She made the reservations and nodded.

That's it – Birmingham. Maybe I can convince Ed to meet me in Houston and then talk him into coming to Venezuela. She looked at her watch: 12:20. *Birmingham should be about two hours away on I-20. If I make good time, might even make the four o'clock flight.*

Ten minutes later, after stopping at a post office to mail a note and packet to her mother in Oshkosh, Wisconsin, Kris turned the Corvette onto the westbound lanes of I-20. *Never been to Birmingham – heard it's nice. Randy Newman liked it.* She started to sing his song to try and keep her spirits up. "Birmingham, greatest city in Alabam' – ." She tried to remember more of the lyrics, but her mind kept wandering back to the scene at the CDC. The urge to learn more about the explosion and the aftermath became irresistible. She turned on the radio.

"...latest on the CDC bombing. About an hour ago, a massive explosion destroyed the fifth floor of Building 2 at the CDC complex on Clifton Road. The fifth floor houses the offices and labs of the Hepatitis Division and many are feared dead. A terrorist bomb is suspected. The radical animal rights group Watchdogs for Animal Rights, or WAR as it is called, was protesting the use of research animals by the Hepatitis Division in a demonstration across from the main CDC entrance when the explosion occurred. It's been confirmed that a WAR leader, Rex Aburcorn, was in a meeting on the fifth floor at the time of the blast. He is among the missing and there is speculation that Aburcorn was a suicide bomber. At this hour Dekalb, Fulton, and Cobb county firefighters continue to battle the fifth floor blaze started by the explosion. Stay tuned for further developments as we continue to cover this breaking story."

Kris turned the radio off and wondered how the FBI might figure out that she was still alive. *They'll find my briefcase, but not me. Seems like it would take time to identify the bodies – maybe a good while, if they were blown to pieces and burned up. The whole fifth floor would be a biohazard site.* The scene that she imagined became too troubling and Kris vowed to not think about it anymore.

Maybe the influenza secretary, Jessie, would come forward when she saw my name on the list of those missing – or maybe she'll ask someone to find me to thank me for helping her out of the building. Exactly how the FBI would discover her escape wasn't clear to Kris, but once they even suspected it, evidence such as the commandeered bike and the building dust on her clothing in her apartment would quickly confirm it. *But they wouldn't know why I left – so I'd be a "fugitive material witness" or a "person of utmost interest." – maybe even a possible co-conspirator. They'd do whatever it would take to find me.* She realized that there would be only a limited window of opportunity for her to leave the country.

An hour later near Heflin, Alabama, Kris turned the radio on again. "This just in. The FBI has confirmed that a suicide note signed by Rex Aburcorn has been found in his apartment in Dunwoody. The full text has not been released and federal authorities only revealed that Aburcorn's intent to punish the CDC's Hepatitis Division was clearly stated. In other developments, firefighters have now extinguished the fifth story blaze, which will allow federal investigators in biohazard protective suits to begin the search for human remains and for clues to the nature and location of the explosive device that was used. We now go live to our reporter at the scene of today's tragedy."

"This is Melissa Blenheim reporting live from the CDC on Clifton Road. Family and friends of the missing CDC staff have been arriving here in the last two hours, clinging to hopes that their loved ones may have somehow survived. I spoke with Jeannie Bauman earlier, whose husband Mike is Epidemiology Branch Chief for the Hepatitis Division. He is among the missing. Here is her statement:"

"I can only s-say that the Hepatitis Division – we are like a family of friends. Please pray for our loved ones, – for Mike – I can't do this. Please –"

The sound of Jeannie Bauman crying brought a lump to Kris' throat. She turned the radio off. Her lip quivered, and tears began to stream down her face. At the next exit, she drove off the interstate onto a frontage road. She stopped the car on the shoulder of the road as her own sobbing became uncontrollable. The outpouring of her pent-up grief continued as she buried her face in her arms on the steering wheel. She looked outside to see if anyone was watching her. A small white church stood up on a hill beyond a line of trees. She felt the need to go there.

She drove into the parking lot of the Mission Hill Presbyterian Church. The main building was a wooden frame structure that shone a bright white in the early afternoon sun. She was still crying as she tried the front entrance door. It was locked, but a side door was open. She entered the sanctuary, which was empty and quiet, lit only by the sunlight coming through the stained glass windows. Her sobbing continued as she knelt to whisper a prayer.

"My spirit struggles on this awful dark day. I cry for my friends and co-workers that are gone. I don't understand why I survived – I would have given up my few remaining days to save any of their lives. Bless their families. Comfort them in their sorrow and the pain of their loss – a loss that I also feel so deeply. I pray for the strength and the spirit to carry on, – for guidance to find answers to this terrible hepatitis. I pray not to harm anyone whom I contact in any way. I know my life is near an end. I hope to rejoin my father. As my body fails, help me to keep a clear mind and control of my actions, – and please allow me to keep my sense of humor – until the very end of my days."

Kris drew a slow deep breath. Her crying had stopped, but she felt emotionally drained. She wondered if she would ever be able to laugh about anything again. She had read once that forced loud vocalization of belly laughter, even when not genuine and nothing funny about the circumstances, caused a release of endorphins in the brain that made the laugher feel better. She had tried it once before, and it seemed to work.

Okay, here goes. God will understand.

Kris closed her eyes and started to vocalize forced belly laughs, guffaws, hoots, and chortles that reverberated through the sanctuary.

"Hah-Hah-Hah, Haw-Haw-Haw – " She had just started to feel better when she opened her eyes to see the pastor of the church standing next to the pulpit and watching her intently. "Ooops!" she said as she put a hand to her mouth.

"How can I help you?" he asked in a calm voice.

"Oh, you must be the pastor, because I'm feeling really sheepish," Kris said. "Believe me, I'm not a nutcase escaped from an asylum. I was at the CDC today and lost many friends in the bombing. I happened upon your church when I was feeling really down. I had to stop to grieve for them and pray for their families." She explained the theory of releasing endorphins with forced laughter.

"Now I understand." The pastor looked relieved. "I thought maybe you'd been possessed by a laughing hyena."

Kris shook her head as she laughed for real.

"I'm Pastor John VandeKamp," he said as he offered his hand.

She took it and held onto it tightly. "I'm Kris."

VandeKamp nodded and offered his other hand as well. "Shall we pray together?"

"Yes," she said. " – please." Tears welled in her eyes again.

A few minutes later, she was about to leave. Kris turned to the pastor and said, "Thank you. I'd like to come back and visit some Sunday."

"I'm glad you came here today," he said. "You are most welcome to return anytime." He paused. "It must be true that our brain's centers for laughing and for crying are close and interlinked. Both of those emotions can be quite therapeutic."

"I agree completely," Kris said. She waved good-bye and went out the door. At the Corvette, she stopped and looked back at the Mission Hill Presbyterian Church. She felt her spirit had been renewed. *I pray I do get a chance to come back here to give thanks.* She put on her sunglasses and got into the car. *I need to call Ed.*

****

The two poker-faced men in business suits entered the orthopedic ward at Dekalb County hospital. They showed their FBI badges and ID cards to the charge nurse and a hospital administrator, who accompanied them to the room of Jessie Clark.

The more senior agent spoke to her first as he displayed his badge. "Good afternoon, Miss Clark. We're with the FBI. I'm Special Agent Steve Garner and this is my partner Jonas Peterson. We're investigating the CDC bombing. I understand that you asked to get in touch with Dr. Kris Jensen. Why is that?"

Jessie Clark looked at them. "She saved my life by getting me off the fourth floor. That's what she said her name was. I wanted to thank her."

Peterson showed her a picture of Kris Jensen. "Is this the woman who helped you?"

She shrugged. "Could be. It was dark, and she was covered with dust. She told me her name. Is she in trouble?"

"No," Garner said, "but we have a lot of questions we want to ask her, if she *is* alive."

"Unless an impersonator helped me, she is. She said she was going to look for her friends when I last saw her going down the stairs. Where is she, then?"

Garner glanced at his partner. "We don't know. Her car is still in the lot at CDC. She's missing, and we thought she had been killed in the blast until you asked someone to find her."

"Why would she leave?"

"That's a really good question," Peterson said. "Did she say how she happened to be on the fourth floor?"

"She said she had used our ladies' room. I seem to remember that theirs on the fifth floor was broken."

"Anything else you remember?" Garner asked.

"Only that I was very thankful she was there."

Peterson said, "Thank you very much for your co-operation. Here's my card. We may want to ask you more questions. If you think of anything else, call me anytime."

"I bet she's alive." Garner said as the FBI agents left the hospital. "Maybe even a co-conspirator. We'll need all her numbers – phone, credit cards, passport. We need to move fast and bring her in. Start with her home residence."

Chapter 18

Kris had the Corvette on cruise control at 70 mph and was about 50 miles east of Birmingham. She had found Ryan Jaskwich's cellphone in the car and had decided to use it as a more secure phone to call Ed, but she was unsure whether it would be safer to call his cell phone or his number at the Orleans Parish Health Department. She opted for the cell, but only got his voicemail prompt. "*This is Ed. – Go ahead. – Leave a message instead.*" Without using her name, she said, "Call me back at this number. Use a safe phone."

While she waited for his return call, she switched on the radio for the latest news on the CDC bombing. "This just in: – Fire rescue teams in biohazard gear have completed their search of the fifth floor and found no survivors. Removal and forensic identification of the remains of the victims of the blast and fire will begin later today. In other developments, federal investigators have found a detonator of the type used to ignite C-4, the plastic explosive now suspected as the cause of the blast. More background is now also known about the alleged bomber, Rex Aburcorn. He was a Vietnam veteran who developed chronic health problems that he attributed to his wartime Agent Orange exposure. He has been a member of several radical anti-government activist groups, and most recently was the Eastern Region President of WAR. Finally, one Hepatitis Division staff survivor has been identified: a secretary named Gina Poluzzi who was off the floor taking an early lunch at the time of the blast. She is being questioned by the FBI. Stay tuned as we bring you live updates . . . "

Kris was smiling as she turned the radio off. "Finally some good news."

She had just washed down a couple of snack crackers with a drink of water when Ryan's cellphone rang. She didn't recognize the number, but it was a New Orleans area code. She assumed it was Ed.

"Kris! I can't believe it's you," Ed said. "The FBI called me earlier to tell me there was an unsubstantiated report that you'd helped someone get out of the building, and to ask me if I had heard from you."

"I'm definitely alive," said Kris. "That's the good news."

"That's great news! So where are you? Why is the FBI having to look for you?"

"Can't tell you right now. I'll explain later. Are you calling from a safe phone?"

"Yeah. A public pay phone here in the Health Department."

"Are you being followed?"

"Now who's being paranoid? Though I *have* gotten the feeling more than once, but I haven't spotted anyone and no one's tried to run me over."

"I need you to take the next flight you can get on and meet me at Houston International. I'll be there in a couple of hours."

Ed hesitated. "What's the rush? An FBI agent wants to interview me at 4:30 this afternoon."

"The Caracas flight leaves tonight. I want to talk to you in person and convince you to come with me."

"What do I tell my Director and the FBI?"

"The usual excuse. Your favorite granny's on her deathbed and you need to rush to her side."

He laughed. "I used that one six months ago and it was actually the truth."

"Then your grandaddy, or another far away-living favorite relative that they can't easily check up on."

"Kris – Tell me the truth. Are you in trouble? Did you do something illegal?"

"No, and emphatic no."

"Okay. I'll meet you."

"Be sure to ditch whoever might be tracking you. Pack a light carry-on bag and don't forget your passport. Text me your airline flight number and arrival time. I'll meet you at your gate."

"No problemo. I've got a million questions."

"They'll have to wait. Don't call me unless absolutely necessary."

"Check. See you in Houston."

Kris hung up. It would be good to see Ed. He was the only person left she could trust or count on.

Her stomach felt queasy again, and her wounded finger started to throb. *These symptoms are only going to get worse. At least I had a little reprieve.* She peeled back the Band-aid on her left index finger. The wound had turned into a rubbery dry ulcer. *Looks just like the others I've seen.* She drank more water. It would be best to try and keep her mind otherwise occupied.

The Corvette was humming along. She decided to use the phone again, to call Dan Stevens. If the FBI hadn't gotten to him yet, he would co-operate if she asked him to keep quiet.

He answered on the first ring and she explained that she couldn't talk about the CDC bombing.

"I'm just glad you somehow made it out," he said.

"I last talked to you Tuesday, I think. What's going on in Corham?"

"LaDonna's in the Medical ICU at UT-Memphis, and they're considering a liver transplant."

"Oh, really? I never did talk to her docs up there. It would seem to me that a transplant might buy her a few days, but in the end it would just be pumping fuel into the inferno." She sighed. "Just three days ago we were chatting with her. Anyone else sick?"

"No, but Bubba Watkins came to see me at the health department today."

"He was Junior's other drug user buddy."

"Yeah. He'd been away for ten days and just found out about the hep deaths. Turns out Junior had told Bubba that he knew about Billy Herman's lust for LaDonna, and that Junior had a plan to get rid of Billy permanently."

Kris nodded. "So I bet Junior got the sparkle heroin he knew was lethal from King Dewey and killed Billy with it –in exchange for a free dragon tattoo, which then caused his own lethal infection. And while Junior was away getting tattooed, Billy assaulted LaDonna and infected her."

"That would explain what happened," Stevens said. "The best-laid crime plans can sure backfire."

"And hurt a lot of innocent people in the process," Kris said. "There are still loose ends in New Orleans – like who supplied the sparkle drug and then paid or forced King Dewey to distribute it. I'm sure King Dewey gave it to the drug user who died at Parish General."

"Let me know if I can help."

Kris saw a sign ahead for the exit to the Birmingham airport. "Listen, Dan, I may not get another chance to say this, but I have the greatest respect and appreciation for you and your staff's work out there in the front line trenches of public health. I could not have gotten this far without your help."

"Thanks. It was a privilege and pleasure to work with you. Keep me posted."

"I'll do my best."

At the Birmingham airport, Kris left the Corvette in the long-term parking lot. It was 3:10 p.m. She was tired from the drive, and the walk to the airline ticket counter wore her out even more. She checked in for the 4:00 flight to Houston and found a ladies' room.

Her urine was much darker. Washing up, she could see that her face, instead of being thinner, was puffier than normal. She looked as tired as she felt. The normally white sclera of her eyes was definitely yellow-tinged, even in the artificial light of the restroom. *That'll only get worse. I'll need to wear sunglasses to keep from spooking people.*

Her flight departed on time. Kris was asleep in her seat even before take-off.

****

In the Atlanta office of the FBI, Steve Garner was sitting at his desk when Jonas Peterson called and said, "Surveillance just got a GPS fix on Dr. Jensen's smartphone. She's on an airplane."

Chapter 19

The two hour flight from Birmingham to Houston International airport was smooth and quiet. Kris awoke to the preparation-for-landing announcement but still felt tired, despite the long nap. As the jetliner rolled to a stop on the runway, a sudden apprehension came over her that someone, either the FBI or one of her enemies, was waiting for her in the terminal. *Or maybe my liver dysfunction has started to mess with my mind.* She decided it was probably just anxiety. Still, to her relief, as she emerged from the walkway with the other passengers, no one in the terminal seemed to pay any particular attention to her.

She sat down to check Ryan's cellphone for messages and found that Ed had texted that he was on a Delta flight scheduled to arrive in 45 minutes. A clock on the wall indicated 7:15 local time. *The Caracas flight departs 11:15, so I should have plenty of time to talk him into coming with me.*

The walk to the arrival gate for Ed's flight tired her out even more. She stopped to rest at an Internet kiosk and sent Cory Flint an e-message with her Caracas flight information. She asked that he text back when and where she could meet with him. When she arrived at the Delta gate to wait for Ed, her fatigue and sleepiness from the antihistamine that she had taken for nausea made her doze off again. She woke up to the overhead announcement of the arrival of the flight from New Orleans.

Ed was among the last of the passengers to exit the walkway into the terminal. He waved and smiled when he spotted Kris. He came over to her and gave her a quick hug, but stepped back with a concerned expression on his face. "Hey, you don't look so good."

"I know. I've been through a lot in the 14 hours since I left you in New Orleans. Let's go find a more private place to talk."

Near the end of the terminal they found a gate that was not in use and sat down in the waiting area.

Ed spoke first. "So tell me about the CDC. How did you get out?"

Kris recounted what happened at the Hepatitis Division meeting, including Aburcorn's strange behavior and the reason she left the conference room. She described how she and Jessie Clark got out of the building and the chaotic scene outside. "I looked up and saw the destruction on the fifth floor. There was nothing I could do to help, so I left."

"Without talking to anyone?"

Kris nodded.

Ed looked puzzled. "But why not stay to help with the investigation?"

"It would've tied me up too long. I've only got a couple of days."

He was even more perplexed. "Couple of days? What does that mean?"

She had to tell him. "Ed, I'm going to die of this hepatitis – the same virus that killed Junior Murphee and the other drug users." She peeled off the Band-aid. "Here, look at my finger. I got a needle stick last Monday after I drew heart blood from Junior's corpse."

Ed was stunned. The visual proof of the ulcer on her index finger left him speechless. He collected himself, then reached out to hold her hand. "So that's the reason you've been sick the last few days?"

Kris nodded again. "Yup, although I did feel bad about blaming my symptoms on New Orleans cuisine."

"So the FBI doesn't know you're sick, or why you left CDC."

"That's right. They don't. By now they probably have evidence of my departure, and are most anxious to find me – "

Ed finished her sentence. "For possible involvement in the bombing. They'll track credit card use, cellphone use. I've heard that they can even use the signal from your smartphone to pinpoint your GPS location."

"I hope so."

"You do?"

"I left it turned on and express mailed it to my mother in Wisconsin before I left Atlanta."

"Clever," he said, "but that won't throw them off for long."

"I know. That's why I've got to leave tonight."

"Kris – " Ed stared down at his hands as he rubbed them together. He looked up at her. "This idea to go to Venezuela – it's crazy. Nothing will come of it. You should be in the NIH Clinical Science Center or at Mayo Clinic for treatment, or at the least be at home with your family in the last few days."

Kris' eyes narrowed. She pointed her index finger at him. "Don't you dare tell me what to do! I'm not dead yet. Whose life is it, anyway? No one knows how to treat this hepatitis. Let them experiment with their poisons on someone else, and my family will just have to understand my decision."

Ed was taken aback at the vehemence of her response. He sat silent as he tried to think of another way to convince Kris not to go.

She leaned toward him. "You'll have to come up with a much better reason than that to get me to stay. C'mon – give me your best shot."

He got up to look out the window at the airport tarmac below, then turned to face her. "Did you know that the world's largest spiders, the goliath bird-eaters with a leg span of 12 inches, live in Venezuela?"

Kris swallowed hard. "You made that up. Even if you didn't, I'm going anyway."

He shrugged. "Actually, it *is* true, but those spiders live in the jungle swamps in the southeast part, not in the western mountain valleys where we're going."

Kris relaxed into exhilaration at his last two words. She jumped to her feet to hug him. "Then it's settled. We're out of here."

As they sat down again, Ed sighed. "Okay. I did bring my passport. What about tickets? Flight info?"

"I already bought you a ticket. We're booked on the 11:15 Continental flight that arrives in Caracas at 6:00 a.m. tomorrow."

He made a face. "I never sleep well on airplanes."

"I've got antihistamines."

"Where are we staying in Caracas?"

Kris shook her head. "We won't stay unless we have to. I want to meet with Cory Flint early tomorrow and have him tell us the best way to get to the Yachabo homeland in El Valle Amarillo. I just sent him another e-mail to ask for his phone number."

"Have you heard from him yet?"

"Not yet."

He put his hand to his forehead. "Kris, c'mon. Let's rethink this."

Kris stiffened and glared at him. "I haven't exactly had much time to fine-tune plans for this trip to the nth degree of your satisfaction."

"Okay. Sorry. I guess if Flint is a no-show, we could find someone else to help us get there. We may have to charter a plane."

"I thought of that. It may be the best way to get there."

Ed leaned forward to get a closer look at her face. "Hey, your eyes have started to get jaundiced."

"I know. You should see the dark tea color of my urine. And look at this bruise!" She pulled up the sleeve of her blouse to reveal a large purple blotch under the skin of her right forearm. She shook her head. "I don't remember even bumping my arm."

"Your face looks a little puffy."

"Talk about puffy, look at these legs." She raised her skirt to show him her swollen legs. "Mine are gone," she said, "replaced by somebody else's!" She threw up her hands in mock amazement.

He didn't laugh or even smile. "What about when you get encephalopathic?"

"Oh, when I get goofy and irreverent? How would you tell?"

"You know what I mean. When you get lethargic, confused, and inappropriate as a sign of toxin build-up due to liver failure."

Kris' face turned serious. "That's one of my biggest fears – when I can't think clearly and start to lose control. Maybe the mission hospital will have a supply of lactulose."

"It's been a while since I prescribed it. How does lactulose help again?"

"It's a sugar taken orally that's metabolized. It binds ammonia in the colon and excretes it, which decreases the blood ammonia level. It's mainly helpful to reverse symptoms in the early stages of encephalopathy, when there's still a little liver function left."

Ed nodded. "It might be sold over-the-counter in Caracas. We can find a drug store and ask."

"But once I'm in a coma, let me go on out. No CPR – it'd be futile, and I wouldn't want anyone to get infected trying to resuscitate me."

He looked glum. "It's still really hard for me to even imagine that happening to you."

Kris shrugged. "I was in denial at first, but now I'm more realistic about what's to come. I've not given up, though. Hey – I'm down but not out. I do want to make the best of the time I have left, and that includes having a little fun. Like Will Rogers once said, 'We're all here for a spell. Get all the good laughs that you can.' I intend to."

"I'll try to keep it light and help get you some of those good laughs."

"That'd be great, but there are some ground rules. We can go over them later on the plane. Let's go check in and get through security before my name shows up on a no-fly list. Oh, by the way, I'm now your wife, Anna Kristen Jensen-Beaufain. That's Jensen hyphen Beaufain. We just got married and I've kept my maiden name, so my ID's the same. Anna actually is my given first name. I've never used it, but I thought now would be a good time to start. "

He offered her his arm. "Yes, my darling Anna. Shall we go?"

Kris took it. "And one more thing. If anyone needs to know about my obvious ill health, I have advanced liver cancer and we plan to consult with an immunotherapy specialist in Caracas."

"Is there one in the city?"

"Yeah, I found him on the Internet, a Dr. Rafael Izquierda."

Ed nodded. "Very good, my dear. Let's be on our way."

In the International terminal, they checked in for their flight and went through the departure security and customs checkpoints without any difficulty. In the waiting area, they found another private place to sit and talk.

"I'm glad we made it through security," Kris said. "I'll feel even better when our plane leaves U.S. airspace."

"If they figure out we left for Venezuela, they might try to intercept us there," Ed said.

"We'll worry about that later. Let me tell you what Dan Stevens said." She related what Stevens had reported from Corham, and smiled at Ed. "So, dear hubby, tell me about *your* day at work."

"I met with Pete Diamond this morning."

"Your detective friend at NOPD?"

Ed nodded. "Found out from him that Hugo was found dead in his apartment by his landlord about a week ago. The Medical Examiner ruled it a natural death from liver failure, so no autopsy was done. His real name was Hugh Goforth and Pete told me he had a long track record of narcotics-related arrests. Hugo's also been shot twice in the past by other junkies for stealing their narcotics."

"Then, maybe Hugo stole some of the sparkle drug from King Dewey and used it not knowing it contained the virus."

"That's plausible, or maybe King Dewey had another reason to get rid of him and just gave him the drug."

Kris shrugged. "Only King Dewey would know. Is Diamond going to interview him?"

"He wants to, but said I needed to be there. Oh, and listen to this tidbit. Pete introduced me to Dominic Russo, who's been an NOPD narc for twenty years. He told me that they had King Dewey nailed in a narcotics sting about two months ago but the DEA got him off the hook. Otherwise he'd be in prison. Supposedly the DEA needed him for an important project, but they wouldn't give Russo any details."

"Do you think Foster lied to us? He should've remembered that when we asked him about King Dewey."

Ed shook his head. "Russo said it was X-Ops people that got King Dewey off. Foster might not even have known about it. Maybe that pickle-puss X-Ops guy – Swanson, I think his name was – knew all about King Dewey but didn't tell us."

"If that's the case, X-Ops must have created the virus beads and distributed the contaminated drug using King Dewey and others like him."

"That would make sense. But why do it?"

"It would have to be as a new deterrent to drug use," Kris said, "to decrease demand. This virus is too rapidly lethal to be secondarily transmitted to more than a few other drug users, so it would never wipe them all out." She paused to consider the ramifications. "But it would work best as a deterrent if they kept the source and transmission of the virus a mystery. They knew CDC would investigate the fulminant case clusters, so they probably shadowed my investigation. When I figured out the King Dewey connection, they got concerned enough to try and get rid of me. Then when we found Renk's sparkle drug, that must have really gotten them desperate because it's the key evidence for a conspiracy."

"But now one of our drug vials has been obliterated in the CDC bombing and the other is in Swanson's possession. If we ask for it back, I bet he'd say it was destroyed as per some standard DEA protocol."

Kris raised her eyebrows. "If this is all true, then you and I are the only ones on to them, and they're not through trying to kill us."

Ed's eyes met hers. "I think you're right. And in a foreign country, they're not going to dick around with a KO anymore."

"Can you handle a gun?"

"Yeah, but I'm not experienced with high powered, military-type firearms."

Kris said, "I've always been an anti-gun type myself, but I would use one to protect you. If they shoot me, it just hastens the inevitable."

"Let's talk to Flint about it. Hopefully he can be trusted."

"I guess we'll find out tomorrow."

****

Jonas Peterson hung up the telephone and walked into the adjacent office at the Atlanta headquarters of the FBI. "Milwaukee just confirmed Jensen wasn't on the Delta flight from Hartsfield. The signal came from a mailsack. She express mailed her phone to her mother in Oshkosh."

Steve Garner put his hand to his chin and rubbed it. "We haven't been able to connect her to Aburcorn in any way, so why would she leave *and* try to throw us off? –if she weren't guilty of something."

Peterson shrugged. "We'll just have to find her to find out."

"I agree. What did you find at her apartment?"

We found clothing that her roommate confirmed as Jensen's that had building dust on it. There was a bicycle in the back that she probably used to get home from CDC."

"Anything to indicate where she went?"

"The roommate, a Miss Janine Jaskwich – " Peterson paused and shook his head. "What a dingbat! Anyway, she reported her brother's Corvette missing from their parking lot. The key was gone from their apartment, so I'm sure Jensen took the 'vette." Peterson chuckled.

"What's so funny?"

"Miss Jaskwich. She's convinced she's dead meat. Going to be immediately butchered by her brother tomorrow when he finds his car gone. She demanded a new identity in the witness protection program, or her blood will be on our hands."

Garner rolled his eyes. "Sounds like my teenage daughter. Did the description of the Corvette go out?"

Peterson nodded. "The post office Jensen used to mail the phone was next to I-85, so she could've headed in any direction."

"Okay. Thanks. By the way, Naomi Wong in the New Orleans office called me to say that her interview with Eduardo Beaufain got postponed. Beaufain gave her some cockamamie excuse about a favorite relative about to croak. Naomi tracked him onto a Delta flight to Houston, but lost his trail there."

"Oh really?" said Peterson. "Think he and Jensen got together?"

"Could be."

"Is she on the no-fly list?"

Garner shook his head. "Not yet. We've got zero evidence to link her to the bombing, and she even saved someone's life on her way out of the building. Yeah, maybe borrowed a bike and a car, but that's it. We'll find her. I doubt she'll leave the country."

****

In the downtown Atlanta offices of the DEA, Agent Bill Swanson looked up as Special Agent Eric Sanders entered the room and closed the door behind him.

Sanders spoke first. "The FBI's confirmed that Jensen somehow got out alive and uninjured, and then left the scene and left Atlanta – without talking to anyone. They're after her as a material witness and possible co-conspirator. Why would she take off like that?"

Swanson shook his head. "Who knows? But it gives us a chance to finish the job on her before the FBI finds her. We need to keep working them for their latest information."

Sanders nodded.

"So tell me again," Swanson asked, "how did you let Beaufain get out of New Orleans?"

"Jones was all set up for the shot, but we never saw Beaufain leave the Public Health building," Sanders said. "He must've hidden in the back of one of their vans. They're coming and going all the time."

"We can't keep screwing up like that. If we're lucky, they've found each other and we can take them both out at the same time. Foster told me she intended to go to Venezuela to investigate the source of the virus. He gave her Corey Flint's name and number as a contact." Swanson closed his eyes and shook his head slightly. "Of all people. Anyway, call Cory and at least find out if she's headed to Caracas."

Sanders made a face. "You know how hard it is to get in touch with that drunk. If he's not at a bar closing it down, he's out spending the night with his latest *chica* and then sleeps all morning."

"Try to call anyway, and send him an e-mail. I've got a feeling our two doctors may already be on their way to Venezuela."

****

A 12:30 a.m. telephone call awakened Steve Garner at home.

"It's Jamison here. We just got an alert that an Anna Jensen, same passport number as Kristen, is on a Continental flight from Houston to Caracas. The plane is over international waters off the Texas gulf coast. Do we call it back?"

Garner sighed. "No, don't. Venezuela's not the easiest country to work with, but we'll catch up with her there. Beaufain flew to Houston, so he's probably with her. Send both their pictures to our contact in Caracas so that he can meet the plane and tail them until we can get a couple of our guys down there. See who's available in Miami, brief them, and fly them down in one of our planes."

"Got it."

Chapter 20

Kris was settled into a window seat next to Ed in the coach section of the Boeing 757. Out the window, she could see the lights of Galveston behind them, while below was only the inky blackness of the Gulf of Mexico. She had taken another 90-minute nap in the international departure waiting area. Because she felt more secure in Ed's presence, she had slept more deeply and was now a little more rested. Just before they boarded the aircraft, she had texted Janie the location of Ryan's Corvette and had found a message from Cory Flint.

Ed noticed that she was awake. "Want to talk, or just go back to sleep?"

"I'm not tired right now."

"Tell me again what Flint said."

"Not much. He said 6:30 a.m. was his middle of the night, but that he would meet us at the airport."

"He must stay up late and like to sleep in. So what do we know about him?"

Kris shrugged. "Not a whole lot. When the DEA was accused of spying and got booted out of the country a few years ago, Flint quit his job as assistant chief of operations and stayed on in Caracas. He does drug control-related consultant work, mainly for the government. Foster warned me he's often difficult to reach."

"How old is he?"

"I got the impression that he was with DEA a long time, so maybe 50 or 60 something."

Ed was silent, then said, "Maybe he can give us an insight into the X-Ops program and how they might have obtained a lethal Venezuelan virus."

"If he does know something, hopefully he'll be willing to talk," Kris said. "It's still painful for me to think about but I wanted to ask you about Aburcorn. Do you think he acted alone?"

"I watched the TV coverage while you were asleep. It was definitely C-4 that was used. How would he get a supply of a highly restricted military explosive without help?"

"I heard animal rights activists have used it before."

"I heard that too, but the bomb experts investigating the building damage now suspect two explosions occurred, each with up to 10 pounds of C-4. Even though Aburcorn was a Vietnam vet, he would've had to have acquired that amount more recently."

"In what unit did he serve when he was in Nam?"

Ed shook his head. "They didn't say."

"If anyone supplied him, it would have to be our friends at X-Ops. A DEA guy was killed – but maybe they sacrificed him."

"That'd be pretty ruthless. So why would Aburcorn agree to a suicide mission like that?"

Kris shrugged. "He looked pretty gaunt. Maybe he had a terminal disease and this was an opportunity to both end his life on his own terms and also make a big statement for his cause."

"That would make sense."

"The only way X-Ops could get away with the bombing would be if they set up someone like Aburcorn to willingly participate in the plot and then plausibly absorb all the blame for it."

Ed nodded.

Kris started to laugh. "It's kind of ironic. I got sick from their virus scheme, and that's what saved me from their bombing scheme."

Ed didn't even smile. "I don't think your hepatitis is so funny."

"But I have the right to laugh about it because I have the infection. We need to go over the ground rules related to humor and laughter domains."

"Domains?"

"Humor and laughter domains are someone's *personal* attributes such as heritage and other background, education and training, health problems, and so on that he or she can legitimately make jokes and laugh about. Yours would include yourself, of course, and your relatives, but also adult men, Hispanics, Cajuns, doctors, Southerners, and whatever health issues you have. Mine would include myself, my family, single adult heterosexual women, Swedes, Germans, Caucasians, doctors, CDC, Wisconsin cheeseheads, and beer drinking. My hepatitis adds death and dying as fodder for laughs."

"I get it."

"It's also legitimate for everyone to joke about what I call Big Powers – big government, big Pharma, big tobacco, the insurance industry, and big professions such as doctors, lawyers, and politicians. The safest subject though is always oneself and if someone is honest, there's usually a deep humor well to draw from."

Ed raised his eyebrows. "So I can't tell a fat joke?"

"You can, but you have to personalize it to make yourself the target."

"How so?"

"You could say, 'I was fat once. Tried to watch what I ate but the food moved too fast for my eyes to follow.'"

Ed smiled. "So no ethnic slur jokes either. Not that I tell them, but the kids I grew up with told them all the time."

"Put-down humor like that is pretty common among children," Kris said. "It comes from peer pressure and often reflects the parent's views. But as adults – it's like the German writer-philosopher Goethe once said, 'There is nothing in which people more betray their character than in what they laugh at.' But I do admit that, according to my mother, my Swedish father – who had a wonderful sense of humor – did tell more than a few dumb Norwegian and stupid Finn jokes. Although maybe that was still legit, within his Scandinavian domain."

Ed sat with his eyes downcast with his hands clenched together. "I'm still not sure how to handle humor related to your – dying of this illness."

She put her hand on his shoulder. "Ed, don't worry about it. That part comes from me. I just want you to be open to it and supportive. We'll have lots of opportunities for laughs in the situations we find ourselves in over the next couple of days. Let's both keep it light. I know you have a good sense of humor. It'll reduce the stress on both of us."

"I'll do my best."

"Good. Listen, tomorrow may be a long, hard day. I need to get some sleep."

Ed yawned. "Me too."

Announcements in both Spanish and English of the aircraft's initial descent for landing at the Simon Bolivar airport in Maiquetia near Caracas roused Kris from sleep at 6:00 a.m. local time. She stretched and looked over at Ed who had a cup of coffee in one hand, and a breakfast roll in the other.

He noticed that she had awakened. "Didn't think you wanted any of this. The coffee's pretty strong."

She shook her head. "I'll just have a drink of your *agua, por favor.*"

"You know more Spanish than you let on. Here's your water."

Just then Kris started to feel clammy and nauseated. She grabbed her purse and blurted, "I need to go to the restroom *now.*"

He got up to let her out and watched with concern as she wobbled down the aisle and almost fall.

Kris returned after about fifteen minutes. "Sorry I took so long. I threw up and then had to clean up after myself. We need to find a drug for nausea other than anti-histamines. I'm out of Phenergan."

"We'll try to get something when we look for lactulose in Caracas." Ed was silent for a moment. "Kris – are you sure you don't want to just head home on the next flight?"

She made a face at him and spoke slowly and emphatically. "I – am – totally – sure." She paused to make sure he got the message. "By the way, my eyes have gotten really yellow, so I'll wear sunglasses a lot. Oh and I've got three new bruises on my legs. Did you remember to pack my shin guards, elbow pads and crash helmet, dear?"

Her facetious question struck Ed him as very funny. He started to laugh and continued until tears started to stream down his cheeks. His laughter made Kris start. After they had both calmed down, he said, "That was one of those good laughs. I do feel less stressed."

"I agree," Kris said. "Also, before I forget, give me the barfbag out of the seatpocket in front of you. I may need it later."

As the aircraft descended over the Venezuelan coastline, Kris could see the lights of Caracas in the distance. The morning sky was light enough to see the outline of bluish-hued mountains behind the city. She wondered what it was going to be like to die in a strange land. She was not afraid of dying. Her concern was the loss of self-control that would precede her death. She also feared abandonment, but she knew Ed would stick with her until the end. She glanced at him and softly touched his arm in thanks for his presence and support.

Kris wondered what her father's last coherent words and thoughts had been before he died in Rhodesia. She had never asked her mother about it because Kris was always afraid it might be too painful for her to talk about. *I should have asked her. Dad probably didn't know what was going to happen to him or denied it. It's so sad when people don't get a chance to say good-bye or to tell someone they love them. Maybe I'll get to ask Dad myself.*

The 757 landed with a jolt and a screech of the tires on the runway, followed by the roar of the jet engines reversing thrust to slow the aircraft to taxi speed. As they stepped off the plane onto the covered walkway, Kris felt the tropical heat and humidity envelop her.

Ed noticed it too. "It should be cooler in the mountains where we're headed."

"I hope so," Kris said.

Inside the International Terminal, they waited in the queue for foreign nationals. The line moved fairly quickly, as it seemed to be just a passport check and stamp. As they waited, Ed turned to Kris and asked, "Do you know what Flint looks like?"

Kris shook her head. "I was hoping he'd be holding up a sign with my name, like those limo drivers do when they pick up a passenger."

When it was their turn to go through the checkpoint, the passport official gave them a perfunctory smile and said, "*Bienvenidos.*" Kris assumed that was a welcome, so she smiled back. The official only glanced at Ed and his passport before he stamped it. He looked at Kris' passport, then at her, again at the passport and said, "There is a problem."

Kris was about to ask what kind of problem when Ed took over in Spanish. "*Que clase de problema?*"

The official answered in Spanish. Ed whispered to her, "He wants to know what kind of illness you have, because you look a lot sicker than your passport picture."

"Remember what I said to say. Don't even hint at any infection."

Ed's answer seemed to satisfy the official. He stamped Kris' passport, much to her relief. But they had hardly gotten three steps past the passport control booth when the official said, "*Un momento, por favor. Vengan conmigo.*"

"Uh-oh. He wants us to come with him," Ed said. "We'd better do it."

The official took back their passports and led them down a hallway without a word in response to any of Ed's questions in Spanish. They took an elevator up one floor. He escorted them down another hallway to a closed door guarded by a burly security type, who scowled at them and who had a holstered pistol in plain view.

Kris whispered, "I don't like this – not at all."

"Me neither," Ed replied.

The passport official nodded at the security guard and knocked on the door. There came a muffled voice response from other side of the door. The official said, "*Si, tengo los dos Norteamericanos.*" Another unintelligible reply came from inside the room. The official returned their passports, opened the door, and gestured for them to enter.

Inside the room, a middle-aged man sat at a table blowing a chewing gum bubble with his eyes locked onto a computer tablet as he scrolled through messages. He was stocky with a reddish bulbous nose and a close-cropped gray beard. He wore an open-collar, short-sleeve tropical flowered shirt, loose trousers and sandals. He looked up at them as they entered and sucked the gum bubble back in. Kris, not knowing what to expect, stopped just inside the room and waited for him to speak first.

The man stood up, smiled, and extended his hand. "You must be Dr. Jensen. Welcome to Venezuela. I'm Coronado Flint. Call me Cory."

Chapter 21

Kris wasn't sure why, but she liked Cory Flint as soon as she shook his hand. She introduced Ed and they sat down at the table. Flint offered coffee; Ed helped himself to a cup.

Kris spoke first. "I'm so glad you – ah – found us. We were just wondering how we were going to identify you in the airport crowd. And we appreciate that you came out to meet us. Dennis Foster said you are *the man* in Caracas."

"Yes – my friend, Dennis. A good man himself. We started out together in the DEA."

"Do you miss it?" Kris asked.

"Nah. I do a lot of similar work, but get paid better. Much more freedom to come and go, dress as I like, or smoke a joint without worry over a drug test. My mother is from a town near Lake Maracaibo and we spent summers there when I was a kid. Venezuela is a country filled with natural beauty, and that includes the women. It was an easy decision to stay. The politics have been tricky, but I've been able to negotiate that, especially after I became a citizen."

Ed pointed a finger at the door. "Who does the intimidator work for?"

"Esteban?" Flint smiled. "I pay him to intimidate people. My work takes me into the barrios of Caracas and a lot of other rough places where I need someone to watch my back."

"Here in the airport?"

Flint shook his head. "The airport is safe. I have a lot of friends and contacts here. Again, it's part of my job. So," he turned to Kris, " – enough about me. Tell me again what brings you here. Something about hepatitis, wasn't it?"

She gave him a brief summary of the investigation, but left out her own infection and did not mention their suspicion of deliberate drug contamination by DEA conspirators.

"But how did you make a connection to Venezuela?"

She related the pathology findings and the case report of the Yachabo Indian. "So I want to get to the mission hospital in their homeland and learn whatever I can about this virus."

Flint had stopped chewing his gum and was paying close attention. "But I think the Yachabo are in the Andes near the Colombian border."

"Yes, in El Valle Amarillo."

"Extremely dangerous area. Lots of Colombian guerilla activity. How would you get there?"

Kris said, "I had hoped you could tell us the best and quickest way."

"You'd have to fly in. The mission hospital probably has a landing strip. Could charter a plane, but it'd be expensive and it might take a few days to find a pilot to fly you in, *if* anyone is willing at all."

Kris shook her head."Don't have that much time."

"You don't?" Flint asked. "Why not?"

"I've got the hepatitis virus. I'll be dead in 2 or 3 days."

Flint swallowed his chewing gum. "Are – are you sure? I'm so sorry to hear that." With a concerned look on his face, he said, ""Your eyes do look yellow and your skin color is not good."

She shrugged. "I'm not dead yet."

"Of course not," said Flint, who still looked very upset by her disclosure.

Flint's openness and his seemingly genuine concern about her illness made Kris doubt that he was one of the conspirators. She decided to tell him their suspicion. "Okay, Cory. Here's the deal. Ed and I are convinced that this outbreak got started by people in X-Ops who deliberately mixed this virus into heroin and distributed it to create a new lethal infection disease threat as a deterrent to drug use."

Flint did not look surprised. "Sounds like something X-Ops might do if they thought they could get away with it. Do you have any proof?"

"We had 2 vials of the contaminated drug," Ed said, "but one is back in the hands of X-Ops and the other was destroyed in the explosion and fire at CDC."

"Destroyed along with all the animal test data that would've proven virus was in the drug," added Kris.

Flint shook his head slowly."I heard about the bombing. Terrible thing. Some animal rights nut was responsible."

"We think X-Ops set up Aburcorn."

Flint looked surprised. "Aburcorn? Rex Aburcorn?

"Yes," Kris said. "Did you know him?"

"Not very well. I remember his unusual name from when I was in Vietnam. He was one of the original Madmen."

"We only know a little about that group, but what you just said implies that you were one too," Ed said.

Flint looked at him. "I was."

"Does that link Aburcorn to X-Ops?" Ed asked.

"Only in that some of the original Madmen later worked for the DEA." Flint popped two sticks of chewing gum into his mouth.

Kris was now even more confident that Flint was not one of the conspirators. "We'd like to hear more about the Madmen later. Right now my burning question is, if we assume that X-Ops mixed the virus into heroin and that it came from Venezuela, who in this country might have given it to them?"

Flint hesitated. He looked down at the table, then directly at Kris. "I did. I'm responsible."

Kris and Ed were both startled by Flint's unexpected admission. The room fell quiet except for the faint roar of a jetliner taking off from a distant runway. Flint appeared wistful and remorseful.

Kris broke the silence. "Ah – would you care to elaborate on that?"

"Sure. About six months ago when I was still on their e-mail list, I received an HCR – that's a highly confidential request – from X-Ops for any information about new biologic agents that target the liver. Two weeks later the Caracas newspaper ran a story about the Yachabo Indian who had died of liver failure. His severe hepatitis was thought to be caused by a variant of yellow fever. I scanned the story and e-mailed it to X-Ops with a suggestion that they contact a Dr. Jorge Cruz directly if they were interested. Cruz was the Indian's doctor, who reported the case to the Health Department. That's the last I heard about it until today."

"That's it?" Kris was relieved to hear that Flint might be only peripheral to the main X-Ops conspiracy.

"That was it."

"Biologic agents," Ed said. "Kind of an unusual request from X-Ops."

Flint turned to him. "Extraordinary. But that describes their mission and methods, so no one questioned the request."

Kris said, "I understand Cruz was killed in a car accident."

"He was," Flint said. "About a month after I e-mailed X-Ops. It was odd, though. According to the newspaper, he wasn't severely injured, but he then died a day or so later in the hospital."

Kris and Ed looked at each other and she raised her eyebrows at Flint. "How about it being a KO?"

Flint didn't have to ask for an explanation of the term. "That's certainly possible."

"There've been two attempts to injure Kris and we think both of those were intended KO's," Ed said.

Kris threw up her hands. "Even though I'm half dead already." She directed her attention to Flint. "Cory – we're sure someone, almost certainly X-Ops conspirators, intend to kill us for what we know."

Flint stroked his beard. "You may be right. I got an e-mail last night from Eric Sanders, he's upper level X-Ops right under Arnett and Bill Swanson. He asked me if you were on your way here."

"What did you tell him?" Ed asked.

"I said yes. I had no reason to lie or not respond."

Kris said, "That means they're on their way."

Flint looked at both of them. "There's a potential threat already. I know and I know Sanders knows of criminal gangs for hire in Caracas who will do X-Ops' dirty work for them. We should assume Sanders has contacted one of these gangs already."

Kris sighed and stared at the floor. "Thanks for the advice, Cory. Any other bright ideas on getting to the Yachabo homeland? Maybe we should at least start to drive in that direction to get out of town before bullets start whizzing around us."

Flint said quietly, "I'll fly you there."

Kris perked up. "The liver-dysfunction toxins have started to play tricks on my brain. I thought I heard you say that you would fly us there."

"I did say it. I have an instrument pilot's license and I'm a damn good bush pilot. Plus have a plane – one the DEA left behind that I bought from the government. I feel responsible for you, and want to help you get there."

Kris was grinning. "I accept your offer. If I didn't have a deadly disease, I'd give you a big hug and kiss right now."

Flint smiled. "We're not there yet. Do you know how to handle a pistol?"

"I can learn, and I'll do what I have to do to protect you two. I should be the designated hit woman anyway. What can they do? Give me the death penalty? Hah!"

Flint turned to Ed. "Tell me. Is she always like this?"

Ed smiled. "Pretty much."

"I have one more question," Flint said. "Why haven't you gone to the FBI with your evidence and suspicions?"

"We were going to when we had proof of virus in the drug from the animal inoculation studies, but the bomb blast wiped out all of that potential evidence in the making."

"So the timing and the damage from the explosion and fire were extremely beneficial for the conspirators."

Kris bit her lip. "That's right – except for me getting out alive." She paused to collect herself. "Although with your testimony about X-Ops' knowledge and access to the virus, along with our circumstantial evidence, I think we now could nail them – but no FBI in Venezuela."

"I wouldn't get the local *policia* involved," Flint said.

Kris nodded. "I agree. So what's our plan to fly out?"

"My plane is based at a small airport half-way between here and Caracas. I'll call ahead to get it fueled up and supplied. We should leave as soon as we can. Do you have more luggage than this?" Flint pointed to their carry-on bags.

They shook their heads.

"That's good, because there's not much extra storage space in the Cessna 172. We'll get you weapons, but not here in the terminal. You two will still need to exit out through customs. Esteban and I will pick you up curbside at the main street entrance to this International Terminal. I'll be driving a dark green Mercedes, but give us at least 15 minutes to get out there. I'll flash the headlights to confirm it's us. We'll wait if we get there first."

Ed said, "Got it."

Five minutes later, Kris and Ed were in the line for customs inspection of their baggage. She whispered, "So did you believe Cory about his limited involvement and knowledge about how X-Ops got the virus?"

Ed looked at her. "I have my doubts. But whether he did more or not, he seems to be on our side now, and I wouldn't want to jeopardize that."

"I agree. By the way, I think he was serious about us being armed. I think I'll keep mine in my purse."

They cleared Customs without a problem. As they made their way through the crowd in the public part of the International

Terminal, they were beset by drivers offering private auto transportation service into Caracas.

Outside the building it was already warm in the early morning sun. Kris put on her sunglasses. They were waiting near the curb when Kris heard a voice behind her call out, "Dr. Jensen."

She looked in the direction of the voice and saw a dark-complexioned man in a white tropical suit. He was waving and smiling as he walked toward them. Although she did not recognize the man, she waved back out of politeness. When he was just a few steps away, he extended his hand to shake hers.

"Welcome to Venezuela. I'm Cory Flint."

Chapter 22

On the sidewalk outside the International Terminal building at the Caracas airport, Kris turned to face the stranger who had just introduced himself as Cory Flint. She hesitated, but shook his outstretched hand. The unexpected appearance of a second man who claimed to be Flint unsettled Kris and made her question her sanity. *Are liver-failure toxins starting to confuse my brain?* She was unsure of how best to respond to the man, so she looked to Ed to speak first.

Ed introduced himself and got right to the point. "We just met someone else who said he was Cory Flint."

The man in the white suit looked surprised. "You did?" He frowned and shook his head. "Beware of that person. He's an impostor."

Kris said, "He was quite believable."

"But obviously a liar." The man beckoned them to accompany him. "Come with me. I have a car waiting. We can talk about it on the way to Caracas."

Kris turned to Ed, who shook his head. "Before we go anywhere, we'll need to see your identification card," Ed said.

"Of course." The man reached into his inside coat pocket and pulled out a gun that he pointed directly at Kris. "Here it is. Now both of you come along quietly, please."

They had picked up their bags to comply when Esteban appeared behind the man in the white suit. Kris caught a glimpse of the silencer-equipped gun that Flint's bodyguard pressed against the man's chest. Esteban said something that made the man lower his gun, which Esteban took from him with his free hand. Esteban looked to Kris and Ed and barked " *Vayan!*" as he nodded toward the green Mercedes at the curb.

Kris was just getting into the back seat of the car when she heard two muffled "pop" sounds. She looked back to see the man in the white suit crumple to the sidewalk as Esteban ran to their car.

From the front seat, Esteban said, "*El Malo es muerto.*"

As the Mercedes sped away from the International Terminal building, Flint looked back at them in the rear view mirror. "You two okay? The guy in the white suit was Carlos Bocanegra. They call him *El Malo* – he's a hit man for the La Palma gang."

Kris said, "He claimed to be you and his English was flawless. If we hadn't met you first, we probably would have gone with him."

"Bocanegra learned English when he lived in Miami for a while. He was a slick, bad-ass killer. Both of you would have been executed somewhere between here and Caracas. He's murdered dozens of people but never been caught. Believe me, the police will be thrilled to find him dead. Once they realize who he is, they won't bother to look for us except to thank us."

Fifteen minutes later, Flint squinted into the rear view mirror. "We're being followed. I expected as much. La Palma operates in two or sometimes three cars. They'll keep after us because they know they won't get paid for an unfinished job."

Esteban spoke in Spanish to Flint, who nodded.

"What did he say?" Kris asked Ed.

"He said to watch out for a roadblock ambush ahead."

"That's right," Flint said. "It's maybe why they've only followed instead of trying to catch up. The gang members up ahead will try to force us to stop. Then they close in and gun us down in a crossfire."

Ed asked, "Do we need guns?"

"Best to each have one." Flint turned to Esteban and pointed back at Kris and Ed in the rear seat. "*Dos Zamorana pistolas por los norteamericanos.*"

Esteban nodded and produced two semi-automatic pistols and two extra magazines, which he handed back to them.

Flint said, "That Zamorana is a 9mm semi-automatic – made in this country, but it's basically a Czech CZ-G2000. Each magazine has 15 rounds and it's a double action trigger."

"What does double action mean?" Kris whispered to Ed.

"Double action just means you have to squeeze harder on the trigger to fire the first shot."

After Ed showed her the safety features of her semi-automatic pistol, Kris held in her hand and inspected it. "Why did they name it Zamorana?"

"Supposedly the name of a fierce Venezuelan Indian war chief," came the reply from Flint.

"Oh." Kris pretended to aim and fire the pistol, then put it in her purse. "So Cory, I take it there'll be no x-ray screening of our carry-on bags at this airport we're going to."

Flint chuckled. "I like her sense of humor," he said. "So – in a few minutes, we'll turn off onto a back road to the Rosita airport where I keep my plane. I called ahead and it should be fueled up, supplied, and ready to go."

He accelerated the Mercedes to lengthen their distance ahead of the car that had been following them. After several minutes of weaving through traffic at high speed, Flint slammed on the brakes to make a sharp left turn onto a dirt road through a line of trees. They roared past a farmhouse and chickens on the side of the road scattered, squawking and flapping their wings.

Kris looked behind them but couldn't tell whether they were still being followed because of the dust cloud raised by the Mercedes.

Flint saw her look back. "I think we lost them."

Kris breathed a small sigh of relief. "Do they know we're headed for this little airport?"

Flint shrugged. "Maybe. If they do know, I hope by the time they get there, we're already airborne. It'd be too easy for them to shoot up and disable the plane."

"Is Esteban coming along?"

Flint shook his head. "Not enough room, and too much weight. Besides, he hates to fly, and I don't expect to need him once we've taken off."

"Will he be all right?"

"They're after us, not him. They won't get paid for taking him out, so I don't think they'll risk ending up dead for nothing."

Twenty minutes later, Flint turned the Mercedes onto the Rosita airport road which ran straight to the airport directly in line with the end of the single paved runway. As they approached, a small plane had just taken off in front of them. It passed directly overhead as it ascended. A chain link fence enclosed the airport grounds, which Flint explained was necessary to keep cows and goats off the runway. Just before the fence, the airport road took a 90- degree right turn and led around to a small office building and a large hangar. Flint drove the Mercedes through an open gate and stopped next to a white Cessna 172 with blue trim that was parked in front of the hangar. A man in orange coveralls came out of the office and walked toward them.

Flint turned around to Kris and Ed. "Here's my plane. The man in orange is Arturo, who's the Rosita owner-operator. Go ahead and put your bags on board. There's a bathroom in the office if you need it. I want to take off in the next 10 minutes."

Esteban showed them where to stow their bags while Flint went over to chat with Arturo. Esteban opened the trunk of the Mercedes and took out Flint's bag, which he gave to Ed to stow on the plane. Esteban next took out a high-powered looking rifle with a telescopic sight and proceeded to load it.

Ed watched him. "*Va a cazar?*"

Esteban smiled and shook his head. "*Solamente* preparando por una batalla posible."

Kris looked quizzically at Ed, who translated: "Preparing for a possible battle."

Flint rejoined them. "Arturo said someone called and asked for me. Not knowing any better, Arturo told them that we were on our way here. We need to leave now."

They climbed into the Cessna with Ed in the right front seat next to Flint. Kris sat in the rear seat behind Flint. Next to her was a storage chest of supplies. After he gave instructions to Esteban, Flint started up the Cessna and taxied it to the right toward the take-off end of the runway. On the way they crossed a grass landing strip, which intersected the main paved runway at an X angle. As they taxied out, Kris asked, "How long is the flight?"

Flint replied, "About four hours depending on the winds aloft. We'll stop to refuel at San Cristobal at the base of the Andes near the Colombian border. I'd like to get some advice there on flying in to El Valle Amarillo and also get an updated local weather report." He stopped the plane just short of the end of the runway and began his preflight checklist. About half way through the list, he happened to look up. "Uh-oh. Trouble."

Kris looked beyond the end of the runway. Two cars were speeding toward them on the airport road.

"That's La Palma," said Flint calmly. "We can't take off over them. They'll shoot up the gas tanks."

As Flint's mind raced through their options, the first car turned at the fence and headed for the hangar while the second broke through the fence and drove onto the runway, headed straight at them.

Chapter 23

Esteban had spotted the two fast-approaching cars on the airport road. He was sure that they carried La Palma gunmen. With the rifle ready, he stood behind the Mercedes parked in front of the hangar and started to fire at the second car when it broke through the chain link fence at the end of the runway.

Flint, at the controls of the Cessna 172 at the opposite end of the runway, had decided to not take off but rather to fast-taxi the plane back to the hangar to consolidate their defense. Ed had his semi-automatic pistol out and ready.

Kris realized the danger. "If they have me, will they let you two go?"

"No."

"Then forget it."

The La Palma car on the runway veered right and skidded to a stop. It was only half on the pavement, but enough to block any take-off attempt. Flint said, "Esteban shot out the right side tires."

As the Cessna came to the grass landing strip, Kris shouted from the back, "Can we take off on the grass?"

"Ah – maybe."

ALEX LETTAU

"Go for it."

Flint decided to try it. He turned the Cessna to head down the grass runway and pushed the throttle to full power. It was a gamble, not only because the Cessna was heavily loaded and would be taking off with a left crosswind, but also because their take-off roll had started from less than the full length of the grass strip. Grass required a longer ground distance to achieve take-off speed than a paved runway.

Flint estimated that the disabled La Palma car would be about 40 yards to their left when the Cessna crossed over the paved runway. He was hoping that Esteban could keep the runway gunmen pinned down enough to prevent them from getting clear shots at the plane. Flint rechecked the flap setting for take-off and watched the air speed indicator gauge closely as the airplane accelerated. The gauge would need to show an air speed of close to 65 mph before he could pull back the control wheel and lift off the grass.

The Cessna crossed over the paved runway with a bump. Flint saw at least one gunman crouched down behind the disabled car start to shoot at them. "Get down," he shouted.

Kris heeded his warning. She ducked just before a bullet came through the left rear window and struck the top of the storage chest in the right rear seat.

Flint glanced at Ed. "She okay back there?"

"Yes."

Flint worried about other hits on the aircraft, but as he scanned the instrument panel, all systems seemed to be operating as expected. The Cessna accelerated down the grass runway.

Kris lifted her head briefly and saw they were still on the ground. She looked to Flint, who was concentrating on the instrument panel. She was sure he knew what he was doing, but she couldn't help blurting out, "Take off. – Take off now!"

Flint heard her and barked back, "Can't yet – not enough airspeed."

The airspeed gauge indicated 58 mph and the fence was only 200 feet away. Just beyond the fence was a line of trees that they would also have to clear.

At 63 mph, Flint pulled back on the control wheel. The Cessna lifted off the grass. The main wheels cleared the fence by a foot, but the trees loomed closer. Flint couldn't bank the plane or pull up too sharply; those maneuvers would cause a loss of lift, followed by a stall and a nose- down crash.

Kris saw the foliage ahead of them and called out, "Trees – pull up!"

Flint ignored her. He pulled back on the control wheel to increase the angle of ascent as much as he dared and angled the plane a bit to the left toward a less dense part of the tree line. As the Cessna closed in on the trees, its airspeed started to drop. The stall warning sounded. To maintain airspeed, Flint had to lower the nose of the plane. A collision with a treetop was imminent.

"Hang on!" he shouted, and gritted his teeth as the nose wheel hit some small branches and the propeller shredded leaves into a cloud of green bits. The contact with the tree branches slowed the aircraft and pitched the nose down slightly, but the Cessna's momentum carried it into an open space beyond the initial tree line. The wind was stronger there, and Flint could descend a bit to regain the lost airspeed. The next tree line was not as high, and they cleared it easily.

Flint exhaled loudly. "Whew. That was close. I need a drink."

Kris said, "Good job, Cory. Sorry about my crazy back-seat flying. Let me know if you ever need a reference for a job as a treetop trimmer."

Flint and Ed laughed loudly.

"What was that alarm that I heard when we were trying to clear the trees?"

"The stall warning horn."

"What's a stall?"

"A stall is a sudden loss of lift of an aircraft. Can be caused by various factors – airspeed too slow, too high of a climb angle and so on. In a stall the nose of the aircraft pitches sharply down toward the ground. It's easy to pull out of high up in the sky, but it's a disaster and crash if it happens close to the ground."

They had taken off to the east. At 2,000 feet, Flint started a 180-degree ascending turn back over the Rosita airport. The oil pressure and fuel gauges registered as he expected and from the cockpit he couldn't see any evidence of damage or leaks from the gunfire aimed at the aircraft. Kris was able to close the small hole in the left rear window with duct tape.

As the plane flew back over the airport at a safe altitude, Flint could see the disabled car on the runway and a body sprawled next to it on the grass. The Mercedes was still parked in front of the hangar, but he didn't see Esteban. The other La Palma car was gone.

Flint picked up the radio and called Arturo, who answered immediately. Both Flint and Ed laughed at something that Arturo said in Spanish.

"What did he just say?" asked Kris.

Ed turned around to her. "Arturo said he's got a few more treetops he wants Cory to trim."

Kris smiled. "What about Esteban?"

"He's fine and in the office with Arturo. I'm sure glad of that, 'cause he's saved our butts twice today already. They're waiting for the police to show up."

Kris flashed a thumbs-up sign. "Everything's come out okay, but it was pretty dicey there for a few minutes."

"Tell me about it. I had my Zamorana out and was ready to start blazing away. Like in a western movie called 'The Shoot-out at the Rosita Corral.'"

"How would it end? I hope not like 'Bonnie and Clyde' or 'Butch Cassidy and the Sundance Kid.'"

Ed shook his head. "Nah, we're the good guys. The ending will be happy, with the baddies vanquished."

"I hope you're right, Ed." Kris said as she sat back in her seat. *But I wouldn't count on it.* Kris started to feel more relaxed as her adrenalin levels subsided. She looked out the windows. To the right in the distance, a jetliner was on approach to land at Maiquetia International airport. Another had just taken off, – with the blue-green Caribbean beyond. To the left and behind them, she could see Caracas with a low mountain range as a backdrop. *Cities always look nicer from high altitude.* Ahead of them was a blend of clouds and bluish haze.

What does lie ahead? Maybe more adventures. Whatever happens, it'll be better than confinement in a hospital bed getting poisoned by some toxic anti-viral drug. That's for sure. As her blood-brain adrenalin levels fell further, she started to feel fatigued again. When the plane hit turbulent air over a mountain ridge, the queasiness came back. She took an antihistamine and quickly fell asleep.

****

At the FBI headquarters in Atlanta, Jonas Peterson sat in the office of Steve Garner, who was at his desk listening on the telephone. Garner hung up the phone and leaned back in his chair. He was silent for a moment, then looked at Peterson and said, "This Jensen-Beaufain lead gets more and more strange. I got a call earlier from Edgar Rodriguez, who's our primary contact in Caracas. He drove to the airport, which is about 13 miles out from the city, to meet the Continental flight from Houston. After the plane landed, he waited quite a while for them to come out into the arrival lobby. Edgar started to think they either weren't on the flight or had been detained. Anyway, they do finally come out and he recognizes Beaufain, but Jensen's totally changed from her picture. He got a close look at them because he pretended to be one of the drivers that hawk rides into Caracas."

"Was she in disguise? How did she look different?" asked Peterson.

"Edgar said she was all puffy and had a sallow complexion. He said that Jensen reminded him of his sister who once had really bad hepatitis. So the two of them go out and stand on the sidewalk in front of the terminal and wait. Then Jensen turns around and shakes hands with a thug named Bocanegra who's a notorious hit man for a criminal gang in Caracas. They talk, but he pulls a gun on her. Then another thug appears who shoves a gun into Bocanegra's ribs and executes him on the spot. Meanwhile, Jensen and Beaufain jump into a green Mercedes and are joined by thug number two – the executioner – and take off. The car is registered to a Cory Flint, who Edgar thought was the driver. Flint's a long-term DEA guy who was based in Caracas, but who stayed and became a citizen when the DEA got booted out of the country a few years ago.

Edgar tried to catch up, but lost Flint on the road to Caracas. He called ahead to have an associate pick up the tail on the green Mercedes on the main road into Caracas, but the Mercedes never showed up. Edgar thinks Flint must have turned off somewhere along the way."

"Bizarre story." Peterson thought a moment and asked, "Any connection with CDC?"

"Maybe. This morning we looked into Flint's background and it turns out that he served in Vietnam the same time as Aburcorn, in the same unit. A vet from that unit, whom we had located to check out Aburcorn, told us the two were close friends ever since Flint saved Aburcorn's life once on the battlefield, for which Flint received a citation."

Peterson raised his eyebrows. "Have they been in contact with each other lately?"

"Not that we've confirmed. Our geeks have taken Aburcorn's home computer apart to try to resurrect the erased stuff. They're pretty sure there's at least one e-mail that came out of Venezuela about a week ago, but they don't have any content."

"We need to talk with Cory Flint," Peterson said.

Garner nodded. "I just got off the phone with the Miami guys – ah – McKeeson and Castillo, who flew down to Venezuela last night. I told them to keep after Jensen and Beaufain, but also to find Cory Flint and to watch out for thug number two. Castillo's fluent in Spanish, so that'll help. By the way, did you find out any more about Aburcorn's medical history?"

"Yeah, I sure did," said Peterson. "He had mental issues, but was never suicidal. The big problem was terminal cancer. Fibrosarcoma, they called it. According to his oncologist, Aburcorn was convinced it was caused by Agent Orange exposure in Vietnam, and Aburcorn was bitter toward the V.A. about insufficient government funding, research and benefits for health problems related to Agent Orange."

"Okay. Thanks. Anything new on Aburcorn's source of C-4?"

Peterson shook his head.

Garner stroked his chin. "Back to Jensen for a minute. I'm not sure we're any smarter over her role. Now it looks like she has an illness and someone wants to kill her. She's chummy with Flint, who used to be a buddy of Aburcorn – which leaves us with even more questions than answers."

Peterson replied, "Here's a thought. Maybe she was sick at the CDC that morning and, lucky for her, had to leave the meeting room just before the fifth floor blew up. The secretary she saved – that Jessie Clark – said Jensen told her she was down on the fourth floor to use the ladies' room. I think Clark corroborated that the one on the fifth floor was out of service."

Garner thought about the suggestion. "Okay. Check the maintenance records for the fifth floor ladies' room and ask the other survivor – Gina something – about whether Jensen looked sick that morning. But we still need to find Jensen. My bad to let her slip away."

"I'm on it."

****

In the downtown Atlanta offices of the DEA, Agent Eric Sanders shook his head at Bill Swanson. "We lost another chance to finish the job. La Palma didn't come through like they have in the past. Beaufain did go with Jensen to Caracas, and the La Palma ace Bocanegra was tipped off when they came through customs and what they looked like. He met them on the sidewalk outside the

International terminal, but Flint's bodyguard took him out. La Palma did catch up with them at a little airport where Flint keeps his plane, but Flint managed to take off and they all flew away headed west-southwest."

Swanson was expressionless. "Sounds to me like Cory's gone completely over to their side. He knows way too much. We'll need to eliminate him along with the other two. Fortunately they're still all together. Where were they headed?"

Sanders shrugged. "Don't know. Cory's mother is from Cabimas, next to Lake Maracaibo, but I don't know why Jensen would want to go there."

"Are we tracking their plane?"

"It's still in the works, but I don't see a problem," Sanders said. "What about an airstrike on them as suspected narco-traffic?"

Swanson shook his head. "Not in the middle of Venezuela. The Venezuelans won't do it for us, and we have no strong basis to invade their airspace. Plus there would be a big stink after it's discovered they were American doctors and no drugs were in the wreckage. *But* if they get anywhere near Colombia, we would be in a much better position to pull it off and get away with it as an unfortunate misidentification of their plane as a drug runner. Keep me updated on their position."

"Okay. Anything useful from the FBI?"

"They're hard after Aburcorn's possible sources of C-4," Swanson said. "Oh, I almost forgot. They must've had a contact at the airport who saw Jensen leave with Cory. Now they're looking at Flint's background – and looking for him. All the more reason to get rid of him."

Chapter 24

After 90 minutes of sleep, Kris awoke to the steady drone of the engine of the Cessna 172. She was disoriented at first, but recognized Ed who had dozed off in the right front seat. Cory Flint was in the pilot seat in front of her, chewing gum as he studied a navigational chart.

"Hey, Cory."

Flint twisted around in his seat toward her. "Ah – you're up. Have a good nap?"

"Not really. Sleep just isn't as refreshing ever since I've had this hepatitis. So where are we?"

"We're at 8,000 feet over the Central Orinoco Plain headed southwest toward the southern end of the Venezuelan Andes. We've got a nice tailwind, so with the plane all trimmed out, it's been a fast and smooth ride. It'll get bumpier in the mountains."

"I can't wait. I brought the barfbags from the seatpockets of the 757 we flew down on. How's the plane been running?"

"Seems just fine. Can't tell there was any damage."

Kris sat up to see what was ahead of them. "How much longer to San Cristobal?"

"I decided to fly 50 kilometers past San Cristobal to stop at the Juan Vicente Gomez International airport in San Antonio, on the Colombian border. It's bigger, so they'll have better information on the weather and the best route to fly in to the Valle Amarillo, which is about 100 miles north in the mountains near the Sierra de Perija National Park."

"If we get that close to Colombia, will there be any danger from the rebels?"

Flint hesitated. "Not by the airport. Lots of military there. But once we're in the mountains, maybe – though I doubt they'd waste a surface-to-air missile on us, and we'd have to fly pretty low for them to take us down with small arms fire. Another risk is to get mistaken for a drug trafficking plane by the DEA or Colombian radar surveillance."

"Now I understand why you said it might be hard to find a pilot to fly us there. Don't you file a flight plan that tells the military on both sides of the border to lay off?"

"Yes, but the drug traffickers sometimes file false ones."

Kris asked, "How does the mission plane get through?"

"It flies on a regular schedule. Everyone knows who they are so they leave it alone."

"Is X-Ops tracking our plane?"

"Maybe so. They do have access to the technology. They'd have to request it from the military satellite or AWACS systems."

"If so, then what's to stop X-Ops from falsely identifying us as drug runners so they can have our military take us out with an airstrike?"

"I don't think they can risk getting them involved to do their dirty work. A criminal gang like La Palma, yes, but not the American military. How would they justify the use of deadly force on an unarmed light aircraft?"

"I don't know but if they can get away with blowing up part of the CDC, they would justify it somehow," Kris said. "Remember, it's usually easier to get forgiveness than permission. What about the Colombians? Do they have an Air Force?"

"One of the largest in South America."

"Wouldn't they be more responsive to a directive from X-Ops?"

Flint shrugged. "Maybe, but my understanding is that when the Colombians intercept an aircraft, they operate under defined rules of engagement. Can't just blow you away. We'll fly low and look out for hostile aircraft, but not too low – the terrain or the guerillas could get us." He chose his next words carefully. "Kris, there's definite danger in this trip to the mission. How about we turn around and take a nice sightseeing air tour of Angel Falls or fly over to the beautiful beaches of Margarita Island?"

Ed, who had awakened, smiled at Flint's suggestions.

Kris sighed. "I know I've put both of you at risk and I pray to God nothing happens to either one of you, but I have no way to get to the Valle Amarillo without your help."

Flint stopped chewing gum. "Then I'd like to know exactly why you need to go there so badly."

"Me too," Ed said.

Kris looked back and forth at them. "Okay – here's the deal. First, I want to confirm this valley is the origin of the virus. I think I can do that just by talking with the mission doctor who's been there five years – mainly because of the entry site ulcer that differentiates this fulminant hepatitis. I also want to pick his brain about his observations of the epidemiology of hepatitis among the Yachabo."

Flint asked, "What's epidemiology?"

"It's the scientific study of disease in a population," Kris said. "It encompasses the prevalence and incidence of the disease, age groups affected, and in the case of infection, how it's transmitted and risk factors for getting it. Also for this virus, whether there's a reservoir in wild animals – which I suspect there is. A killer virus can't sustain itself in a human population when it's so lethal and not easily transmitted."

"So how would this knowledge help you?" Flint asked.

"I don't expect it'll help me personally, but the more you learn about a new infectious disease, the better equipped you are to control and prevent it. Epidemiologic information complements the basic lab virology. For example, if we were to identify persons with immunity, the virologists would try to identify the protective antibody against the virus which then could lead to development of a vaccine." She looked down at her ulcerated fingertip and her bruised and swollen arms and legs. "I honestly don't expect to leave the valley alive. It's my hope that Ed will take what we learn back to the States and help start a larger field investigation in conjunction with the Venezuelan Health Department."

"So-o-o," Flint said, "this trip is a grant-a-last-wish miracle flight, like for kids with terminal cancer."

Kris smiled and nodded. "And I thank you so much for granting my wish. Now then, how much farther to the San Antonio airport?"

Flint glanced at his watch. "It's 10:30. We should be there by 1:00 this afternoon. After we land, I'll get the plane refueled while you two can stretch and go for refreshments. Then once I have the mountain weather forecast and find out the best route to fly up to the Valle, we're off again."

As they flew on over the Central Orinoco Plain, Flint pointed out Lake Maracaibo in the far distance to their right. He reminisced about boyhood trips to his mother's home city of Cabimas. "My Puerto Rican father, Rafael Flintana, changed his last name to Flint when he moved to Miami. My parents spoke Spanish at home, but I was raised in South Florida so I always spoke English. Sounds odd, but it was natural in our house."

"So how did you come to work for the DEA?" Kris asked.

"I got interested in illegal drug control while in Vietnam. I started with the DEA right after the war ended and spent the first few years in D.C. When a position opened up in Caracas, I lobbied hard for it, and I've been there ever since."

"Cory, we want to know more about the Madmen," Ed said. "What can you tell us?"

"It's a group that got started in Vietnam. Drug abuse among our troops affected morale and was putting our guys' lives at risk. We did what we could to stop it."

Kris asked, "What happened to the group after the war?"

"It stayed intact as an informal organization. Some of us went into the DEA, others into law enforcement. The rest acted as eyes and ears in the community as their contribution to our common goal of controlling illegal drug use. There's been some attrition in numbers but it's still active as a semi-secret network."

"So we shouldn't bother looking for a website?" Kris asked.

"That's right."

Ed asked, "Do the Madmen ever, ah – do extra-legal dirty work for the DEA and law enforcement? I mean, like actions outside the law to achieve the end."

Flint nodded. "Definitely. There's a few Madmen I'd even call vigilantes."

"Ever heard of a Gareth Miller in New Orleans?" Ed asked.

"Met him once. I understand he's one of the leaders of the Southeast region."

"Was."

"What do you mean?"

"He's dead. His nurse daughter got accidentally infected with this hepatitis virus, and we think Miller was killed via KO to keep him from telling us about the X-Ops conspiracy."

Flint was visibly upset by the news. "I'm sorry to hear that. How is his daughter doing?"

"I haven't heard for a couple of days, but I expect she'll die this weekend," Kris said.

Flint sighed. "I was also introduced to Miller's wife. I don't remember her name, but she was such a kind Christian woman. I'm so sad for her."

"We've met Corinne and feel the same way," said Kris. Ed nodded agreement.

Flint was silent, then said, "Please get me the bottle of Jack Daniels out of the storage cabinet next to you. I need a shot."

Kris wasn't happy with the idea of the pilot of their airplane drinking alcohol, but opened the cabinet anyway. When she did, a piece of broken glass fell out and bourbon whiskey dripped onto the seat. She noticed a hole in the door and a bullet lodged in the back wall of the cabinet. "I'm afraid Jack already took a shot for you. I can get you a slug, but it won't be the kind you want."

Flint looked back at the cabinet. "I see what you mean. There's also a metal hip flask in there. I'll take that instead."

Kris found it and handed it forward.

"Thanks, Kris. Before I take a swig, anyone else want a hit? Cups are in the cabinet."

Ed shook his head.

"I'll pass," Kris said. "I need to be good to the liver cells I have left."

"I understand. Any other questions about the Madmen?"

"No, but have you ever heard of Dewey Duarte?" Kris asked.

Flint nodded. "Sure. Just about everyone in Nam at the time heard about him and the Trang Son incident. You know about that?"

"We do."

"Everyone was aware of the drug problem, and the incident was kind of a last-straw catalyst that got the Madmen organized to fight it."

Kris said, "I heard Duarte got off."

"True, but the Madmen have never forgotten and have monitored him ever since. Duarte knew he'd be in big trouble or even killed if he were ever busted for any narcotics violation."

"My understanding is that he's been a regular user, but never got caught until a narcotics sting a couple of months ago," Ed said.

"Then he should be in some kind of trouble with the local Madmen."

Ed shook his head. "We heard X-Ops got him off the narcotics charge so he could participate in a special project with them. We assume it was a deal to have Duarte help distribute the virus-contaminated drug."

"Gareth Miller and the Madmen may have been involved in any such deal with Duarte," Flint said.

Kris nodded. "But I'm sure Miller never found out that Duarte was later responsible for infecting Renk, who then infected Miller's daughter." Kris paused to think back on her decision to withhold information from Miller. "If I'd told him about Renk, maybe Miller would have confessed any involvement with Duarte and X-Ops – and be alive today. Then again he may have gone out and killed Duarte himself."

Flint shrugged. "Don't second-guess yourself. As for Duarte, he's doomed regardless."

"Why is that?" Kris asked.

"He knows too much, so he won't outlive his usefulness to X-Ops."

Two hours later, Flint had the Cessna on final approach to the Juan Vicente Gomez International airport in San Antonio. The air over the foothills at the southern end of the Venezuelan Andes had been turbulent, and the Cessna had dipped and risen abruptly so many times that Kris' nausea control efforts had been overwhelmed. She had been retching into the airsickness bags for the last 15 minutes. Flint felt sorry for her, but could do little except to get them on the ground.

The landing was smooth. Flint taxied the plane to the general aviation section of the airport. He got out first and walked around the Cessna to inspect for gunfire-related damage incurred during their hurried departure from the Rosita airport. There was a bullet hole in the tail section, but it hadn't seemed to affect the rudder function or the aerodynamics of the flight, so he wasn't worried about it. Flint left to arrange for refueling and to get a weather forecast while Ed helped Kris across the tarmac to the general aviation lounge and the women's restroom.

She put her hand on his shoulder. "Thanks, Ed. I'm okay from here. Could you please get me a bottle of fruit juice and some cookies or crackers?"

He nodded. "Meet you back here."

In the restroom, Kris took off her sunglasses. She was not surprised to see that the normally white sclera of her eyes were a deep yellow and, even in the artificial light her skin had a bronze hue. She was still weak and a little dizzy from having vomited, but the cool dry air and a nice fresh breeze out on the airport tarmac had settled the nausea. She washed her face and brushed her teeth and felt even better. Thirsty and a little hungry, she sat down with Ed, who had found a small table in the lounge and was munching a candy bar. After she had eaten two chocolate chip cookies and a tropical fruit drink, Kris felt even more energized.

"I feel so much better. Maybe I was hypoglycemic."

Ed nodded. "I think that can be a problem in liver failure. I'll get you more cookies, candy bars, and juice to keep your blood sugar up while we head north. I expect it'll get bumpy again. Hope you do better than just now."

"Better get a couple of plastic bags just in case."

Flint came to join them with a cup of black coffee in hand. He took a sip and stroked his beard. "There's bad news and good news."

Kris put her hand to her forehead. "Please let the good news not just simply be that there is no more bad news."

Flint shook his head. "The good news is that the plane is fully functional and that the mountain weather will be clear for the next few hours before thunderstorms move in. I also got the GPS routing for the best approach to El Valle Amarillo."

"Did you tell them where we're going?" asked Kris.

Flint shook his head. "They didn't seem interested. I would guess that the staff here have learned to give out information without asking questions. I did file a flight plan to Maracaibo, which is about 100 miles northeast of where we're going."

"So what's the bad news?" Ed asked.

Flint turned to him. "Lots of Colombian guerilla activity in the mountains, both in Colombia and across into Venezuela. They've been shooting at planes they don't recognize. And – ah – "

"What else?" prompted Kris.

"The Colombian Air Force shot down a drug trafficking plane yesterday. The drug runner pilot didn't comply with orders to land and ignored the warning shots."

"What does that mean for us?"

"I would hope the Colombians would only act on intelligence info."

"Like from X-Ops?"

"Maybe."

Kris looked at Ed and then squarely at Flint. "I can only speak for myself. I have complete confidence that you can get us there."

Ed nodded agreement.

Flint sipped his coffee and was silent. He took a deep breath and said, "If it were just us, the plane and the mountains, there'd be no problem."

It was obvious to Kris that Flint thought the trip was too risky and wanted out. "Cory, I'm a short-timer. It's easy for me to accept the risks, but I can't make you and Ed do the same. You both have years of life ahead of you."

"I'm not bailing," Ed said.

Kris smiled her appreciation at him and turned back to Flint. "I've come too far to give up now. If you do back out, I understand completely. Don't feel guilty about it. I'm so grateful for what you've done for us already. Ed and I will find another way to get there."

Flint looked relieved. "Okay. I *am* going to head back to Caracas. I'll ask the staff here about other pilots who might be willing to take you, or a driver-guide to get you there overland. Let me first go get your bags out of the plane. I wish you the best of luck." He got up and left without another word.

Ed muttered, "That was a quick exit. What a rat!"

"Like a rat deserting a sinking trip?"

"Yeah."

"Don't be too hard on Cory. He's risked a lot for us already."

After a moment, Ed said, "You're right. He has. Now, about our options. I think overland would be too rough. You're in no shape for a hike or a burro-back ride. It'd be hard even if a four-wheel drive vehicle could get all the way through. We need to fly in."

"Yes," said Kris. "Maybe the mission pilot is based here. What about hiring him?"

"That's a great idea. I'll go find out." Ed left to inquire at the general aviation desk, but returned two minutes later. "The mission pilot *is* based here, but he left yesterday to fly to Caracas to visit his mother. Won't be back for a week."

Kris sighed. She leaned back in her chair and closed her eyes to try to conjure up another plan. She was mulling over renting a car and driving north to the town nearest to the Valle, when Ed nudged her. She opened her eyes and saw Flint standing before them. Instead of their bags, he held his hip flask.

"I had a little session with Jack Daniels and we decided to take you up to the Valle after all."

Kris grinned. "Great! Just one thing – who's the pilot in command? Cory or Jack?"

Flint smiled. "It'll be me." He sat down and his facial
expression turned sad and reflective. "Years ago, my favorite little
niece came down with lymphoma. Elena was only five years old.
She'd always wanted to visit Disneyland but never got to go before
she died of the cancer. I've always regretted that I didn't help fulfill
her wish." He wiped away a tear. "I don't want to make the same
mistake."

Kris reached out and touched his shoulder. "Thanks,
Cory."

****

At the FBI headquarters in Atlanta, Steve Garner looked up as
Jonas Peterson entered his office with a piece of paper in hand and
said, "You need to see this."

Garner asked, "What've you got?"

"Our geeks just un-deleted this message out of Aburcorn's
e-mail server. It was sent a week ago from Flint and reads: The
government is responsible for your cancer. This is your chance to
strike back. Do it for me and the animals. Your friend, Cory.
Sounds to me like Flint encouraged Aburcorn to be a suicide
bomber."

Garner nodded. "That *would* make him a co-conspirator.
Any possibility it was faked by someone who pretended to be
Flint?"

"Sure, if they got access to Flint's e-mail account. But who
would that be?"

Garner turned both palms up. "I dunno. But I just don't see
that Flint had the means or a motive to mastermind the bombing of
a major government facility. It would probably be whoever

provided Aburcorn with the C-4 and the detonator system. Still no leads among the animal rights groups?"

Peterson shook his head.

"I'm sure there's somebody other than Flint involved. But now we do have enough on him to get the Venezuelans to search his house and confiscate any computers they find. In the meantime, I'll check into whether Flint's recently been in the U.S."

"Any lead on how he disappeared?"

"Castillo found out that Flint owned a small airplane that he kept at some dinky little airstrip off the main road from the international airport to Caracas. He and McKeeson are on their way over there to look for him." Garner drummed his fingers on his desk. "Did you check with the other CDC survivor about Jensen's health?"

"Yeah. I talked with a Gina Poluzzi. She confirmed not only that Jensen looked sick that morning, but also that the fifth floor ladies' room was closed. Toilets being replaced."

Garner raised his eyebrows. "Then maybe your theory of how and why she survived is right, but we're still left with the question of why she ran off and is hanging out with Flint. We need to find them. They're our only solid leads so far. We'll ask the Venezuelans for help, and hopefully they'll co-operate."

****

In the Atlanta headquarters of the DEA, Agent Eric Sanders walked into the office of Bill Swanson and closed the door behind him. Swanson looked up and said, "Hope you've got good news."

"Couple of items. Jones called in from New Orleans about our loose end."

"You mean Duarte? Loose cannon is more like it. Are we rid of him?"

Sanders nodded. "The King abdicated his throne with a smile on his face. Heroin overdose and DOA at Parish General."

"Good. It was a mistake to ever use him. Make sure the Madmen know. Was there anyone else who shadowed Duarte besides Miller?"

Sanders paused to check his notepad. "Ah – a part-time guy named John Faissoux. Lives in Slidell, east of New Orleans."

"Call him about Duarte so he can pass it on to the Madmen network. Feel him out, see if Miller ever mentioned the project to him. I doubt Miller did. He was a hothead but he knew when to keep his mouth shut – at least until his daughter got sick. Too bad about him and his kid, but in every war there's collateral damage. By the way, did Jones recover Duarte's project drug supply?"

"He got all the vials."

Swanson gave a thumbs-up. "Good work. What's your other item?"

"We tracked Flint's plane to an airport in western Venezuela near the Colombian border. Place called San Antonio."

"You sure?"

"Yeah, but I don't know if they're staying or just stopped to refuel," Sanders said. "They were there as of 30 minutes ago." Sanders' cellphone buzzed. He listened, then switched it off and smiled at Swanson. "That was an update. They took off again headed due north into the mountains."

Swanson gave two thumbs up. "Send the plane's description, location and heading to the Colombian Air Force Command and Control Center along with the message that we advise interception of Flint's plane as suspected narco-traffic. Flint would have to land at the nearest airport where we can have them held. You and Jones need to head down there to tie up those last loose ends. If Flint tries to evade the intercept, the interdiction procedure allows the Colombians to shoot him down. Let's hope he does and they do."

Chapter 25

Kris was thankful that the take-off and climb-out from the runway in San Antonio were smooth and uneventful in stark contrast to the nerve-wracking departure from Rosita airport. She was also relieved that Flint had stowed the hip flask and didn't seem impaired from the bourbon. As the Cessna ascended to the north, Flint pointed out the Colombian city of Cucuta off to the left and the rugged mountain peaks of the Venezuelan Andes in the distance on the right. The weather was clear and the air much less turbulent, so Kris was able to relax and enjoy the spectacular scenery.

After they had reached a cruising altitude of 8000 feet, Flint said, "It'll take about an hour to get there. A straight shot would be faster but would cut through Colombia. We should stay inside Venezuela because if X-Ops sics the Colombian Air Force on us, I don't think they're allowed to pursue an intercept in Venezuelan airspace."

Forty minutes later, Flint announced that they were only about 20 minutes from El Valle Amarillo. He reduced power to start a descent. Kris had dozed off again but awoke quickly, excited finally to get close to the place of origin of the virus. She remembered a question she'd wanted to ask. "Hey, Cory. Does the name 'Yellow Valley' have anything to do with hepatitis?"

"I have no idea."

She noticed that Flint had stopped chewing gum and that his attention was fixed on the left front windscreen.

"Uh oh," Flint said.

Kris and Ed simultaneously asked, "What?"

"To the left – two specks on the windscreen. They're not moving."

"A couple of bugs that we hit?" Kris asked.

Flint shook his head.

"Okay, so what are the two immobile specks on the windscreen?"

"Two approaching aircraft. If they don't move in your field of view, they're on a collision course. Likely Colombian jet interceptors."

"I thought we were in Venezuela."

"I'm sure we are."

"What now?" Kris asked.

"I'll wait to see what they do and say after they get closer, which won't be long. They move pretty fast." Flint reached to set the radio to the emergency frequency.

Only 10 seconds later, the outlines of the fast-approaching jets were more clearly visible. They continued to close on an intercept course with the Cessna's flight path until the jets streaked past, one in front and the other below them.

Flint remained calm. "That was just to get our attention. Those are Colombian A-37 jets. Good tactical fighter planes. We had an earlier version flying in Nam."

The radio came alive with a series of questions in Spanish. Flint responded to each of them.

Ed turned to interpret for Kris. "They wanted to know who we are, where the plane is registered, our point of origin and intended destination. Cory told them he's taking two American doctors on a sightseeing air tour of some National Parks and Lake Maracaibo with a flight plan filed for Maracaibo airport."

"And I pointed out that we've been in Venezuelan airspace since we left San Antonio," Flint said as they waited for the jet pilot to respond. "They're circling behind us, – probably calling their command center for instructions."

After a couple of tense minutes, the radio crackled in Spanish again to which Flint replied, "*Entiendo. Muchas gracias.*"

The A-37s flashed past them banked to the left and headed west back to their base in Colombia.

"What did they say?" asked Kris.

Flint said, "That we'd been reported as suspected drug traffickers. We must have not fit their profile, otherwise they'd have forced us to go land somewhere in Colombia."

"You think they believed we're doctors?" Ed asked.

"I think it helped to play the American doctor card. A while back, a Peruvian jet shot down a missionary plane they had misidentified as a drug runner. A woman and her baby were killed and the whole regional air interdiction program was shut down for several years."

"So, are we off the hook?"

Flint shrugged. "They've sent notification of the drug trafficker report along with our description, position, heading, and destination to the Venezuelan border security, and said we can expect to be inspected in Maracaibo. But when we land at the Mission in the Valle Amarillo, I doubt the Venezuelans will come looking for us."

"Yeah, but X-Ops had to be the source of the drug trafficker report," Ed said. "The question is will *they* come looking for us?"

Flint looked at him. "I guess we'll find out."

The Cessna's descent to a lower altitude allowed Kris a closer look at the terrain. In the distance to the left and right, rocky mountain tops towered above them. Below were densely forested ridges and deep ravines with no visible evidence of human existence. "Looks primeval and impenetrable down there. No houses, no roads, nothing. How do people get through to the Valle?" she asked.

"There are trails through the forest. People get around on foot or by burro."

"It must be sparsely populated."

"By humans, yes," Flint said. "But lots of birds, insects, snakes, and other wildlife."

Kris thought, *I'm glad we're flying over it.*

At the lower altitude, the Cessna had started to pitch up, down, and sideways. "It's bumpier down here because of the tricky wind shifts, but once we clear the bald ridge up ahead, the mountain pass leading to the Valle is just beyond."

As they approached the ridge, a downdraft dropped the Cessna several hundred feet and Flint had to apply full engine power to clear the ridge at a safe altitude. As they flew 1000 feet over the rocky crest, a bullet fired from an AK-47 rifle tore through the outer hull of the Cessna just below the left door and struck Flint's left thigh, fracturing his femur.

"Ahhh – my leg!" Flint clutched at his thigh. When he saw blood on his hand, he knew he'd been shot. A glance at the ridge below confirmed his suspicion. Men in jungle fatigues with rifles aimed at the Cessna. "Guerillas firing at us. Get down!"

Flint maintained full power and banked the plane to the right. He nosed the Cessna down to increase their airspeed to get out of rifle range as quickly as possible.

Another bullet shattered the rear window next to Kris and struck the ceiling of the cabin. A third hit Flint in the left flank, contused his kidney and lodged in the muscles of his back. Flint groaned and gritted his teeth. "I'm hit. You two okay?"

Both Kris and Ed shouted "Yeah."

Flint was unaware that two other bullets had already hit the engine compartment. One had punctured the oil reservoir tank and the other had ruptured the fuel line. Just as they flew beyond the range of the AK-47 rifle fire, the engine started to sputter and misfire for insufficient fuel. The wing tanks were nearly full of fuel, but it was not getting to the engine. The fuel problem and the dropping oil pressure were both indicators of imminent engine failure. A crash would follow. Flint started to scan the terrain in front of them for the safest place to put the airplane down. The sun glinted off water at the bottom of a ravine ahead, so he decided to try for a water landing. Then the engine quit and would not restart.

The Cessna cabin became eerily quiet, except for the whistle of air rushing past the broken left rear window. "Lost the engine. Going to glide down into a river ahead. Buckle in as tight as you can." Flint was sweating, but his calm demeanor and instructions kept Kris and Ed from panicking.

"You can do it, Cory," Kris said.

Flint remembered the blankets. "Kris, get the blankets under my seat, give one to Ed. fold them and cover your faces just before we hit."

"Got 'em."

As the Cessna glided downward, Flint muttered to himself, "Need full flaps." He moved the lever to fully lower the wingflaps. This would help keep their airspeed from getting excessive as the plane angled down toward the small river just visible between overhanging tree branches. He would try to keep their airspeed just above stall speed and hoped that the wings mushing into the overhanging branches would dissipate at least some of the Cessna's downward crash energy before they hit the water and riverbed. When he estimated twenty seconds to impact, he opened the left door and shouted to Ed, "Open your door and leave it cracked like this."

"Got it."

The stall warning sounded, so Flint nosed the plane down a bit. He banked slightly left, aiming to hit branches equally near the middle of the river. He shut off the fuel pump and electrical switch. "Cover your face and hang on!"

The green foliage loomed larger, then filled the windscreen as the Cessna struck the overhanging branches with a loud thwack sounds and jolts of deceleration. The left wing struck a larger branch, and the differential in impact resistance rotated the Cessna toward the left riverbank. The nose and fuselage plunged into the river, generating a huge spray of water, before thudding to a stop against the sandy riverbank.

It was quiet, except for the river water gurgling and eddying around the downed Cessna. Kris was dazed and aware of pain in her left arm, chest and hip. She felt weak and unsure of where she was or what had just happened. She noticed a blanket on her lap and that she was strapped in by a seat belt. Her feet felt cool, and she realized they were in water. Someone was calling her name and shaking her arm.

"Kris – Kris – are you okay?"

She turned toward the voice and recognized Ed. "W-what happened?"

"Our plane was shot down by guerillas. We just crashed into a river."

Kris began to become more aware of their situation, and to remember the events leading up to it. "All I could think about as we were going down was what that intern at Parish General said about Renk being treetop level with all engines out."

"Are you hurt?"

"My left side – just muscles bashed up, I think. Am I bleeding?"

"All I see are a few tiny glass cuts on your face."

"What about you? And Cory?"

"I'm fine. A little sore and stiff. Cory's slumped over, bleeding from his forehead. He's alive but not moving. I need to get both of you out and onto the riverbank."

"I smell gas."

"Me too, but I don't think there's a fire risk. Everything's too wet."

The Cessna had come to rest on the fuselage with the left wing down, so it was a struggle for Ed to get Kris from the left back seat out the right side door. Once out and on her feet, she started to pass out. Ed had to catch her and carry her to the riverbank, where he laid her down on a blanket. Kris came to within a few seconds.

"Woo. I feel so much better lying down. Everything turned white just now. Blood pressure must've bottomed out."

Ed was worried that Kris' low blood pressure might be from internal bleeding. Liver failure would cause a depletion of blood clotting factors and result in a bleeding tendency. Kris' skin bruises were an indication that the process had already begun. Blunt injury to her liver or spleen in the crash could cause those organs to bleed uncontrollably into her abdomen and be rapidly fatal. He started to poke and palpate her upper abdomen to see if she was tender over those organs.

"What are you doing? Oh, I know – doctors can't help but mash on patients – myself included. We're all a bunch of mashers."

"You don't seem to be tender over the liver or spleen," Ed said.

"I don't have abdominal pain, but I am thirsty. Please get me something to drink, but go help Cory first."

Ed went to check on Flint, who was awake but confused and mumbling. There was no hope of getting him out through the left door which was wedged shut against the riverbed. He guessed Flint's weight to be at least 250 pounds, and Ed knew he couldn't drag him out. Flint would have to help get himself out. Ed pondered briefly over how to wake him up more. He got a cup out of the storage cabinet, filled it with cool river water, and splashed the contents on Flint's face.

Flint sputtered, shook his head, and wiped his face with his hands. "What are you doing? Trying to drown me?"

"Cory – just trying to wake you up. It worked."

Flint moved in his seat and winced. "Damn, my left thigh and back are killing me."

"I think you got shot."

"I did? Shit. Where's that Esteban when I need him? Who shot me?"

Ed realized that Flint must have had a concussion to account for his confusion and amnesia. He shook Flint's arm and said, "Cory, we got shot down by guerillas. You flew the Cessna down into the trees and this river and saved our lives."

Flint looked at Ed, at the damaged Cessna, and at the river water soaking his feet. He sighed and said, "I need a drink."

That reminded Ed of Kris' request. He retrieved two bottles of water out of the storage cabinet and handed one to Flint.

"No, you idiot. I need the bourbon. There's another full hip flask in there." When Ed hesitated, Flint pleaded. "Please. I need it for the medicinal anesthetic effect."

Ed figured that the alcohol might help get Flint out of the plane. He retrieved the flask of bourbon and gave it to Flint. "I need to go check on Kris."

Flint nodded as he held up the flask. "Jack will keep me company."

Kris was still lying flat on the riverbank as Ed brought the water. She looked up at him and said, "Every time I sit up, I get *really* faint." She gulped down the two bottles of water. "Thanks. How's Cory?"

I think he's had a concussion and got shot at least once. He's in a lot of pain, but will have to help himself get out."

"I can't help you with him. My left arm and leg are so sore." She remembered her propensity to bruise. "Oh Lordy. I bet my whole left side turns purple."

"I'll get you more to drink. You need more fluid volume. Want a hit of bourbon before Cory drinks it all?"

"I would if I didn't have a bad liver."

Ed sloshed back to the Cessna. Flint had already finished the bourbon and announced he was feeling a little better.

"Okay. Then let's try to get you out of there."

Flint was able to use his arms and right leg to flop into the right seat. His lower back and left trouser seat were blood stained, and he bellowed in pain with any movement of his left thigh. With Ed's help, Flint got out and stood up holding onto the door of the plane, although he couldn't bear any weight on his left leg.

He grimaced and said, "It has to be broken."

Ed took Flint's left arm over his shoulder and got him up on the riverbank next to Kris. He went back to the Cessna and retrieved Kris' purse, Flint's bag, the storage cabinet, and the juice that he had purchased in San Antonio.

She drank the fruit juice. "I feel better, but still really weak. My body's turned to mush. And look how yellow I've gotten," she said as she raised her arms for the others to see.

Flint was oblivious to her as he stared at the wreckage. "Sorry about the crash."

Ed shook his head. "Cory, – a pilot friend once told me that any landing that you walk or crawl away from was a good one. You saved our lives."

"I agree," said Kris. "So Cory, how do we get out of here? Is the plane sending an emergency signal out to guide the rescue team?"

Flint shook his head and laughed. "I turned everything off to avoid detection. The radio should still work. If not, we're in a real fix. No one will start to look for us until we are overdue in Maracaibo. Even then, a search plane could fly right overhead and not spot the Cessna because of the trees. Ed will have to –. " Flint stopped in mid-sentence and raised both arms in the air.

Kris turned in the direction Flint was facing. Out of the forest had come a dozen soldiers who were shouting in Spanish as they aimed their rifles at them. Ed already had his arms up, and she raised hers.

Chapter 26

As the soldiers surrounded them, Kris kept her arms up and whispered to Ed, "This is not the rescue team."

"No, I would guess they're Colombians – probably the guerillas who shot us down. They didn't immediately kill us, so maybe we can convince them to help us once they take what they want."

One soldier had already started to loot the Cessna. Two others helped themselves to sandwiches and cans of cola out of the storage cabinet. Another demanded Flint's wallet.

Kris watched and whispered, "Some of them are just kids."

"Tough, experienced kids," Ed said as he handed over his wallet in response to a rifle muzzle poked against his left chest.

Two guerillas were eyeing Kris and her purse. The closest stepped forward to grab it when a voice commanded, "*Espere!*"

The guerilla stopped and turned to the one who had just spoken, who was clearly in charge. The guerilla leader stepped forward and pointed to Kris' raised left hand with the ugly dry ulcer on the index fingertip. He turned to the others and said, "*Mire el dedo y el piel. Ella tiene el muerto amarillo de las montañas y va a morir pronto. No le moleste.*"

The guerillas who had menaced Kris both murmured, nodded, and stepped away from her.

"What did their leader say?"

"He said you have the yellow death of the mountains and ...ah...will die soon."

"Oh. Then we're in the right place."

A hint of a smile showed on Ed's face. He shook his head slightly in admiration. He thought, *I'm really going to miss her when she's gone.* Kris' expected death was still difficult for him to accept, even though her physical changes were undeniable.

The guerilla leader demanded to know who they were and why they were in the area. He became especially suspicious of Flint when one of his men discovered an old DEA identification card in his wallet. The soldiers had searched the Cessna for drugs, but found only Flint's stash of four bottles of Jack Daniels and a couple of handguns, all of which they confiscated.

When Flint explained that Ed and Kris were American doctors headed for the mission hospital, the leader came over to Ed and said, "*Me llamo Enrique. Necesitamos un medico. Tiene que venir con nosotros. Si usted resiste, vamos a matar sus amigos.*" He pointed at Kris and Flint as he spoke.

Ed looked panic-stricken and turned to Kris. "Their leader, Enrique, is demanding I go with them as their doctor. If I resist, they'll kill you and Cory and then force me to go anyway. I have no choice."

Kris bit her lip. "It's okay. We'll figure something out. Better go."

Ed still looked distraught. "I have to. I'll do anything and everything to get back as soon as I can."

Enrique barked orders to two of his men, prompting Flint to mutter, "Shit."

Two guerillas positioned themselves near the open Cessna door, aimed their rifles, and shot up the instrument panel and the radio. The bullets created sparks that ignited residual fuel in the engine compartment. There was a *whump* sound as flames enveloped the whole front of the Cessna, generating a thick cloud of black smoke that rose up through the trees.

Enrique called out to his men, "*Vamos. Va a llover.*" The guerillas got up to go and took all the extra provisions. Two of them used their rifles to prod Ed to move, as they could tell that he was extremely reluctant to leave. Kris heard him say something to Enrique in Spanish just before they disappeared into the forest.

"What did Ed say?" she asked.

"He protested them leaving us without food or water. The good news is that water won't be a problem."

"Why not?"

"See the floodwater marks on those trees?"

Kris nodded.

"A heavy rain in the mountains above us probably turns this quiet little river into a raging torrent five feet deep where we are right now. Thunderstorms are forecast, and Enrique just told his men that it's going to rain."

"Great. Here's good news - bad news for you. We get found - but it's by X-Ops."

Flint only grunted in response. Then he started to sing: "Roll me over, in the clover..."

"Are you drunk?"

"I got a little buzz going."

Kris was upset, although not really at Flint. She could use a shot herself. She missed Ed. He'd been her rock. Suddenly he was gone, and she hadn't really gotten a chance to say good bye and thank him. Kris was afraid she would never see him again. She turned to Flint. "How long might they hold Ed?"

"They've been known to abduct and hold hostages for ransom for years."

"Will they hurt him?"

Flint shook his head. "Not if he co-operates."

"So how do we get out of this fix?"

"I dunno. Maybe the smoke will attract someone's attention. The guerillas took the flare gun. I can't even get up on my feet."

"I'm not much better off," Kris said. "Though at least I can sit up now for a couple of minutes before I get dizzy. Let me see what's left in the storage – Cory! – a snake. Get it!" She pointed to a small bright green snake that had slithered atop the cabinet and was flicking its forked tongue at her.

Flint looked serious. "Good news – that's a non-poisonous Andes mountain water snake. Bad news – they come out and seek higher ground before a flood. Watch him."

He threw a stone which missed the snake and hit the cabinet instead, but it was enough of a disturbance to make the snake slither down. It moved quickly away from the river and disappeared into foliage, on its way to higher ground.

"You weren't kidding about the snake's behavior, were you?"

Flint shook his head as thunder rumbled in the distance. "Good news – we'll be able to tell the water is rising. Bad news – it can come down as a wall of water."

"I am just not going to listen to you anymore," said Kris. She slid over to the storage unit to see if she could salvage anything useful. "Here's a whistle." She raised it to her lips and blew a sound that was a shrill tweet at first, then a lower-pitched screechy growl.

Flint started to laugh. "Good news – it'll get someone's attention. Bad news – that was the mating call of a female jaguar in heat."

At that comment, Kris started to giggle. She stopped when she saw a small human face peering at them from behind a bush only 30 yards away. The face disappeared. "Hey!" Kris shouted. "Please help us!"

Flint turned in the direction she was looking. "What did you see?"

"A face, dark hair – like an Indian. Short stature. Any pygmies around here?"

"No. Try the whistle again."

Kris blew it again. This time it was a long shrill whistle. The subsequent silence was broken by a loud rumble overhead, followed by a crackling crescendo of thunder. She saw another green snake slither out of the river and head for higher ground in the same direction as the previous one. It grew darker and the air seemed cooler. A gust of wind swayed the treetops. Rain began to drip down off the leaves of the trees above them.

Flint looked nervous and fidgety. "We need to get to higher ground. Look at the river."

The water flow was faster and deeper already, washing almost up to the broken left rear window of the Cessna. The river water color had changed into an opaque reddish brown. Kris gasped as she watched the increasing force of the flow of water push the airplane wreckage 10 yards downstream until it caught on large boulders. Rain started to come down hard, and the river roared even louder.

Flint yelled at Kris, "Let's go – now!" He turned away and started to drag himself in the direction the snakes had taken.

Kris realized the rationale for his choice of an escape route. "No!" she shouted. "Not that way! Well, all right." She zipped shut her purse and slung it tightly over her right shoulder, and belly-crawled right after him as fast as she could.

Within the next few seconds, the river overflowed its banks. Kris felt cool muddy water flow under her as she crawled into the underbrush after Flint. She was already soaked, and started to shiver. She had to stop briefly when a big black beetle and an even larger spider, both being washed downriver, sought refuge on her left arm and shoulder. "Oh no, you don't," she said as she knocked them off her.

Floating debris bumped against Kris' tender left side, making her wince. The current deepened and its force strengthened, and started to push her downstream. Kris had to grab bushes and saplings to pull forward and push with her feet to make any progress and not be swept away. She was weakening against the torrent of water cascading down the ravine. Ten yards ahead of her, she saw Flint grim-faced and locked onto a small tree trunk with both arms and his good leg. The water was up to his waist. He couldn't help her. Totally exhausted, Kris held onto a sapling with both hands. She felt her grip weakening, then couldn't hold on any longer. *So this is how it ends*, she thought just before she passed out.

Chapter 27

Kris never felt the hand that grabbed her wrist and pulled her to safety out of the raging river. She was only barely cognizant of the strong arms that carried her and laid her on the back of a pack animal. It was her face in the wet fur of her beast of burden and a noseful of its ammoniacal stench that served as the smelling salt that woke her up.

Kris opened her eyes. Somehow she hadn't drowned in the flash flood. She was covered with a blanket and riding crossways on the back of a pack animal, maybe a mule or burro. A strong dark-skinned arm and hand supported her. It belonged to a man whom she assumed was a Yachabo Indian. She was so weak that her arms and legs flopped in rhythm with the animal's up and down movement as they followed a trail through the forest. She tried to look up to see where they were going, but couldn't keep her head up. Her face plopped into the pungent fur again.

"Woof" was her reaction as she got another noseful and snapped her head back. She patted the animal's side and whispered, "I'm going to name you Rosebud and I'm going to give you a bath when I get stronger."

Pain-related grunts and curses made Kris look back. She saw Flint being transported on another pack animal that followed behind Rosebud. She was thankful the Indians had been able to rescue him. She was sure it hadn't been easy, as big as he was and unable to use his left leg. She caught the eye of the Indian beside her. She thought he might understand Spanish so she said, "*Muchas gracias.*"

He seemed to understand as he smiled an acknowledgement.

Kris pointed a finger at the Indian and asked, "Yachabo?"

He grinned and pointed at himself "Yachabo – Mesala."

Kris assumed "Mesala" was his name. She pointed at herself and said "Kris."

The Indian pointed back and said, "Kiss."

With that response, Kris decided to change the subject but didn't know how else to communicate. She called back to Flint, "Hey – Cory."

"Yo."

"Are you okay?"

"I'm sober and my leg is killing me. Otherwise okay. How about you?"

"I'm so weak I'm flopping around like a wet noodle. Do these guys speak Spanish?"

"A couple of them do. They're taking us to the mission hospital."

"Good news. No bad news – right?"

"Right."

"How did they find us?"

"The midget you spotted was a boy from their village, which isn't too far from where we crash landed. He got curious about the rifle fire and the smoke from the Cessna. When he saw where we were and the thunderstorm brewing, he ran home to alert his parents."

"Smart boy. He saved our lives."

"I saw you being swept away and I was about to give up myself when five Indians showed up. They fished us out and others went to get the mules and blankets."

"How much farther to the mission hospital?"

"I have no idea."

Kris appreciated Rosebud's strength and surefootedness more and more as the trail wound through the forest. At times it descended at a steep angle down to the Valle Amarillo. As they approached the valley floor, the forest thinned out and the trail passed through several open meadows. The rain had long since stopped, but several of the creeks they crossed were swollen with the same reddish brown flood water as in the mountain ravine.

It was late afternoon. All Kris wanted was fresh, dry clothing and a warm, clean bed to sleep in for a few hours. She had thought about Ed several times, and prayed for his safety. She couldn't imagine the guerillas would just let him go. If he somehow escaped, he wouldn't know the way back to the ravine and to the hospital, unless the Indians guided him. She had expected and wanted him to be there by her side when she lapsed into the final irreversible coma that she knew was coming in the next day or so. If she hadn't gotten the needlestick and the infection, she wondered whether her relationship with him might have blossomed into a serious romance, or even marriage and children. *Maybe. He's definitely someone I could go for.*

Her reverie was abruptly terminated when Rosebud lost her footing on a loose rock and stumbled. Mesala had to grab onto Kris' arm to keep her from falling off.

The Indians finally stopped in a clearing at the end of what looked to Kris like a road.

"Someone's coming out from the mission to get us," Flint called to her.

"Sounds good, but how did they know we're here?"

"The Yachabo sent a runner ahead to alert the mission people."

After a few minutes, Kris heard a car and looked up to see it was actually a pick-up truck coming up the road toward them. She pushed herself back and slid off Rosebud, but got dizzy when up on her feet and had to hold onto Rosebud's neck for support. The mule stood patiently as Kris leaned and held onto her. Kris wished she had an apple for her as a thank-you reward.

As she waited, one of the Yachabo brought Kris her purse, which she had assumed had washed away in the flash flood. She was delighted to have it back and gave a smile and nod of appreciation to the Indian who returned it. She had had it on her shoulder while struggling against the floodwater. It must have still been there when she was pulled from the river. When she pulled the zipper to open it, the contents were damp but seemed intact.

The dark green Dodge pick-up truck drove up to the end of the road and came to a stop with a squeal of the brakes. The name *Mision de Santa Maria* was painted on the side and mattresses were set up in the cargo bed. Through the open truck window, Kris saw that the driver was a middle-aged man with reddish-brown hair and a pale, freckly face. He got out of the pick-up along with an older woman dressed in a crisply starched blue and white nurse's uniform. The man headed toward Kris with a concerned expression while the woman went to check on Flint.

"Hello, I'm Robby Paterson, the doctor for the Santa Maria hospital," the man said in a soft Scottish accent.

Kris extended her hand. "I'm Dr. Kris Jensen."

"We heard the Agora villagers had found two people in the Noravo Ravine. That's a death trap. What happened?"

"We were flying in to your mission hospital and got shot down by Colombian guerillas. Crashed into the ravine."

"Oh my Lord. Are you hurt?"

"Bashed up my left side. Mainly stiff and bruised. Nothing broken."

"We'll check you thoroughly at the hospital. You look jaundiced. You say you're a doctor?"

Kris nodded. "Internal medicine, now an epidemiologist specializing in viral hepatitis."

"Then what kind of liver disease do you have?"

"I have a rapidly progressive viral hepatitis. I heard it's called 'the yellow death of the mountains' around here."

Paterson looked puzzled. "I know what you mean, but you've only just arrived. How could you have gotten that?"

"It's a long story. I – ." Kris started to feel faint. She looked pale, felt clammy and began to slump to the ground.

Paterson stepped forward to catch her and ease her down. He spoke in Yachabo to the Indians standing nearby to get them to help get Kris onto one of the mattresses in the back of the pick-up truck. He checked her pulse and blood pressure, which were okay once she was recumbent.

Kris came around quickly once off her feet. "Sorry, I just passed out on you, didn't I?"

Paterson said, "Yes. You need a saline drip at the hospital."

"You mean IV fluids because my circulating volume is low."

"Exactly. Sorry about this rather primitive ambulance."

"It's already more comfortable than Rosebud's back," Kris said as she pointed to the mule.

"Good. Excuse me please." Paterson left to check on Flint. He returned shortly thereafter with the older nurse. Kris sat up as they approached. The nurse had a stern expression and her hair was tied back in a severe bun. Kris' first impression was that she was stiff, humorless, and no-nonsense. Her German accent came as no surprise.

"I am Sister Helmtrude," she said and offered her hand with a nod of respect.

"Pleased to meet you. I'm Kris Jensen."

"You are a doctor, I understand."

"Yes."

"You look more like a patient than a doctor."

Kris smiled. "I'm sure I do." Sister Helmtrude's bluntness reminded Kris of her German mother.

"Helmtrude, we should get back to the Mission before dark and before the rain starts again." Paterson turned to Kris. "The road is rather bumpy, I'm afraid, but I'll go slow."

"I'll be fine. How far is it?"

"Only about 10 miles but it'll take us 30 minutes."

The Yachabo loaded Flint onto a stretcher and placed him on the mattresses next to Kris. Mesala and two other Indians rode along in the back of the pick-up with them. Kris was exhausted and wanted to sleep but the many bumps and jolts along the way prevented it, even though Paterson did his best to slow down for each of them. While lying on the mattress, Kris got a good look at the Indians starting with their bare feet. All had tough leathery skin and scars on their legs. The Yachabo standing next to Mesala had an odd looking oval depressed scar on his distal calf that almost looked like a brand on a steer. Kris wondered whether it was some type of ritual tribal scarification.

As they approached the Mission, the roadbed became smoother and Kris started to doze off, but she became more alert when she realized that they had entered the Mission grounds. They drove past a white church and then a school with an adjacent small soccer field marked by two opposing rectangular goals. The pick-up truck stopped with another squeal of the brakes in front of a complex of single-story buildings. Kris looked up at the sign over the main door, which read *El Hospital de Santa Maria.*

So this, then, is my final resting place.

****

At the FBI headquarters in Atlanta, Jonas Peterson sat down again in Steve Garner's office for a briefing prior to the daily 4:00 p.m. meeting of the CDC Bombing Task Force.

Garner began, "Here's the latest from Venezuela. Flint did fly off with Beaufain and Jensen from that little airport near Caracas, but not before a gun battle that left a drug gang member dead. Flint's bodyguard, who was the executioner at the airport, is in police custody for questioning, but he couldn't or wouldn't tell them where Flint was headed."

"What about Flint's computer?"

"They found one computer and did get into his e-mail. Found a message from Jensen that asked him to meet her early this morning when their plane arrived from Houston, but didn't say why. No messages to or from Aburcorn, but they're still looking."

"Okay, so how do we find them?" Peterson asked.

"There's more. We'd asked the Venezuelans for help and they told us Flint filed a flight plan from San Antonio in western Venezuela right on the Colombian border to Maracaibo in the north. But then the Colombians report to the Venezuelans that two of their jets intercepted Flint's plane as a suspected drug trafficker, but then let them go mainly because they were in Venezuelan airspace. Now Flint's plane is overdue in Maracaibo, and no one knows where he is. Either he landed someplace else or they crashed somewhere in the mountains. The Colombian Air Force denies shooting them down."

"Why would Flint traffic in drugs?"

Garner shook his head. "I don't think he would. He had a spotless career with the DEA. He's had a problem with alcohol. That's it."

Peterson mulled over the information. "Then who reported him as a drug trafficker? That could've gotten him killed."

"Oddly enough, it was our DEA. We've requested the basis for it from them, but so far DEA's not co-operating. I did get from the State Department that Flint hasn't been back in the U.S. since his mother died five years ago. That supports there are others involved."

"What's next?"

Garner said, "Castillo's en route to San Antonio where Flint refueled to see what they may have told people at the airport about their destination. McKeeson stayed in Caracas to investigate Flint's e-mails. The big problem will be to find them if their plane crashed. The intercept occurred in a remote area with mountains, dense forests and jungles, not to mention being an area infiltrated and

controlled by Colombian guerillas, FARC mostly. I wouldn't
expect much from Venezuelan search and rescue."

"Do we have justification to use our military?"

"I would think so. Jensen, Flint and Beaufain are all key
people in our investigation. Dr. Jensen is a Lieutenant Commander
in the USPHS, so technically she's military and AWOL. I'd have to
get it cleared by State and the Pentagon, though. Then the
Venezuelans would have to cooperate."

Peterson looked at his watch. "We better get over to the
meeting."

****

In the Extraordinary Operations Division of the DEA Headquarters
building in Washington D.C., Agent Bill Swanson sat with his
chief, Peter Arnett.

Swanson spoke first. "Haven't yet wrapped up the
unfinished business."

Arnett scowled and asked, "What happened with the
intercept?"

"Flint stayed in Venezuelan airspace and the Colombians'
criteria to force a landing weren't met, so they let him go. Then the
FBI found out from them that we had fingered Flint as narco-
traffic, and now the FBI wants us to tell them why."

Arnett rubbed his chin. "Just tell them we got tips from
reliable informants based in Venezuela. If the FBI asks about Jensen
and Beaufain, deny any knowledge that they were with him."

"What if they find out we tracked his plane?"

"If they do, tell them it's routine for suspected drug
traffickers. So where is the plane?"

"It dropped out of sight in a remote mountainous area. I'm sure they crashed."

"Why? I thought Cory was an experienced pilot."

Swanson shrugged. "He is – or was. The Colombian jet pilots deny shooting at them. Could have been mechanical failure, or maybe Flint misjudged tricky mountain winds. Another scenario is that they were shot down by groundfire from Colombian guerillas."

"Have we spotted the plane?"

"Not yet. Probably won't. The area is a dense tropical forest, and now there's cloud cover from thunderstorms."

"Could they have landed anywhere?"

"They appeared to be on an approach to a mountain valley called 'El Valle Amarillo.' There's a mission there with a landing strip, but we looked hard at satellite images of the mission grounds and saw no airplane. We think they went down in an area called the Noravo Ravine. It's a natural drainage funnel for rainwater coming off the mountains and with the thunderstorms in the area, there was probably a flash flood in the ravine shortly after the plane disappeared. They're all likely dead, but I don't know that for sure."

Arnett frowned. "Send in a team to make sure. We need to get to them before the FBI does. I want their dogtags in my hand."

"Sanders and Jones are already on their way."

Chapter 28

Kris and Flint were placed in beds in adjacent rooms in a small
private wing of the Santa Maria Mission hospital. Kris had blood
drawn for lab tests, and had gotten cleaned up and changed into a
set of surgical scrub clothes. After an examination by Paterson and
insertion of an intravenous catheter for fluid administration, she
quickly fell asleep. Paterson tried to obtain additional medical
history from her, but she kept dozing off. He gave up and returned
two hours later with her chart and lab reports in hand. He was
pleased to find she was now easily aroused from sleep, stayed
awake and was lucid.

"Feeling better?"

"Much, thank you. How's Cory?"

"Mr. Flint? He was shot twice, but his vital signs are stable.
The main problem is a left femoral shaft fracture, most likely from a
bullet rather than the crash as there are metal fragments in his
thigh. He also has blood in his urine, though I'm not sure why.
Could be a contused kidney from blunt injury or damage to the
urinary tract from a second bullet in his back. We gave him
morphine. He's asleep."

"Two things you need to know. Ed told me Cory was initially unconscious, so he at least had a concussion in the plane crash. Also I suspect he's a heavy drinker, so watch out for symptoms of alcohol withdrawal."

"I'm glad you told me. We'll do neuro checks on him. Who's Ed?"

"He's a public health doc from New Orleans who was with us in the plane. He came through the crash intact, but he was forced to go with the guerillas to be their doctor. I'd *really* like to somehow find out if he's okay. Do you know of any way to contact the guerillas? Their leader was named Enrique."

"Colombians show up here every so often when they need medical treatment. They appreciate and respect what we do, so they generally leave us alone. I've heard of Enrique but I have no way to contact him, much less have any influence on his actions." Paterson raised her chart in the air. "We need to talk about you and your lab results."

Kris nodded. "How bad are they?"

"Bad. Your bilirubin is 22. The SGOT is over 3000 – that is as high as our lab can measure. We can't do blood ammonia or a prothrombin time."

Kris shook her head. "You won't need them. I expect to deteriorate into a hepatic coma over the next 24 to 48 hours – and I want no CPR or other resuscitation attempt."

"Understood."

"If I become encephalopathic, I do want to get lactulose."

"No problem. We have it." Paterson paused. "Dr. Jensen, could you please now tell me how you might have acquired our local fulminant hepatitis and why you came here for – ah – your final days?"

"I'll be glad to explain."

"Before you do, let me get the Sister," Paterson said. "She wanted to know also. She's just down the hall."

After he returned with Sister Helmtrude, Kris began with the X-Ops plot and how they acquired the virus and then summarized her investigation, the subsequent events, and finally her reasons for coming to the Santa Maria Mission.

Paterson listened with rapt attention. After she had finished, he said, "That is a remarkable story." He looked at Helmtrude. "Don't you think?"

Sister Helmtrude nodded. "Ja."

He turned back to Kris. "Let me add a little background. The Yachabo who died in Caracas was a young man named Nadeiko, about 20 years old and rather a rebellious type. About six months ago, he developed the primary ulcer on his leg followed by early symptoms of hepatitis but refused to just go home to die in the village. Nadeiko was convinced that the white's man's medicine in the big city could cure him of the yellow death. He knew Jose Banda, our mission pilot, who happened to be here for the biweekly supply visit. He talked Jose into taking him back to San Antonio and then to fly him on to Caracas, where Jose has family. Two weeks later, when Jose came for his next visit, he reported that Nadeiko had died. The parents were quite upset, not only because their son was dead but even more so because his death occurred away from their home village."

Kris said, "I don't even want to think about how far away I am from my home village. Why is that an issue for the Yachabo?"

Sister Helmtrude answered, "It is one of their strongest tribal beliefs that death must occur in the home village so as to appease the ancestors."

"It's a belief we have to respect," Paterson said. "When the Yachabo come to visit a relative in the hospital, they count the number of tubes attached to the patient. If it's three or more, such as a nasogastric tube, an intravenous line, and a urinary drainage catheter, the Yachabo interpret that many tubes to signify that the severity of illness is such that the patient is at high risk of dying. They'll abscond with the patient in the night for a one-way trip back to the home village. Such premature removal of patients from the hospital has resulted in unnecessary deaths."

"If that's true, have you ever had any patient die of this yellow death hepatitis in the hospital?"

Paterson and Sister Helmtrude looked at each other. Paterson shook his head, but Helmtrude said, "The only one was Sister Rosa, about 15 years ago. Rosa was a Spanish nurse who came as a volunteer. She was athletic and enjoyed hiking the trails in the mountain forest. She noticed the ulcer on her arm and within a few days became jaundiced and died before we could arrange to evacuate her. It was frightening to all of us back then, because Rosa had had hepatitis B and yellow fever vaccines before she came here. But no one else of our staff has ever gotten it before or since Rosa." Sister Helmtrude looked directly at Kris. "I am sorry to say this, but your appearance disturbs me because the day before she died, Sister Rosa looked exactly like you do now."

"I know what's in store for me." Kris raised her bare right foot high up off the bed and wiggled it. "But I'm not dead yet." She smiled and they both smiled back. "So – another question. How long has this hepatitis been plaguing the Yachabo?"

Paterson said, "A long time. Maybe hundreds of years. This place was originally called 'Valley of the Yellow Devil' in reference to the hepatitis, but when it was appreciated that the disease was more associated with the mountain forest, the devil part of the valley name got dropped."

Sister Helmtrude added, "This Mission was first established about 125 years ago because of the misconception that the Yachabo were devil worshipers."

Kris said, "That's fascinating. But just how common is this hepatitis among the Yachabo? Are there ever any survivors?"

"I simply don't know," Paterson said. "I hear about hepatitis cases, but the Yachabo rarely come to the hospital or even to our village-based clinics for its evaluation or treatment. I guess they've long since realized that we have little to offer. We do have one of the tribal elders staying overnight here in the hospital after foot surgery earlier today. He might have better answers for you."

Sister Helmtrude nodded. "He would be quite a good person to ask, because we have heard he is also an important native healer or 'root doctor' as we call them. If he is willing and you are able, why don't we go ask him in the morning?"

"Are you kidding? That's why I'm here. Can we go see him now? Who knows what kind of shape I'll be in tomorrow."

Sister Helmtrude looked at Paterson. "Ingasa *is* still awake. I just checked on him. Said he can't sleep in our mushy soft beds and wants to sleep on the floor."

Paterson shrugged. "Go ask him if he would agree to answer a few questions."

The Sister nodded and left.

Paterson turned to Kris. "So how do you plan to pass on the information that you gather?"

"Ed's not here, so I had hoped to borrow a tape recorder from you. And, ah – " Kris paused and bit her lip. "While I'm still able, I'd like to record a last message to my mom and one to my brother Eric." She started to sniffle. A tear rolled down her cheek.

Paterson found a tissue for her and said, "I have a recorder you can use and lots of blank tapes."

"I'd appreciate it. Thanks," she said as she used the tissue to dab at her eyes and wipe away the tear track. "You know my father was a missionary doctor in Africa. Mission work, along with Mozart and railroad trains, were his passions. We were in Rhodesia when he died of an Ebola-like infection." More tears welled up and flowed down her face. "Sorry. I seem to be losing it."

Paterson gave her the box of tissues and reached out to hold her hand. "Sometimes it's best to just let it out." He waited to allow her to collect herself. "I share your father's passion for the mission – and for Mozart. I'd love to hear more about your father when you are up to it."

Kris drew a deep breath and blew her nose. Her mood brightened when Helmtrude returned to report that the Yachabo elder was quite willing to answer questions.

Paterson said, "How about I take you in a wheelchair?"

"Good idea. I'm ready."

Ingasa was sitting up with his bandaged foot elevated as they approached his bed in the semi-private men's ward. Kris smiled and gave him a deferential nod when she was introduced by Sister Helmtrude, who spoke fluent Yachabo. Ingasa was small in stature and his facial skin was wrinkled by age and outdoor exposure, but his eyes were bright and clear. He had scrutinized Kris from the moment she was wheeled into his presence. Even before Kris could ask the first question, he said something that that softened Helmtrude's stern countenance. She turned to Kris and said, "He says you should immediately return to your home village."

"Tell him I understand." She pointed at herself and raised her left index finger to show him the ulcer. "And ask him what the Yachabo call this disease."

Helmtrude spoke to Ingasa and translated his reply. "He says it is the yellow death of the mountain forest."

"How many Yachabo die every year from it?"

Helmtrude translated the question, then raised her eyebrows at Ingasa's response. "He says four to six per year, mostly in the rainy season. I had no idea it was so common."

Paterson shook his head. "Nor did I."

Through a series of questions, Kris learned from Ingasa that the hepatitis primarily affected adult men and sometimes their wives shortly thereafter, which she assumed was via sexual transmission. Children were also occasionally affected, boys more so than girls. There had been one case in a newborn whose mother had become ill just before birth. The primary ulcer most often occurred on the leg, sometimes on the arm, and rarely on the head or neck. The ulcer was not associated with any specific type of insect bite.

Kris said, "Tell him his information has been most helpful. One last question: are there ever any survivors of this disease?" She had expected his answer to be a simple "no," but the translated question led to a lively verbal exchange that lasted several minutes.

Helmtrude finally gave Ingasa's answer simply as, "A few."

Kris said, "Oh really? But what was all the discussion about?"

"We had a little argument over the merit of their root medicine versus what we offer here at the hospital. He said their root medicine saves about one in 10 of the hepatitis cases, but must be given early so that is why they never bring those patients to us because it is a waste of time. That's when we got into it. For most medical conditions, it is the attempt at a root cure before coming to the hospital that is the waste of time. Our treatments get delayed sometimes at great harm to patients."

Paterson said, "I agree. It's a bad problem. The only positive is that root healers are skilled in handling psychiatric illness, which we then never see but would be ill equipped to deal with anyway."

"I understand. But now I have more questions about survivors. First, did they all have primary ulcers? Next, have they remained in good health or have they ever gotten yellow with hepatitis again? Finally, are there any survivors around whom we can talk to and examine?"

Helmtrude translated the questions and summarized Ingasa's replies. "He says the survivors all had ulcers. Most remain healthy but some stay sickly and later die from another yellow illness. He knows of two healthy survivors, one in the Yuka village and one in the Agora village whose name is Kurka." She turned to Paterson. "Wasn't Kurka one of the Agorans who brought Dr. Jensen and Mr. Flint from the ravine?"

He nodded. "In fact, he rode back to the mission with us. Must be staying on the grounds somewhere." He turned to Kris and waved his extended index finger back and forth. "But we're not going out to look for him tonight."

She didn't argue. She asked Helmtrude to thank Ingasa. As Paterson wheeled her back to her room, she mulled over the epidemiologic information gleaned from the Yachabo elder.

Her thoughts were interrupted by the onset of pain in the right upper part of her abdomen, which was followed by a wave of nausea. The dizziness returned, and she was thankful to be in a wheelchair. "I think I'm going to need Phenergan or something for nausea," she said to Paterson as she climbed back into bed.

"A pill or hypo?"

"I'll try a pill first."

Helmtrude went to get the medicine while Paterson left to retrieve the recorder and tapes from his office. By the time they returned, Kris' pain and nausea had abated but were replaced by a sense of profound weakness.

"Woo – just now, I started to get really weak. My arms and legs feel like a ton of swollen mush." She turned to Helmtrude. "But, the nausea's let up, so I'd like to hold off on the Phenergan."

Helmtrude had brought the Phenergan pill in a medicine cup. She put it on the bedside table next to where Paterson had placed the tape recorder.

Kris said, "Now then – want to hear my thoughts on what Ingasa told us?"

They both nodded. Paterson picked up the recorder, loaded a blank tape and handed it to her. "Why don't you dictate and we'll listen."

"Good idea." She cleared her throat and clicked the record button. "This yellow death hepatitis virus is linked to the mountain forest so that its primary transmission almost has to be vector-borne, by that I mean transmitted from an insect. Unlikely to be a tick which stays attached and would've gotten noticed. More likely a small biting fly. There also has to be a virus reservoir in some forest animal that's adapted to this virus and maybe maintains it in a carrier state. We know that small animals like ducks and woodchucks can carry a virus similar to hepatitis B. The secondary person-to-person transmission of this virus by sex, by contaminated sharp object and at birth to a newborn is typical for any bloodborne virus."

"So why do some patients survive?" asked Helmtrude.

"This mountain forest animal virus most likely kills off human liver cells so fast that the entire liver is wiped out before our immune system has time to react and mount an effective response to the virus. In New Orleans with the help of a pathologist, we looked at liver sections from a drug user who had died of the virus and there was a complete lack of white blood cells and inflammatory response – only necrotic dead liver cells. Maybe Ingasa's root medicine inhibits the virus and slows down the liver destruction long enough for the immune system to kick in with white blood cells and antibodies that target and eliminate the virus. Ingasa's sickly survivors probably had so little functioning liver left that, even though the virus was gone, they still died of hepatic insufficiency. It's conceivable that the well survivors not only retained enough liver function but also developed protective antibodies and are now immune to re-infection."

Helmtrude asked, "Should we try to obtain that root medicine to treat you?"

"I think it's too late. Remember, Ingasa advised me to return to my home village. The only treatment that might be worth a try at this point is transfusion from a well survivor. *If* survivors really are immune, transfusion of their blood might transfer specific anti-viral antibodies to me that might slow or even stop the virus and its destruction of my liver."

Paterson shook his head. "Transfusion would be impossible. The Yachabo believe that their blood is the essence of their vitality bestowed upon them by their parents and ancestors. They will only donate to a blood relative, and even then only after a lot of convincing. Giving it away to someone unrelated is forbidden. I don't think it's ever happened." He turned to Helmtrude for corroboration.

"Dr. Paterson is quite correct. It's another Yachabo belief that we have to work around. I would add that our laboratory has only basic blood type and cross-matching technology."

Kris said, "I think I'm type A – or maybe it was O? Rh negative, anyway. Maybe we wouldn't be able to persuade Kurka, but I'd still like to speak with him. Could you find him tomorrow morning and bring him here?"

Helmtrude said, "We will try."

"Thanks." Kris yawned. "I am *so* tired. I still need to record messages for my family. I'll see you in the morning."

Paterson placed his hand gently on her shoulder. "I hope you rest well. Your night nurse, Carmen will let Helmtrude know if there're any problems overnight. I'm on back-up call tonight."

He gave instructions in Spanish to Carmen who was standing in the doorway. They then left Kris to go reassess Cory Flint and to check in with the night staff for the other patient wards.

After she recorded the messages to her family, Kris nodded off almost immediately.

That night, vivid dreams disturbed her sleep. In the first, a ferocious animal with large yellow eyes chased her and Eric through a tropical forest. As they ran, her brother stumbled and fell. The beast pounced on his leg and sunk its teeth into the flesh of his calf. He cried out to Kris, *Help me – I'm dead meat.* She awoke in a sweat and was temporarily disoriented about her surroundings.

In another dream, she was floating on her back in a lake. The gray-green, bloated bodies of Junior Murphee and Homer Renk drifted close by. She looked down and saw that her own body was just as bloated and gray-green. Junior Murphee winked at her and Renk said, *We've been waiting for you to join us,* as he reached to grab her. She pushed against his arm and kicked her legs to get away. They disappeared and when she felt the bed below her, she knew it hadn't been real. She remained restless through the night, with a recurring dream of Ed and her own family turning yellow and dying.

As the first early morning light came through the window, she opened her eyes and saw a huge black spider crawling on the bedsheet toward her face. She seemed unable to move her arms or legs to knock it away, so she yelled for help.

The door that connected to Flint's room was ajar. He awoke when he heard her cry out. "Kris – what is it?"

"A huge spider on me!"

Flint looked around and his eyes widened. He shouted back, "Oh my God! There're spiders all over my room and they're on my bed." He thrashed his arms and bellowed, "Get them off me!"

Chapter 29

At 6:30 a.m., Robby Paterson was asleep in the one-story cottage that served as both his home and office at the Santa Maria Mission. He awoke to a rapping on his bedroom window, which was the way the nurses had been instructed to alert him to an overnight problem in the hospital that required his attention. He got right up and opened the front door.

Anna, one of the night shift nurses, stood on the doorstep. "*Lo siento. Venga pronto, por favor. Sus pacientes, los dos Norteamericanos se comportan como estan loco.*"

"*Gracias. Voy a venir dentro de poco,*" he said, and got dressed. As he trotted the 50 yards to the hospital, he considered reasons why Dr. Jensen and Cory Flint might start to act crazy. It made the most sense that she was encephalopathic from early liver failure, and that he was in alcohol withdrawal.

In the private ward, Sister Helmtrude was already supervising three nurses who were trying to hold down an agitated, writhing Cory Flint. Kris had soft restraints on her arms and legs and was yelling at her nurse.

Helmtrude acknowledged Paterson's arrival. "Good morning. Glad to have you join us."

"What's been going on?"

"Carmen reported both were restless all night. Dr. Jensen became confused, so we gave her a dose of lactulose about ten p.m. She got another dose at three this morning and then we had to put restraints on her. About 6:15, they both became extremely agitated and thrashed about. They were shouting something about spiders in the room and on them."

Paterson liked to ruffle Helmtrude's feathers on occasion. He looked concerned and said, "Were they bitten? I thought you and the nurses kept the hospital a spider-free zone."

Helmtrude stiffened and frowned at him. "Of course we do. They were hallucinating."

"Oh. – Right. They must have been. Vital signs?"

"Both have somewhat elevated blood pressures and heart rates. He has a 101 degree fever."

Paterson went over to Flint, who was in restraints and was tremulous and wide-eyed. He was still babbling about bugs in the room. "It looks like DT's. I saw plenty of cases during my medical training in Glasgow."

"DT's?"

He turned to look at the Sister. "The Yachabo don't drink alcohol, so I guess you've been spared the privilege of caring for it. DT stands for delirium tremens, the most serious form of alcohol withdrawal. Can be life-threatening. He'll need strong sedation. Let's give him 4 mg of IV lorazepam, but let me check him first."

Helmtrude sent a nurse to get the sedative. While Paterson examined Flint, she walked to the connecting door to look in the next room at Kris who was agitated and protesting her restraints.

Helmtrude shook her head slightly, turned back to Paterson and said, "Shouldn't we evacuate these two? Maybe to the hospital in Maracaibo where they are better equipped to handle them."

He looked up. "Yes, but you know how difficult that is to arrange. As for him, we can manage the DT's. His wounds look good and his hematuria has stopped. He does need a rod in his femur, and it's been a while since I did one. We don't have the right orthopedic equipment for the procedure, and regardless, there's no urgent need to get it done. As for Dr. Jensen, it was her expressed wish to remain here with the full expectation that she would die here. I think we should respect that. Don't you?"

She was silent, then said, "You're right, but it's so painful and difficult to watch a young person deteriorate before our eyes."

He said, "I agree, but we'll be with her to comfort her. That's all she expects from us. I wouldn't want to abandon her to strangers in Maracaibo who couldn't do anything more for her there. But you've dealt with dying patients before. What is it about her case?"

Helmtrude's expression turned sad and wistful. "Long ago my parents took me and my older sister Helena on a mission trip to India. Helena was married and pregnant, but her husband had to stay behind in Berlin. Helena was a newly trained nurse and frequently went out into the slums of Calcutta to minister to the poorest of the poor. We had all taken gamma globulin shots beforehand, but Helena became ill with a rapidly progressive hepatitis and died in my arms within a week."

He winced. "How terrible and tragic. It likely was hepatitis E, which has a high mortality in pregnancy."

"Yes. We learned that years later. Then Sister Rosa's death brought back all the sad and painful memories, and now this girl Kris does also." She bit her lip and a tear tracked down her cheek.

Paterson had never seen Helmtrude show such emotion. He put his arm around her shoulder and said, "Whatever happens, we'll help each other see it through."

She whispered, "Thank you."

He glanced at Flint, who had been given the lorazepam and was already calmer. Shouts came from the adjacent room. "Let's go check on our other patient."

Kris was awake but not happy with the nurse standing next to her bed. "Please untie me," Kris pleaded. "There's nothing wrong with me!" She noticed Paterson and Helmtrude. "Whoa, Nelly. Here we go. Here comes the rooster of this effing henhouse, the one with the big cock-a-doodle. Wait, no. This isn't a henhouse – it's the cuckoo's nest, because that's Nurse Ratched with him."

Helmtrude looked puzzled. "Do you have any idea what she's talking about?"

Paterson knew and was trying not to laugh. "I think the liver toxins have clogged up her social filter and rendered it nonfunctional."

"What do you mean?"

"The encephalopathy allows her to express uncensored raw and crude thoughts, ones that she is normally much too polite and respectful to ever verbalize."

"Oh."

Kris was getting impatient. "Come over here, Big Boy, and introduce yourself."

He moved closer and said, "I'm your doctor. Now which doctor am I?"

She showed a sly smile and said, "You're not the witch doctor. You're the *good* doctor, the one who's going to turn me loose."

"Can't do that just yet. Who's the President?"

"Of what?"

Paterson shook his head. "Can you give me the date?"

She smiled and shrugged. "Well, Handsome. I wish I could say I'm free for a date with you but I'm not." She raised her wrists as much as she could against the restraints to show him.

Helmtrude was amused by the repartee between them, but she felt it was time to intercede. "Dr. Paterson, I don't think you are getting anywhere."

"No. But her responses do reflect her confused state of mind."

"I agree. When do you think the lactulose might start to work?"

"Usually not until there's been a bowel movement."

Helmtrude shook her head. "None yet."

"It's been about four hours since her last dose. Let's give her some more lactulose now. It tastes nasty, but I'd like to avoid a nasogastric tube. Was she able to swallow it last night?"

"Yes, but with difficulty. She only took it because I think she understood it was a medication to help her."

"Were you here with Carmen to give it?"

Helmtrude yawned. "I was up about five times last night. It'll be your turn tonight," she said as she left to get the lactulose.

Kris had dozed off. Paterson took the opportunity to examine her while she was resting quietly. Her whole left side was purple with bruises and from bleeding just under her skin. The greenish-yellow hue to her skin had deepened overnight, and with the intravenous fluids she'd received, her arms and legs as well as her abdomen were even more swollen. By the time Helmtrude returned, he had decided he would try to administer the lactulose himself rather than subject one of the nurses to the coughing and sputtering of potentially infectious oral secretions. He did take personal protective precautions that included a gown as well as gloves, mask, and eye protection.

Helmtrude handed him the cupful of lactulose. He woke Kris up and had the wrist restraints removed to allow her to sit up and drink.

She smiled and said, "That's better, honey." She saw the cup in his hand. "Is that for me?"

He smiled back. "Yes, and I want you to drink it quickly. Gulp it down."

She started to drink it, but made a face and spit the lactulose out onto her gown. She spat several more times, trying to get the taste out of her mouth, then looked up and said, "What was that shit? A poison?"

Paterson looked around for Helmtrude, but she had left the room. He walked over to the day nurse Angelina, who spoke English and for that reason had been assigned to care for Kris. He whispered, "She won't swallow it. We'll tie her down again and I'll put down an NG tube."

A small dose of intravenous haloperidol was administered to calm Kris down prior to the nasogastric tube insertion. She strained and bucked anyway, but the plastic tube slid easily into her nasopharynx, down the esophagus and into her stomach, and the lactulose dose was administered via the tube shortly thereafter. Still sedated, she quickly fell back to sleep.

"We'll leave the tube in to give her low protein-high calorie liquid feeding at least until she wakes up. Keep her head and upper body elevated to thirty degrees."

Angelina then reported the discovery that Kris had moved her bowels while she was straining against the NG insertion.

Paterson said, "Good. I'll be back in a couple of hours. Let me know if she wakes up sooner." He wrote orders on her chart, peeked in at Flint who remained asleep, and left to start his ward rounds.

Helmtrude was walking toward him on the covered breezeway that led to the main hospital. She stopped and said, "Sorry to leave you. Angelina was there to help, so I went to the chapel to pray for them. How did it go?"

"Quite well. I placed an NG tube for the lactulose and she's had a BM. Right now she's sleeping off the wee bit of haloperidol we gave her. Once that wears off, I hope she comes around, which would mean she has viable liver left." He paused. "Oh, and remember to try to find Kurka."

"I saw Mesala outside the church just now and I asked him about Kurka. Mesala said he set off early this morning to walk back to the Agora village."

"How long ago did he leave?"

"I'm not sure. Maybe an hour ago."

"We might still catch up with him on the road with the pick-up."

Helmtrude frowned. "Dr. Paterson. First of all, gasoline is too expensive for such wild goose chases. Second, who is to drive? You have three new sick patients admitted last night to see this morning. Third, she is in no condition to talk to him."

"But I'm hopeful she will be later this morning. Why don't you have Sister Antje drive? She's has a bit of experience and she speaks Yachabo."

"Sister Antje is a terrible driver. I would have to go with her."

Paterson pointed a finger at Helmtrude. " *You* need to learn to drive. You should go with her anyway. You can better explain to Kurka why he needs to return. Don't mention blood donation, or he may refuse to come at all."

"What do I tell him?"

"The truth. A sick American needs to talk to him about his hepatitis treatment and recovery. Drop Ingasa's name if you have to."

Helmtrude sighed. "Okay. Let me find the Sister."

"Better get going."

Ninety minutes later, Paterson interrupted his rounds to return to the private ward. Angelina had sent a message that Kris had awakened and seemed to converse and behave more appropriately. By the time he arrived, she had already fallen back to sleep. She remained in restraints and was receiving nutrition via the nasogastric tube. He gently shook her arm and said, "Good morning."

She opened her eyes and answered, "Hello, Dr. Paterson." She wiggled her wrists to acknowledge the restraints. "I must have been acting up last night. I kind of remember some pretty wild dreams."

He motioned for Angelina to release her. "You got encephalopathic last night, so we started lactulose given every four hours. It seems to have worked. You needed nutrition also."

"That I can drink, so – can I have the NG out?"

He nodded and Angelina handed him gloves for its removal.

As he pulled it out, she gagged but the administered tube feeding stayed in her stomach. She said, "Ugh. I always wondered what it felt like to have an NG. Now I know. Where's the Sister, and how's Cory doing?"

"He's in DT's, but quieted down on IV lorazepam. The Sister left in the pick-up truck to try to catch up with Kurka, who started walking back to his village early this morning. I thought they would've been back by now."

"Any news about Ed Beaufain?"

"Sorry, –no."

Sister Helmtrude poked her head in the door and Kris waved at her. She smiled at Kris' obvious improvement. "Glad to see you're better. Kurka agreed to return with us, but only if we let him ride in the cab. He's right here, but he's afraid to enter your room."

"Tell him Mesala wasn't afraid of me when they brought us from the ravine."

Helmtrude relayed her statement and then his reply. "He said Mesala is stupid and that you need to go see Ingasa."

Kris sensed an opportunity. "Tell him I want to see his healed leg ulcer and hear more about Ingasa's medicine first." She heard conversation in the hallway and then Kurka came into the room, but stayed near the door. He was slight in stature, as were most of the Yachabo, but looked healthy. She smiled and said, "Tell him my name is Kris and that I won't bite him."

He smiled back after he heard Helmtrude's translation and moved a few steps closer.

"Ask him to show me his yellow death scar."

After he heard Kris' request, he came even closer and proudly pointed to the deep brand-like scar on his right calf that she had noticed on the ride in to the mission.

Kris looked closely at the scar. She wanted to palpate it but did not, to avoid the risk of spooking Kurka. She only commented, "It seems to be a bit of a badge of honor for him. Now ask him to tell me all about Ingasa's medicine – when he started it, side effects and so on."

Helmtrude relayed the questions and listened patiently to Kurka's lengthy reply. "He started it the day after he first noticed the leg ulcer," she said. "He had to chew and swallow the plant leaves four times every day. It had a bitter taste and made him sick many times. Also had dizziness and diarrhea. After a week, he started to feel better and only had to chew and swallow leaves twice daily for seven more days. His eyes only turned a little bit yellow. He says he is fine now and his blood is strong."

Kris was glad that Kurka brought up the subject of his blood. "Tell him he does look healthy, – and ask him what it is about his blood that makes it strong."

Helmtrude translated the comment and question, then his answer. "It is the redness."

"Tell him Ingasa said it is too late for the plant medicine to treat me, but we think that Kurka's blood is so strong that it might help me."

Helmtrude translated and Kris noticed Kurka start to look nervous and suspicious. Kris whispered to Paterson. "Do we have any chips to bargain with him? Like a ride on the mission airplane?"

Paterson shrugged, "I have no idea what he might want."

Helmtrude said, "Kurka wants to know what you mean by his blood helping you." She added as an aside, "You better have a good answer. I think he is about to run out the door."

Kris looked at her. "I can see that. Tell him everyone's blood has two parts: the redness and a yellow watery part. We want to take some of his blood and separate off the yellow watery part. We will then give all of the redness back to him. We think the yellow watery part has strength to help me fight the yellow death disease."

Helmtrude said, "All right, I'll try to explain it that way."

While she was translating, Paterson whispered to Kris, "We've never transfused anything other than fresh whole blood. To separate plasma from the red cells, we'd need a centrifuge that can handle a whole unit of blood. We don't have one."

"We'd have to figure out a way. Can I offer him a ride on the airplane?"

"I don't see why not. The Mission owns it."

Helmtrude said, "Kurka said you are not his relative. It is therefore forbidden."

Kris decided to gamble on an assumption and countered, "But only the redness is forbidden. He will get all of it back."

Kurka listened to the translation, stood silent and then replied. Helmtrude turned to Kris. "Now he says he wants to go back to the village to consult with the elders about it."

"Tell him that would take too long. It's important that we do this very soon. We won't tell anyone that he did it, and we'll give him a ride in the mission airplane if he agrees to it."

Helmtrude looked at Paterson, who nodded his assent. "Okay," she said, "here goes."

Kurka listened closely and again stood silent looking at Kris as he mulled over the offer. He chattered at length in Yachabo, which Helmtrude translated. "He doesn't want to go on an airplane. Too dangerous. He saw the wreck wash down the ravine. But he will do it on several conditions: First, we tell no one. Second, he wants to keep watch on his red blood through the whole procedure. Third, he wants to learn to drive the pick-up truck."

Kris said, "It's all okay with me, but it's not my truck."

Paterson said, "We agree to his conditions."

Helmtrude told Kurka of their acceptance of his three conditions. She turned to Paterson. "But what if he's a different blood type? And how do we separate off the red cells?"

"Get Sister Nita to come over from the lab, and find Hermano Guillermo to help us figure out how to rig up a large volume centrifuge."

****

The unmarked Blackhawk helicopter hovered over the upper reaches of the Noravo Ravine as three men in military fatigues lowered themselves by rope down through the trees to the river. They assembled next to a large boulder.

Eric Sanders spoke first. "We'll search while we work our way downstream. I'll be point man in the middle and Cam will flank on the left." He turned to the Colombian mercenary with them, "And you Diego, on the right. We're looking for bodies or wreckage of the Cessna. Indians are in the area 'cause I saw one of their villages from the air a couple of minutes ago. No shooting unless you have a clear hostile target. The chopper will wait at the bald ridge we just passed over for our pick-up call. Let's move."

Thirty minutes later, Cameron Jones spotted the wreckage of the Cessna wedged between two large trees and a rocky outcropping 20 yards from the left riverbank. He called the others over. When they arrived, he pointed up at the intact tree canopy and said, "It didn't crash here. Must've washed down in a flood."

Sanders looked up and nodded. "Yeah, but that means we'll have to keep looking for bodies downriver." He opened the right cockpit door and reached in with his hand to rub off soot residue. "There was a fire, and look at all the bullet holes in the instrument panel. I bet FARC shot out the radio so it couldn't be used. That means someone was still alive."

Jones forced open the left door and looked inside. "There's a blood stain on the pilot's seat. Flint must've got hurt."

Sanders sighed. "Yeah, but we need dogtags. Let's move on downriver."

After searching for several miles downstream, they had found only the storage cabinet. As the river widened and flowed into the valley, they stopped to rest in a clearing.

Sanders said, "Let's quit and call in the chopper. I want to stop at the Indian village and see what they can tell us." He turned to Diego. "What tribe lives here?"

"The Yachabo."

"Do you speak their language?"

Diego shook his head. "But there's usually someone who speaks Spanish."

****

Two hours later, Bill Swanson was in his office in the DEA building in Washington D.C. and picked up his cellphone on the first ring. "Eric, What'd you find out?"

Sanders said, "We found the plane in the ravine. Didn't find any bodies in it or any when we searched downriver. Then we heard from the local Indians that they rescued two people from a flood yesterday. They took an injured woman and a man, who I assume was Flint, to the mission hospital in the valley. The Indians didn't know anything about a third person, so Beaufain either died in the crash and his body washed away or he was abducted by FARC. We'll try to find out if they took him."

"You and Jones need to finish the job."

"I know. We will."

Chapter 30

Guillermo Perez was a Venezuelan lay leader in the church as well as the Santa Maria Mission engineer and an all-around handyman and mechanical problem solver. Shortly after being summoned by Paterson, he left his shop and headed for the private ward. His enthusiastic, boisterous greeting of Angelina in the hallway heralded his arrival.

Paterson smiled and said to Kris, "You almost always hear Guillermo coming before you actually see him."

An obese, middle-aged man in blue coveralls burst into the room. Guillermo had a full black beard streaked with gray and an unlit stub of a cigar in his mouth. When he saw Helmtrude, he stopped short, took out the cigar and gave her a solemn nod of acknowledgement. He smiled at Kris, strode over to Paterson, slapped him on the back and said, "*Hola, Doc. Mucho gusto.*"

Paterson replied in English, which Guillermo understood although his spoken English was somewhat broken. "Guillermo, it's always a pleasure. Let me introduce you to Kris Jensen. She's an American doctor and has hepatitis. She needs a plasma transfusion and we need your help to centrifuge the blood for it."

Guillermo nodded to Paterson and said, "Of course. I will make it happen." He turned to Kris and reached out his hand to her. "I am Brother Guillermo. My pleasure to meet you."

Kris liked his friendly, outgoing manner and was encouraged by his confident can-do attitude. She shook his hand, smiled and said, "Pleased to meet you, also. Thank you for helping."

Guillermo returned the smile and looked to Paterson. "Okay. Now explain please exactly what you need."

Paterson described the large volume of blood that needed to be spun down and the inadequacy of the small laboratory centrifuges.

Guillermo paid close attention. He glanced at Helmtrude twice as he listened. The cigar stub had found its way back between his lips, and he took it out again. "How big are the blood collection containers, and what kind of material are they?"

Paterson said, "We used to use one-liter glass bottles, but I think we're now using sterile one-liter plastic bags. Isn't that right, Nita?"

The Sister who supervised the laboratory had just come into the room. She nodded in response.

Guillermo rubbed his hands together and removed the cigar stub again. "So – we will need a large spinner for this job." He looked down, drew a deep breath and exhaled slowly through pursed lips as if gathering up his courage. He turned to Helmtrude and declared, "Sister, to do this we will have to convert your washer-dryer to a centrifuge."

Kris heard a gasp, but couldn't tell from whom it came. She glanced around the room. All eyes were on Helmtrude who looked quite distraught and was speechless. Paterson whispered to Kris that the washer-dryer was Helmtrude's pride and joy. It had just arrived on the most recent supply truck, which delivered heavy-duty goods and supplies to the Mission three times a year.

Helmtrude stammered, "B-But what if there's spillage? Is there no alternative?" When Guillermo shook his head in reply, she closed her eyes and muttered, "*Ach, mein lieber Gott im Himmel.*"

Paterson didn't speak or understand German so he waited for her to say more. When she did not, he ventured, "Was that a yes?"

Helmtrude glared at him, but her expression softened when she noticed Kris with her hands together as if in prayer and mouthing the word "please." She sighed. "Ja, Ja. Take it. Use it. Just clean it up after."

Kris said, "Thank you, Helmtrude."

Guillermo spoke to Sister Nita. "I will need a few empty blood collection bags to fill with water and extra blood that you can give me to test the system."

Paterson added, "The blood would need to have been anti-coagulated."

Sister Nita nodded. "I think we have some that we were going to discard." She left to collect the supplies while Guillermo went with Helmtrude to look over the washer-dryer to figure out how to convert it to a centrifuge.

After they had all left the room, Kris said to Paterson, "I like Guillermo. I'm confident he'll rig up a centrifuge for us."

"I'm sure he will. He's a talented engineer and innovator. We're lucky to have him."

"By the way, where did Kurka go?"

"He went to look over the pick-up truck that he'll learn to drive," Paterson said. "Maybe that'll work out. We could use a regular driver."

"When will he have the blood drawn?"

"I was going to wait until Guillermo was ready to spin it down."

"But we don't know how long that will take," Kris said. "Kurka might change his mind."

"You're right. No good reason to wait. I'll tell Sister Nita to go ahead when she gets back."

"Sorry to ask, but could you find Angelina and send her in? I need help going to the bathroom."

Paterson said, "Of course. Let me get her for you. I'll be back in a bit."

Thirty minutes later Paterson returned and found Kris talking with Sister Nita. The lab supervisor turned to him with a look of concern on her face and said, "Dr. Jensen's not sure if she's blood type A or O."

"The Yachabo are 100% type O. That means Kurka is type O, a universal donor. So why is there a problem?"

Sister Nita replied, "It wouldn't be a problem to transfuse his red blood cells, but his plasma will likely have both anti-A and anti-B type antibodies. If she has blood type A, Kurka's anti-A antibodies will destroy her red cells. She's already anemic, so a major hemolytic transfusion reaction like that could kill her."

"Let's rephrase that to say could slightly hasten the inevitable," Kris said.

Paterson asked, "Can't we pre-test for the compatibility of his plasma and her blood?"

"Sure. We would mix a sample of her blood and his plasma in a test tube, then spin it down. If the supernatant fluid is red or even pink, that means red cell lysis occurred in the test tube and would occur in her bloodstream also."

Kris said, "I'm embarrassed to not know my blood type, but I don't see an alternative. Even if we were to find another Yachabo donor, wouldn't he or she also be type O and pose the same problem?"

Sister Nita and Paterson both nodded.

"So let's just go ahead and give me Kurka's plasma, and substitute a prayer for the mixing pre-test."

Paterson looked at her. "Are you sure?" After she nodded, he turned to the Sister. "Go ahead and draw Kurka's blood. In fact, take two liters if he'll allow it. Won't hurt to have extra plasma."

"Where is he?"

"I think he's in the garage looking over the pick-up truck. Hopefully Guillermo will have the – ah, washer-centrifuge ready soon."

"He had already welded an adaptor to the holding trays when I brought him the blood and the collection bags." Nita started to giggle, then stifled herself with her hand over her mouth.

"What?" prompted Paterson.

"I shouldn't say this, but Sister Helmtrude was fluttering about like a mother hen clucking and squawking over a few scratches to the washer and the mess he was making of the laundry room."

Paterson smiled. "I'll go over there shortly and usher her back to the wards until he's done."

Sister Nita left to find Kurka and Kris asked, "So how's my next door neighbor doing? Awfully quiet in there."

Paterson said, "I've kept him sedated. Gets too agitated when I don't. DT's can last several days, as I'm sure you know."

Kris was silent, then said, "I'm just sorry Cory won't be back to himself soon enough for me to thank him and say good-bye. I couldn't have gotten here without his help. I just hope he'll be all right. I also feel bad that his plane got wrecked."

"Let me reassure you that Mr. Flint will get over his DT's. And who knows, maybe he'll stay sober because of it. He's stable with respect to the gunshot wounds. He does need a rod in his femur, and for that we'll probably evacuate him to Maracaibo. Lastly, I imagine he had insurance coverage on the airplane. We're required to have it on our mission plane."

Kris turned to him. "Thanks. That makes me feel a little better." She looked out the window at the mountains in the distance. "Then there's Ed. I keep hoping I'll see him peering in this window looking for me."

"That's your abducted doctor friend?"

Kris nodded.

"You really miss him don't you?"

"Yeah, I sure do," Kris said. "We'd been through a lot together these last few days and had gotten pretty close. It doesn't look like I'll get a chance to thank or say good-bye to him either."

"Maybe you could record something. I'll try to make sure he gets it."

"I did already, when I taped messages to my mother and brother. Ed's become like family to me. I just hope he's okay." Kris started to laugh.

"What's so funny?"

"I just had a flash mental image of Ed sitting on a log in the jungle eating a bug, and I thought – Oh Lordy! I hate bugs, so that's a fate far worse than death, at least in my mind." She shrugged. "I thought it was funny. And it is." She started to laugh again.

Paterson went along. "That *is* funny. About a year ago, we actually did treat a guerilla here for gastroenteritis from a beetle he'd eaten."

Kris laughed harder. "Gives a whole new meaning to 'you've got some bug,' doesn't it?"

Paterson started to laugh. "Yes and to 'I think I know what's bugging you'."

They both laughed so loud that Angelina came in to see what the ruckus was about. They calmed down and were trying to explain that the word "bug" could also mean an infectious germ when they were interrupted by a loud voice in the hallway.

"Mother-of-pearl!" came the exclamation from just outside their room.

Paterson said, "I hear Guillermo."

A moment later the blue-coveralled engineer was in the doorway, holding a box and looking exasperated. He tore the cigar stub from his mouth and said, "Dr. Paterson, you must do something about that woman."

"Sister Helmtrude?"

"Of course. She was all over me, inside my skin, again and again about nothing. It took me twice the time to finish the job. Unfortunately my centrifuge did not work." He reached into the box and took out a one-liter plastic collection bag full of red liquid, which he held up to show them. "See? It did not separate the red blood cells even a little bit."

Paterson inspected the bag. "Maybe it didn't spin fast enough or long enough."

Kris also looked at it. "Wait, how much blood did you use and what did you add it to?"

"I added 200 ml of blood to 800 ml of water."

Kris was relieved to hear him say so. "Then what happened is that water is hypotonic to the red blood cells. That caused all the red cells to break up and release free hemoglobin, which would be impossible to spin down."

Paterson said, "She's right. Try it again with normal saline instead of water. I'll come along and take Helmtrude with me back to the ward."

Guillermo said, "I thank you for that favor." He turned to Kris. "And I thank you for the information. I am glad to have a reason for it not working."

Paterson looked at his watch. "I'll be back later. We'll need to give you more lactulose in an hour."

"I so look forward to it. Could I get something for nausea? I'll drink some of that tube feeding when the nausea settles."

Paterson nodded approval to Angelina for Kris' medication, and left with Guillermo.

An hour later, Paterson returned to the private ward with Sister Helmtrude and found Kris asleep. He had a drink cup of lactulose in one hand and a nasogastric tube in the other. He gently woke her up and offered her a choice. She opted to drink it.

"I'll need a chaser, though."

"What is that?" asked Helmtrude.

"Something else to drink to kill the bad taste. Like we used to drink beer after a shot of peppermint schnapps in college to get a buzz."

"Schnapps is a German liqueur. I remember growing up in Berlin, my uncle Uli liked his schnapps and his beer too. Sometimes he got a schwips, which is like a buzz. But we don't have alcohol here. No buzzes."

Kris smiled. "I know. I'll chase the lactulose with tube feed."

Just as Kris was drinking down the chaser, Sister Nita arrived and reported that they had drawn two liters of Kurka's blood and that Guillermo had the two collection bags of blood in the washer-centrifuge re-configured to a continuous spin cycle. She added, "Kurka is so excited about driving the pick-up, he wants to give us three liters."

Paterson said, "Good work. If we can get 500 ml of plasma out of each liter of his blood, that should be plenty. Then give the red cells right back to Kurka. I imagine his tank is a little low after giving up that much blood."

Sister Nita nodded. "It is. He almost passed out when he got up to follow after Guillermo and the blood bags. I had to give him a liter of intravenous normal saline. He's fine now, and watching his blood spin in Guillermo's washer centrifuge."

Paterson turned to Kris. "I want to go see how Guillermo is coming along. You okay for now?"

"I just stay really tired, and the nausea won't go away."

"More Phenergan might just knock you out."

"I may need it anyway."

He turned to Sister Nita. "Oh, and before I forget. Draw baseline hemoglobin and chemistries on her now. We'll start infusion of the plasma as soon as Guillermo has it separated."

Thirty minutes later Paterson returned with two 500 ml bags of Kurka's plasma. Kris was lethargic and confused again. Sister Helmtrude had stayed with her and said, "She's been retching and threw up all the lactulose and the tube feed. There was also fresh blood mixed with the vomitus."

Paterson frowned. "An upper GI bleed would be a disaster right now. Kurka's plasma should contain some clotting factors to help stop any bleeding, but she would need the whole 500 ml and maybe a lot more fresh plasma if she really started hemorrhaging." He paused and looked around at Sister Helmtrude, Nita, and Angelina. "Let's start the plasma, and then I think it's time for a prayer."

Sister Helmtrude motioned to Angelina to proceed. The day nurse hung the plasma bag up on the stand, filled the IV tubing with plasma, connected it to the access port on Kris' forearm, and opened the stopcock to start the infusion. Kris was oblivious, as she had fallen back to sleep.

Paterson watched the plasma drip in for a few seconds, then said, "Let us pray," and they joined hands in a semi-circle around the bed.

"Dear Lord God, our Father Almighty in Heaven – please hear our prayer for Kris Jensen, who is here with us far from her home. She came to this place, not for herself, but only to give of herself. She came to help us understand and treat the hepatitis that has so long plagued the Yachabo, the same terrible infection that now ravages her body. We pray with all our hearts that this plasma will stop the virus. We pray for guidance in our treatment decisions for her, both day and night until she is well again. If she passes from this earth, we pray for her soul and that she be re-united with her father in Heaven. In the name of the Father, the Son and the Holy Spirit, we pray. Amen."

Sister Helmtrude whispered, "She's in God's hands now."

Paterson looked at her and said, "Yes, but we have to believe that He works through us." He turned to Angelina. "Let's give her a small dose of haloperidol and then put an NG tube down to give the lactulose and to monitor for gastric bleeding. We'll also put a Foley catheter in to monitor urine output."

After placement of the catheters and administration of the lactulose, the infusion of the first bag of plasma was almost complete. Angelina watched it go in and asked Paterson, "How will we know if she's having a transfusion reaction?"

"She could develop fever, abdominal pain, free hemoglobin in the urine, or kidney shutdown, or just go into shock. It may be hard to tell, because all of those can happen to her for other reasons. We'll need to monitor her vital signs and urine output every hour or so, as well as her hemoglobin level every two or three hours. We'll treat complications that come along the best we can."

"What about the second bag of plasma?"

"Let's wait and see how she does with the first – " He was interrupted by someone coming down the hallway shouting for him and Helmtrude.

Moments later, a breathless Sister Antje appeared in the doorway. "Dr. Paterson, Sister Helmtrude. Come quickly. Three soldiers are here looking for Dr. Jensen and Mr. Flint. They have guns!"

****

The FBI headquarters building in Atlanta was closed for the weekend. Jonas Peterson used his ID to access the back door and then checked in at the security barrier. He told the guard, "Agent Garner is expecting me upstairs in his office."

Steve Garner had left his door open and he waved Peterson in when he arrived. "Sorry to have you come in on a Saturday. Let me update you on a couple of items before the conference call."

Peterson sat down and pulled out a notepad. "I'm ready."

Garner rubbed his chin. "We got approval from both the State Department and the Pentagon to go after Flint's plane, so at the El Condor Air Base in northeastern Colombia, we have two search-and-rescue units, a med-evac team, and a couple of Cobra gunships assembled and ready. The hang-up now is the Venezuelans who maintain use of our military teams is an invasion of their sovereignty. They say they'll handle it themselves, but the truth is they haven't even started to look for Flint."

"Can't we just go in anyway?"

"We could and would for a quickie evacuation from a specific location. Problem is that search and rescue might take days to spot a wreck in that terrain. A confrontation with the Venezuelans over our uninvited presence might get ugly."

"Anything on satellite images?"

Garner shook his head. "We've scrutinized the sector where the intercept took place and north from that point, but the cloud cover and the dense forest make it almost impossible to spot wreckage. We'll try anyway."

"Did Castillo come up with any leads at the San Antonio airport?"

"Only that Flint inquired about the weather and the best approach to a mountain valley called El Valle Amarillo. Nothing there except a Catholic mission. We got a good satellite view of the valley and no plane. He had to have crashed. Castillo's on his way to the El Condor base to join the search-and-rescue team. What did you learn from the DEA?"

Peterson glanced at his notepad. "I spoke with Special Agent Bill Swanson. He's second in command of X-Ops under Peter Arnett. He said they got tipped by reliable informants based in Venezuela that Flint was running drugs, so per their protocol they tracked his plane, but when the Colombian jets broke away, they stopped tracking him."

"That's strange. The Colombians didn't do anything except tell Flint to proceed to Maracaibo. If DEA really thought he was running drugs, why not track him all the way there?"

"Swanson wasn't co-operative. It was like pulling teeth to get him to tell me anything."

"They're withholding something. We may have to go through our Chief."

Peterson nodded. "Yeah, I got the feeling there was more behind it than Swanson let on. By the way, what time is the conference call with the State Department?"

Garner looked up at the clock on the wall. "Right now."

Chapter 31

Paterson and Sister Helmtrude hurried to the front of Santa Maria hospital. Waiting outside the door were three men in military fatigues. Two of them carried AK-47 rifles and looked to Paterson like typical FARC guerillas. The third man was taller and lighter-skinned, and armed with a holstered pistol. When Paterson and Helmtrude emerged from the hospital, the taller man stepped forward and extended his hand. "*Buenos dias. Habla usted ingles?*"

Paterson nodded as he shook the man's hand. "Yes. I'm Dr. Robby Paterson and this is Sister Helmtrude, the hospital Nurse-Matron. What can we do for you?"

"I'm Dr. Ed Beaufain. I'm looking for my friends Kris Jensen and Cory Flint. We heard the Yachabo brought them here after our plane crash."

"Dr. Jensen told me of you. They're here, but both quite ill."

Ed looked relieved. "Thank God. I was afraid they hadn't survived."

"We'll take you to them." Paterson glanced at the guerillas. "But, ah – are you still a hostage?"

Ed shook his head. "Carlos and Pedro just guided me here. Without them I'd be wandering around lost in the mountain forest. Pedro will head back, but I'd like Carlos to stay and get checked out for his chronic diarrhea and weight loss."

"No problem. The Sister can take him over to the outpatient clinic for lab work and I can see him over there later. Are *you* okay?"

"Yeah. Just bug-bitten, tired, dirty, and hungry. But I'll be fine."

"Ready to go see your friends?"

Ed grinned. "I sure am." He turned to the guerillas and explained the plans.

Pedro nodded and patted Carlos on the back. He waved good-bye, then headed back to the mountains while Carlos left with Helmtrude for an evaluation at the outpatient clinic.

On the way to the private ward Paterson asked, "How did you find out your friends were here?"

"We went to the crash site and found the plane had washed 50 yards down the ravine. The wreckage was being scavenged by a couple of Yachabo Indians, one of whom spoke Spanish. He told us that a white man and woman from the plane had been rescued from a flash flood and taken here. I was so happy to hear that, I deeded them the plane on the spot. So, how bad is Kris?"

"She's been in and out of encephalopathy since last night. So far she's responded to lactulose, but we just had to give her another dose. A gastric bleed this morning probably caused a relapse of her confusion."

"Why is that?"

"Blood in the gut is a protein load that gets digested and absorbed. That raises the ammonia level."

Ed frowned. "Is she still bleeding?"

"I hope not. She's gotten vitamin K and we just gave her fresh plasma, which should help restore her clotting factors."

"That'll help for a while, but she'll need more."

"There *is* good news. The plasma was from an Indian who may have antibodies to her virus."

Ed perked up. "Oh really? Some hope, then."

"The main concern now is that she may have blood type A. If she does, the Indian's plasma will hemolyze her red cells."

"Has that happened?"

"We were just observing her for it when you showed up."

`They arrived at the private ward and first went in to check on Flint, who was snoring loudly.

Ed asked, "How is Cory?"

"He's recovering from the gunshot wounds, and will need a rod to stabilize his broken left femur. Right now he's heavily sedated while he goes through DT's."

"Sounds like you've had your hands full with them. I'll try to help as much as I can."

Paterson shrugged. "It *has* been a bit of a strain on our staff and resources, but then, that's why we're here – to care for sick people." He paused. "I haven't spoken to Mr. Flint much, but we've gotten to know and appreciate Dr. Jensen for her compassion, good humor and dedication to her investigation of the hepatitis. In less than a day, her knowledge and the information she obtained from a Yachabo root healer have taught me more about the virus than I'd learned in the five years that I've been here. Kris is someone very special, and we're more than happy to do anything we can for her." He pointed to the connecting door. "Let's go see her."

As they entered her room, Kris was in soft restraints and appeared to be asleep. Paterson introduced Ed to Angelina, then went to the bedside. "How is she doing?"

The nurse shook her head. "Not well. Her temp is 102 and her blood pressure is only 80 over 50. The nasogastric drainage doesn't have any blood in it, but look at her urine. It's turned completely red."

Paterson frowned. "Not good, but not necessarily a hemolytic transfusion reaction. The red urine could just be red blood cells and not free hemoglobin. Give her 500 ml saline as an IV bolus and draw another hemoglobin and chemistry panel. Once the lab has spun the red top tube down, have them tell us if her serum is reddish or even just pink."

Angelina left to get the bottle of saline and the supplies to draw blood. Paterson knelt down to take a closer look at the urine collection bag. He sighed and said to himself, "At least her kidneys are still making urine." He looked up across the bed and saw Ed hold her hand and whisper with his eyes closed as if in prayer. When Ed was finished, Paterson stood up and said, "We've all been praying for her."

When Angelina inserted a needle in Kris' arm to draw her blood, she woke up, pulled her arm back, and said, "Hey, stop stabbing me!"

Angelina had difficulty drawing blood for the tests, as Kris resisted and moved despite the restraints and Paterson's weight on her arm. The blood trickled into the collection tubes. Finally Angelina announced, "I think I have enough. Let me get this to the lab."

With the needle out of her arm, Kris looked up and noticed Ed standing next to the bed. Before he could say anything, she said, "Whoever you are, you look a lot like that rascal Ed Beaufain."

He took and gently held her bruised and swollen hand. "Kris, it's me – Ed. The guerillas let me go early this morning. I've been so worried about you."

Kris sat up to focus her full attention on him. "Ed?" she whispered. "It *is* you. I thought I was hallucinating." Her lip quivered and she bit it. A tear tracked down her cheek. "I didn't expect to ever see you again."

Ed wiped his own tear away. "Yeah. Me too."

She squeezed and held his hand. "I never got to tell you how much I appreciate your coming to Venezuela with me – and all your help and support. Promise me you'll carry on the investigation after I'm gone."

"I promise. But you're not gone yet."

"No, I'm not. But in this – ah – lucid interval, I want to let you know how important you are to me. How much I care for you, and I want to say a meaningful good bye while I'm still able to. I expect that when I get encephalopathic again, I'll speak my mind, but Lord knows what'll come out of my mouth."

Paterson had been listening in as he removed her restraints. "The encephalopathy did clog up your social filter earlier this morning."

"Oh, you mean I was goofy and irreverent?"

Paterson smiled. "I would say so."

"But sometimes she acted like that before she got sick," Ed said. "How do we tell the difference?"

She winked at him. "You won't. It means I get to say anything to anyone at anytime." She paused to sniff the air around her a couple of times, then wrinkled her face in disgust. "Ugh! Someone in here reeks of jungle rot." She pointed to Ed. "It's Bug-breath here. He needs a hosing down with bleach – and maybe a de-lousing." She looked to Paterson. "Quick! Break out the surgical masks and gowns before we catch any of his cooties or we asphyxiate from his fumes."

Ed was laughing. "See? There she goes again."

Kris looked puzzled. "What are you talking about? What did I just say?"

They all laughed. Then Paterson said, "There's a shower and clean scrub clothes down the hallway on the left."

"Okay. I can take a hint."

As Ed was about to leave, Angelina returned from the lab with Sister Nita, who had a concerned look on her face. The lab director said, "I'm afraid her serum is red. Her blood must be hemolyzing from the transfusion."

Paterson's face turned serious as he asked Kris, "Do you feel any different?"

She shrugged. "I stay nauseated, weak and washed out."

"Any abdominal or flank pain?"

"My upper abdomen hurts, but not any worse than before." She looked down at her bruised and swollen arm. "Was the blood sample hard to get?"

Paterson nodded and said, "We haven't been able to draw blood from your IV access, so we had to find a new vein – which we did, but you were squirming around quite a bit so it took a while to get enough blood."

"Maybe the blood got hemolyzed in the process of being drawn and we should test another sample."

Paterson said, "That's certainly possible." After re-examining her swollen arms and hands, he shook his head. "You're so edematous now I'm not sure we can find another vein."

Ed spoke up. "I can do a femoral stick. I was always good at it." He looked at Kris. "Okay with you?"

She nodded. "Just be careful."

Ed put on gloves and cleaned the skin over Kris' proximal left anterior thigh. After he palpated the location of the femoral artery, he inserted a needle attached to a 60 ml syringe into the adjacent femoral vein. He drew up the blood sample quickly and cleanly and filled two red top and a blue top centrifuge tubes. He placed the needle, syringe, and tubes into a small basin and passed it to Sister Nita who was waiting to take them to the lab. He turned to Angelina. "Please hold pressure on this site for another five minutes while I go take my Chlorox shower."

The nurse put on gloves and took over the application of pressure to Kris' femoral vein. She looked upset, so Kris asked, "What's wrong?

"Do I need a shower also?"

Kris smiled and shook her head. "He needs one because he smells like the jungle he slept in last night."

Ed returned to the room just as Sister Nita reported that the repeat serum sample was not red but only a dark yellow-green from the high bilirubin level associated with her jaundice and liver failure. She added that her hemoglobin had dropped to 7.5 grams.

Paterson looked at Kris. "With no hemolysis, we can go ahead with the second bag of Kurka's plasma, both for the antibodies and the clotting factors. We can't afford any more bleeding." When she nodded agreement, he turned to Ed. "Angelina will start the plasma and I have to get back to the wards. Can you keep an eye on our two patients?"

"No problemo."

Kris waved to Paterson as he left. "I'm pretty tired, but tell me a little bit about what happened with the guerillas."

"The worst part was leaving you and Cory helpless on the riverbank. From there we hiked in the rain along a forest trail for a couple of hours to get to their base camp. On the way it was obvious to me that even if I escaped, I'd never find my way back. So I figured my only real option was to be friendly and cooperative, and somehow convince them to let me go."

"What did they need you for?"

"They had a few sick people back at their base camp. There wasn't a lot I could do without meds or diagnostic tests. I did drain an abscess and set a fracture. Told several others to just go back to Colombia and get evaluated at a medical clinic. By the way, Enrique said they lose two or three soldiers a year to the yellow death hepatitis. That's why they got spooked and left you alone."

"So why *did* they let you go?"

"I convinced them that we came here to help solve the yellow death problem. But in the end it was Jack who swayed them."

"Jack Daniels? I remember they took Cory's stash of three or four bottles. Did you get drunk?"

"We got a little snootful. It was kind of a guy thing. Sat around a campfire, drank, and told a few jokes."

"I hope you stayed within your humor domains."

He laughed. "I did."

"You sure? Tell me one of your jokes."

Ed paused and scratched his head.

"Trying to remember a clean one?"

He smiled. "They loved the one about the father who wanted to teach his young son about the danger of alcohol."

She knitted her brow. "I don't know that one."

"A father drops a live earthworm into a glass of water and it wriggles around vigorously. He drops another into a glass of vodka and it immediately stiffens, dies and sinks to the bottom. The father asks his boy, *What does this show you?* The boy studies the two glasses and says, *If you drink alcohol, you won't get worms.*"

Kris laughed.

"Then a couple guerillas who got tooted ate two beetles and said, 'If we drink alcohol, we won't get 'The Bugs.' That's their name for beetle-related diarrhea."

"Ugh. Why eat them?"

"They say they're tasty, plus I think there's a little macho element to it."

"I had a vision of you eating bugs."

He shook his head and made a face. "Anyway, Enrique told me last night they'd let me go early this morning with a couple of his men to guide me back. They even returned one of Cory's handguns. "

"How did you find out we were here?"

"From the Yachabo." He looked up as Angelina brought the second bottle of plasma, which she hung on the IV pole next to the bed. She filled the infusion tubing and attached it to Kris' IV access port. He watched and said, "I wonder how long this will take to work."

Kris shrugged. "*If* it does at all, it'll be hours, I would guess. It's not like the movies where as soon as the patient gets the antidote, they tear out the IV and jump out of bed, restored to health."

"Hmmm. Too bad. So why might there be antibodies in this plasma?"

Kris summarized what she had learned in the conversations with Ingasa and Kurka. Ed listened and asked, "Why didn't you try the root medicine?"

"It sounded like it had a lot of side effects and it didn't work at all when the Yachabo patients were already pretty sick. But you should take some of it back with you to try to get the active component identified. Maybe it'll turn out to be a useful anti-viral drug. If it is, make sure the Yachabo get credit and royalties."

"I promise."

"Listen, Ed, I'm exhausted. I'll fall asleep even with this tube in my nose. Have Angelina keep the tube feed drip going and re-dose the lactulose when it's due," Kris said. "Oops. I forgot. I'm the patient and not the doctor."

He smiled. "When I was a resident in training, I always listened to patients, because who knows? They might be right."

"You were smart to do so."

"Anything else that I can do for you?

She thought for a moment. "You could get me some music."

"What kind of music?"

"My father's favorite Mozart opera was *The Marriage of Figaro*. I heard it many times when I was little and I became enamored with several of the arias. I want to listen to *Porgi Amor, Dove sono,* and *Deh vieni, non tardar.* Paterson said that he was a Mozart aficionado. I'm sure he has *Figaro*."

"I'll have to write those down." He found paper and a pen at the nurses' station and came back and made notes. "I'll ask him, but shouldn't we wait until you wake up to play it?"

"No," she said. "Play it when you have it here. I'll hear it."

"Okay. You can listen to it again when you wake up."

She looked at him and sighed. "If I don't wake up, thank you for everything, and take care of yourself."

Ed gave her hand a squeeze. He looked straight at her. "You *are* going to wake up."

"I'm not so sure. I'm so tired. I feel like the end is near – but at least for now, I'm still pretty much in control of my – ah – faculties. That was something I prayed for a couple of days ago." She laid herself back down on the bed and yawned. "Remember that childhood prayer, *Now I lay me down to sleep?*"

"I know it well."

"The *If I should die before I wake* part finally seems to have relevance."

Ed nodded. "I know what you mean. I read once that that prayer may have had its origin centuries ago in Europe when there was a risk of sudden death from the black plague. Dying is a scary notion, especially for children. My four year-old nephew Ricky was frightened by that part so I went on the Internet, and found a less scary version for him."

"Do you remember it?"

"I do. It goes: *Now I lay me down to sleep, I pray the Lord my soul to keep. Thy love be with me thru the night, and keep me safe till morning light.*"

"I do like that one better."

"There's more: *Should I be granted extra days, I pray thee Lord to guide my ways.*"

"Perfect. Say it again for me after I close my eyes."

She smiled as she listened to him repeat the prayer, and fell asleep almost immediately. He stood next to her and watched her for a few minutes until he was sure she remained peacefully asleep. After a quick check on Flint, he returned and moved a chair to Kris' bedside. He sat down to watch over her. He wondered about what was to be, and he reflected on what might have been.

An hour later, as Ed was about to doze off himself, Paterson returned from his ward rounds with a brown bag in hand. Ed got up, rubbed his eyes and said, "It's been quiet. Both of them are asleep with stable vital signs. No sign of bleeding in Kris, neither her GI tract nor the urine."

Paterson nodded, "Good." He handed Ed the bag. "I figured you'd be hungry so I brought you a snack from the kitchen."

"Thanks."

"You look tired. There's an empty bed in the room across the hall. Get a bit of rest. It's going to be a long night for both of us. We can pass the quiet time in shifts."

Ed sighed. "Yeah, you're right. But please do get me up for any change in her condition, whether better or worse." He turned to go, but glanced back at Kris. "Do you think we should wake her up to check on her?"

Paterson shook his head. "Not for a few hours, anyway. I don't know what we would do differently right now based on her responsiveness. If she gets agitated or seems to be in pain, we would treat those symptoms, of course."

"I do want her to be pain-free," Ed said. "Maybe we just should take out the NG tube and *only* focus on comfort measures." He looked over at her, then turned back to Paterson. "I just don't know. What do you think?"

"Did she say what *she* wanted us to do?"

"Actually, she did tell me to leave the NG tube in."

"Then we should keep on with the tube feeding and the lactulose."

"But at what point does this all become futile?"

Paterson looked over at Kris and said, "When there's uncertainty about how much to support patients who are critically ill, my approach is to just continue to do what I can for them. Patients eventually either get better or they don't. Decisions about the intensity of treatment and the goals of care become easier to make." He put his hand on Ed's shoulder. "And a tired brain may not make the best decision. Get some sleep. I'll keep you posted."

Chapter 32

For the next four hours, Kris slept and remained calm except for an attempt to pull out the naso-gastric tube in her sleep. This prompted Angelina to re-apply soft wrist restraints. The nurse also administered another dose of lactulose via the tube and kept the feeding supplement infusing.

Kris' blood pressure, pulse rate, respirations, and temperature remained in a range satisfactory to Paterson. With her vital signs stable, he decided to try to wake her up to assess whether the encephalopathy had progressed to a deeper, less-reversible hepatic coma. He started with a moderate shake of her shoulder while he called out her name. Getting no response, he shook harder and called out louder, but she still didn't rouse.

Paterson didn't like to do painful sternal rubs, but the stimulus to arouse had to be sufficiently noxious to adequately assess her responsiveness. He rubbed his knuckle on her central upper chest. At first she didn't react, but as he was about to do it again, harder, she grimaced and opened one eye.

"Stop that. It hurt!"

"Sorry. I wanted to wake you up. Do you know where you are?"

"Venezuelan torture chamber," came the slurred reply.

Paterson gave a nod. "Partial credit for that answer. Who am I?"

She mumbled, "I dunno. The Grand Inquisitor?"

He didn't answer or ask another question, and she fell right back to sleep.

To Paterson, her degree of responsiveness was lower and suggested progression of the encephalopathy over the last four hours. Before proceeding further, he decided to have Ed help assess her. He went out into the hallway to ask Angelina to get Ed up. When he saw that she was busy giving a report to Carmen who was coming on as the night duty nurse, he decided to get Ed up himself. After no response to several knocks on the door, he went into the room. Ed was snoring. Paterson had to shake him hard to rouse him from a deep sleep.

As soon as Ed realized who had awakened him, he sat right up and asked, "Everything all right with Kris?"

"I'm not sure. I want you to come help evaluate her."

"I'll be right there." He yawned. "Felt good to sleep in a bed again. I was out."

"You were. I was about to do a sternal rub."

When Paterson returned to Kris' room, Sister Helmtrude was standing next to her, holding her hand. When she saw him come in, she asked, "Have you been able to wake her up?"

"Yes, just a few minutes ago, but only briefly with a hard sternal rub."

Helmtrude winced at the thought. When Ed joined them, she said, "Good evening, Dr. Beaufain."

Ed smiled to acknowledge her, but his attention was directed to Kris. "Why is she back in restraints?"

"She tried to pull her NG out in her sleep."

"Do you think she's worse?"

"I think so," said Paterson. "It was harder to wake her up just now, and when I did, she was confused despite the lactulose, which Angelina gave about an hour ago. On the plus side, her vital signs have been relatively stable, and there's been no sign of bleeding although we do need to recheck her blood chemistries and hemoglobin level."

Helmtrude looked upset. "When will Kurka's plasma start to work?"

Paterson shrugged. "I have no idea *when* it will, *how much* it will, or even *if* it will help her. And we have no way to test for a response. "

Ed frowned. "Then what do we do next?"

"If her hemoglobin is less than 7, we transfuse her. We have several nurses who are type O who I think would be willing to donate blood."

Helmtrude agreed. "Ja, but how would we give it? Angelina just told me her IV has stopped working."

"I could do a cut-down to access a large vein for transfusion, if needed," Paterson said. "Need to check her hemoglobin first, though, and it'd be best to start a new IV than to do a fingerprick or another femoral stick."

"I could put in a butterfly needle access," Ed said. "I was always pretty good at it when I was a resident on the pediatric ward."

Paterson said, "Go for it. That would get us a blood sample and be usable to give her IV meds if needed."

Carmen brought the supplies. Within a few minutes Ed had the butterfly needle inserted and taped securely into a small vein on the back of Kris' right hand. It disturbed Ed that she had not moved or reacted at all when the sharp needletip stuck the skin of her hand. The blood samples for hemoglobin and basic chemistries were easily obtained, and Helmtrude took them to the lab.

Paterson left to check on Flint and returned 10 minutes later when Helmtrude came back to report that Kris' hemoglobin was 7.2 and that the chemistry panel results would be ready in another 20 minutes.

Ed spoke first. "So, no transfusion for now." He looked over at Kris, who appeared to be sleeping peacefully. "Do we really need to wake her up again?"

Paterson shook his head. "No. Let's wait for a couple of hours." He turned around to Carmen to give a verbal order for the tube feeding supplement. "Why don't – "

"Doctor!" Carmen had interrupted him and was pointing at Kris.

Paterson spun around. Both of Kris' arms were twitching. Moments later her teeth were clenched, and her whole body was rhythmically convulsing. "She's seizing. Get me IV lorazepam now!"

Helmtrude and Carmen ran out to get the drug while Ed and Paterson supported Kris to keep from hurting herself. Two mg of intravenous lorazepam given via the butterfly needle access aborted the seizure. Kris' arms, legs and body went limp. Her mouth fell open to reveal that she was bleeding from having bitten her lower lip. Paterson already had gloves on. He applied pressure

301

to the lip with a piece of gauze to control the bleeding. He looked at it more closely and said, "It'll need a couple of stitches." He turned to Ed. "Sure glad we had the butterfly in."

Ed looked upset and nodded slowly.

Paterson could see that Ed was depressed over the turn of events. "I wouldn't give up hope yet. But now we'll have to wait several hours at least for both the post-seizure effect and the drug to wear off before we can re-assess her mental status."

"What do you think triggered the seizure?"

"Not sure. Her blood sodium, calcium, or magnesium could be low. Those electrolytes we can try to correct. I hope it's not brain edema." Paterson turned to Helmtrude. "Go tell Sister Nita to add a calcium level to the routine chemistries." He explained to Ed, "Our lab can't do magnesium. If her renal function is still okay, we'll give her IV mag."

Before she left, Helmtrude said to Paterson, "Don't forget to tell Dr. Beaufain about the Colombian."

Ed looked to Paterson. "Carlos? What did you find out?"

"He tested positive for Giardia, so we started treatment late this afternoon. He wants to head back to rejoin his guerilla unit tomorrow, but asked to stay here with you tonight."

"Do we have any more beds on this ward?"

"No, but he said that all he wants is a blanket on the floor and a roof over his head to stay dry in case it rains."

"No problemo. He can stay in my room."

Carmen brought the suture tray. Paterson put on a gown, gloves and eye protection in preparation to sew up Kris' lower lip laceration. Ed was again disappointed that she didn't seem to react when Paterson inserted a needle into her lower lip to inject anesthetic. Shortly after he tied the last suture, Sister Nita came by to report that Kris' kidney function and electrolytes were all in the normal range.

Paterson frowned as he removed his cover gown and gloves. "Then maybe brain edema caused the seizure, but we'll give her magnesium anyway. If she has another seizure, we'll use phenytoin to control them."

"Any way to treat cerebral edema?"

"The only effective treatment would be a liver transplant."

Ed decided to change the subject. "How is Cory?"

"His liver must not be in the best shape, either. He's still out from the sedative we gave him last night. He's a little more responsive this evening, but pretty much still sleeps all the time. I expect he'll be more awake by tomorrow."

"I'm glad to hear that."

Paterson looked at his watch. "I have to go over to OB to check on a woman in labor who may need a C-section. It's now 7:45. I'll come back at 10:30 and we'll try to wake her up then."

Ed nodded. "I'll be right here."

"Let Carmen know if you need me." Paterson left to write orders for the magnesium, which the nurse started to infuse shortly thereafter.

As Kris lay in an apparent coma, Ed kept a vigil at her bedside. He helped Carmen monitor the vital signs, but the hours passed slowly. He checked on Flint a couple of times but only got a slurred, mumbled response to each attempt to arouse him. As Ed waited and watched over Kris, he was resigned to her impending death. The seizure and her deeper level of coma had brought him to the realization that it was perhaps only a matter of a few more hours. He thought about pulling the NG tube out, but decided that she was probably no longer aware of it anyway, so he left it in. He wondered about funeral arrangements for Kris and thought about the possible ongoing threat to himself or Flint from X-Ops. There would be danger, but they should have plenty of police and FBI protection once they returned home. For the present, he'd keep his gun ready and handy. He went back to his room to confirm that it was fully loaded, and left it under the pillow on his bed.

In the corner of the room on the mattress that Ed had set up, Carlos was asleep with his arms wrapped around his AK-47 rifle. Ed would ask Carlos to guard the back outside door whenever Ed got to bed that night.

Paterson returned to Kris' room around 11:00 and found that Ed had dozed off in a chair next to her bed. He shook him awake and said, "Sorry to be late. I just got done with the C-section."

Ed rubbed his eyes and yawned. "It's been quiet. Vitals signs okay. No apparent bleeding."

"And no seizure activity?"

"Not a twitch. Maybe the magnesium helped."

Paterson whispered, "I hope so," as he stood next to Kris, watching her breathing pattern. The rise and fall of her chest was her only visible movement. "Have we checked her pupils lately?"

Ed shook his head.

Holding a penlight that he took out of his shirt pocket, Paterson used the thumb of his free hand to gently retract each of her upper eyelids. He briefly flashed light at each pupil to assess its size and responsiveness. "Pupils are mid-position and quite reactive," he said.

"That's good. Shall we try to wake her up?"

Paterson nodded. He first gave her right shoulder several vigorous shakes as he yelled, "Kris – wake up!" directly into her left ear. After no response and two more unsuccessful attempts, he rubbed her central sternum with his knuckle progressively harder. The hardest rub, which he was sure would be quite painful, elicited only facial twitching and a brief guttural grunt. He stopped and turned to Ed. "Either she's in a deeper coma, or the lorazepam and that seizure she had are still depressing her level of responsiveness."

Ed was silent, but his face and demeanor showed his intense disappointment. He sat down on the chair and stared at the floor.

Paterson put his hand on his shoulder. "Let's reassess her in about an hour. Either she'll get better or she won't." He paused to give Ed a chance to reply, but he remained silent with his head down. "I've got paperwork to do in my office. I'll be back about midnight and we'll try again."

Ed looked up. "Wait. I almost forgot. Kris asked for Mozart opera music to be played for her whether she was awake or not. I wrote down the arias from *Figaro* that she requested."

He handed the piece of paper with his notes to Paterson, who looked at it and said, "No problem. I have the CD. It's one of my favorites. I'll bring a portable player when I come back."

Shortly after midnight, Paterson left his office to return to the private ward. He was carrying the CD player, glad for an opportunity to do a little something for Kris Jensen. He had no real hope that she would survive the night. He checked in with Carmen at the nurse's station and got her report on Kris and Flint before he went into the room. Ed was at her bedside.

Paterson said, "Carmen tells me all has been quiet."

"Pretty much status quo."

Paterson set up the CD player on Kris' bedside table. "*The Marriage of Figaro* is loaded and ready to go. Play it now?"

"Why not?"

"We'll start with the overture and then skip to the arias she requested. Are you at all familiar with this work of Mozart?"

"Can't say that I'm an opera buff, so – ah – it's all Greek to me."

"Actually, it's in Italian," said Paterson. He moved another chair to Kris' bedside and sat down. As the overture played, he described to Ed the music of Mozart and the importance of *Figaro* among the composer's operatic works.

As she lay on the bed, Kris' mind took her back to the big, soft, forest green couch in her father's study at her childhood home in Oshkosh. It was a snowy Sunday afternoon in the middle of a Wisconsin winter. As the wind howled against the frosted window, she was curled up on the couch with a cup of hot chocolate. Her father was at his desk and had just placed his LP recording of *Figaro* onto the turntable of the record player that sat on a filing cabinet next to his desk. He settled into his brown leather desk chair, lit his pipe, and leaned back to listen to the music.

Late Sunday afternoon was a special time that Kris often shared alone with her father because her mother generally took a nap and her brother Eric much preferred to play basketball at the Holy Saviour Lutheran church gym. Her father took a sip from his cup of hot chocolate and smiled at her. "This is *Porgi amor*, that you like," he said as the intro music to the aria started. She nodded and closed her eyes to listen. As the aria came to a close, she next heard him say, "This is the Countess singing, *Dove sono.*" Then came her father's voice again. "This is Susanna singing *Deh vieni, non tardar.*" As the love song came to a close, Kris said, "Daddy, it's so beautiful."

Both Paterson and Ed had been listening to the music and not paying attention to Kris until she spoke out after the third aria. Ed turned to Paterson with his mouth open and eyebrows raised. "Did you hear her say that?"

Paterson nodded. Both of them jumped up from their chairs to stand and lean over to look at Kris, who had her eyes closed but was smiling. Paterson reached out and gently shook her shoulder. "Kris?"

She opened her eyes and looked at them with a puzzled expression. "What happened to my Daddy?"

Ed took her hand and said, "He's in heaven, and you're still down here on earth with us. Thank God."

Kris focused on their faces. "Okay, now I remember. I guess I was asleep and dreaming." She turned to look at the CD player. "Thanks for getting *Figaro* for me." She yawned but was unable to cover her mouth, due to being tied down. She looked at the restraints. "I must have been acting up again. Can I have these off?"

Paterson nodded. "Absolutely." Carmen had come into the room to listen to the music and he motioned for her to help him remove them. "So, how do you feel?"

"With these," she said, wagging her freed-up hands at him. She shrugged. "Okay – not clever, but I'm only half awake. I do feel better than I have for days though." She reached up and felt the stitches on her swollen lower lip. "How did I get a fat, hairy lip?"

"You had a seizure and bit it. I had to put in sutures to stop the bleeding."

"Oh. Thank you." She reached up and touched her lower lip again, then brushed her hair back a bit with her fingertips. "I must look like a mess."

"That clinches it."

Kris looked at Ed. "What?"

"They taught us in medical school that when a female patient starts to care about her personal appearance, it's a sure sign of improvement."

She smiled at him. "There's a bit of truth in that. I really do feel better. Kurka's plasma must be helping. I'll take being a sickly survivor." She turned to Paterson and pleaded, "Could you please take the NG tube out? And the Foley catheter ?"

"Why not? And that'll get you off the Yachabo critical list."

Ed looked puzzled by Paterson's last comment. Kris explained to him the Yachabo tube number-based severity of illness scoring system. She added, "I did use to tell my hospital patients, 'You know you're getting better when you have fewer tubes hanging off your body.'"

Ed nodded. "We called it the tube titer."

After Carmen had removed the urinary catheter and the nasogastric tube, Kris raised her right hand to display the IV needle that Ed had inserted. "The butterfly too?"

Paterson shook his head. "That'll need to stay, in case you have another seizure."

"Okay. Makes sense." She yawned. "I'm still really tired and need to go back to sleep, but I want to listen to a little more of *Figaro* first."

"I need to get some sleep myself," said Ed, "but I'm going to have Carmen get me up in a couple of hours so I can check on you again."

Kris yawned again. "Okay."

Ed gave her hand a squeeze. "I'll see you in a couple of hours." He left to instruct Carmen.

Paterson watched him go. "Neither one of us expected you to improve, especially after the seizure."

"I really do feel better."

"You look better to me," he said. "Livelier, I'd say. If you continue to improve or at least remain stable, we'll need to evacuate you and Mr. Flint either to Caracas or back to the States."

She nodded. "I agree. Hey. Why don't you just call the FBI. They'll come pick us up." She laughed. "Just kidding. However you want to proceed would be fine with me."

"Let's wait and see how the two of you are doing in the morning. We'll decide then."

"Sounds like a plan."

Paterson left and she listened to *Figaro* for only a few minutes before she fell right back to sleep.

Two hours later, at 2:30 a.m., Kris awoke promptly when Ed touched her shoulder and said her name. She opened one eye and said, "It's not time to get up yet, is it?"

He smiled. "No, not yet. Just wanted to check on you. Go back to sleep." Undisturbed, she dozed off again. He stood over her for a few minutes to be sure she was calm and stayed asleep.

Ed was now optimistic about Kris' survival. He instructed Carmen to awaken him only for a problem or deterioration in Kris' status. He woke Carlos up and asked him to keep watch at the back outside doorstep. Carlos went willingly with his rifle in one hand and a pack of cigarettes in the other.

Ed wanted to get at least three more hours of sleep before sunrise. He went back to bed just before 3:00 a.m., but his sleep was light and vigilant, from lingering anxiety and a gnawing expectation that he was about to awakened. In the pre-dawn twilight, he awoke to a choking-gagging sound, followed by a thud that came from the hallway outside his room.

He sat up to listen, but all was quiet. When he turned on the bedside light, his watch read 5:30 a.m. He started to wonder if it had been a dream, but thought that he heard whispered voices. He got up to check with Carmen.

Chapter 33

Ed turned off the bedside light and moved quietly to the door. He opened it just enough to peer into the darkened hallway toward the lighted nurses' station. Carmen was on the floor on her back, motionless, with her mouth gaping open. Her neck was crimson with blood, which had pooled around the back of her head and shoulders. Ed was sure she was dead. Because he thought that her killer could still be in the building, he resisted the urge to rush to her side.

Across the hallway, the door to Kris' room was closed. Ed listened but heard nothing. Fearing for the safety of Kris and Flint, Ed closed his door and moved quickly back to his bed to retrieve the handgun he'd gotten from the guerillas. He wondered what had happened to Carlos, who had promised to keep watch until dawn.

Ed went to the front window of his room and pulled the curtain aside. In the dim early morning light, he could make out the legs and boots of Carlos sprawled motionless on the ground just beyond the doorstep. Gun in hand, Ed hurried to the door to check on his friends.

Armed with a hunting knife, Cameron Jones had entered Kris' room through the connecting door. She was asleep on her back with the bedside lamp lit as Jones approached. When he was next to her bed, he hesitated, then stopped. Because she looked so much different from the pictures of Kris Jensen that he had seen, he retreated to the connecting door and whispered to Eric Sanders, "Is that her?"

"Has to be. Flint's in this room."

"If that's her, she's got some bad disease or infection. I don't want her blood on me."

"So take her out with a pillow while I cut Flint. Then we'll search the rest of the rooms to be sure."

Kris awoke to a pillow pressed hard against her face. She grabbed at the pillow with both hands to get it off her, and in the attempt, felt the strong arms of the person trying to kill her. She pulled and clawed at the arms, but felt herself weakening.

She remembered the butterfly needle in the back of her right hand. She moved her arms down over her stomach and pulled the needle out with her left hand. With a firm grip on the plastic butterfly base, she used the needle to repeatedly stab at the arms holding down the pillow.

Jones cursed her. "Damn you, bitch." He let go of the pillow and backed off to get away from further needlesticks. "I'm going to finish you off." He reached for his gun.

When Ed stepped into the dark hallway to go across to Kris' room, he saw a masked soldier with a rifle guarding Carmen's body at the nurses' station. At first the soldier didn't notice Ed in the dark end of the hallway, but when he did, he raised his rifle to fire. Before he could do so, Ed fired two quick shots that hit the soldier in the chest and the forehead. The Colombian mercenary staggered back and fell to the floor.

Kris had pulled the pillow away and was gasping for air when she heard the two gunshots outside the room. Jones had his gun drawn to execute her, but when the two shots rang out, he turned to face the door and the more immediate threat of someone with a gun in the hallway. He knocked over the bedside lamp to darken the room and called out to the Colombian mercenary, "*Diego! Esta bien?*" Hearing no response, he started toward the connecting door to regroup with Sanders.

Kris decided to get out of the line of any gunfire. She slid off the side of her bed onto the floor. Jones saw her disappear from view and growled, "I'm not done with you yet, bitch."

Ed stood outside Kris' room, looking toward the soldier he hoped he had just killed. He wondered how many more were in or around the building. When he heard the voice of someone in Kris' room, he had no choice but to go in. He kicked open the door and immediately fired three shots at a man silhouetted in the light from the connecting door. Before Jones collapsed to the floor from bullets to his neck and heart, he fired back twice, hitting Ed in the abdomen and right thigh.

Ed, bent over from abdominal pain but still standing, kept his gun aimed at Jones' body, sprawled immobile on the floor. Ed decided that the downed gunman was no longer a threat, so he turned his attention to the bed. When he saw it empty, he whispered, "Kris –where are you?"

A shot fired by Sanders struck Ed in the right temple and dropped him to the floor.

Kris was about to answer Ed when she heard the last gunshot, and then the thud of someone falling hard to the floor. She peeked out from behind the foot of the bed. Ed lay face down just inside the hallway door. *Oh my God!* She wanted to crawl to him to help him, but she'd expose herself to whoever shot him. She groped around for something that she could use for a weapon and felt her purse on the lower shelf of the bedside table. She reached in and found the Zamorana semi-automatic pistol that Esteban had given her in the car after they had left the Caracas airport. *I just hope this thing still works.* She released the safety.

Eric Sanders' knife had just cut into the right side of Flint's neck when the X-Ops agent heard the two gunshots in the hallway. He drew his gun and left Flint, who was now awake and gagging and clutching at his neck wound. As Sanders approached the hallway door, he could see Diego dead on the floor next to the nurse. Sanders didn't respond to Jones' call to the Colombian mercenary, so as not to alert whoever killed Diego as to their number and location. When the gunfire erupted in the next room and Jones went down, he crept into position next to the connecting door. It was an easy shot to take out the gunman, who Sanders hoped was Beaufain.

He didn't see the woman on the bed, but from what he had heard Jones say, he knew that she was still alive. To let more light into her room, he opened the connecting door all the way. As he stepped over Jones' body, he approached the bed with his gun drawn. He couldn't see her yet, but he knew that she hadn't escaped out the door. He was also pretty sure that she wasn't armed; the man he had just shot still had his gun in his hand. Sanders squatted down beside the body to get a closer look at his face. Satisfied that it was Beaufain, he muttered, "Two down, one to go." He stood up. With his gun held ready, he slowly moved around the foot of the bed to view the other side. He lowered his weapon when he saw Kris lying on her back on the floor with just a pillow in front of her. He could see what Jones had meant by her changed appearance.

"Dr. Jensen, I presume."

She looked him in the eye and said, "Yeah. Agent X-Ops, I presume."

He nodded. "Yeah. Agent Sanders – here to finally take you out."

As he raised his arm to fire his gun, she offered up the pillow in her left hand. "Want to use the pillow instead?"

He shook his head. "Nope."

"I do." With her right hand hidden behind the pillow, she fired five shots from the Zamorana pistol into Sanders' chest and face. Through the cloud of feathers blown out of the pillow, she watched him sink to his knees and slump to the floor.

Chapter 34

Sanders wasn't moving and didn't appear to be breathing, but Kris kept her pistol aimed at him as she sat up and poked at his chest with her foot. When he didn't react, she reached to take the gun from his hand and placed the weapon up on the bed. Holding onto the bedrail, she got up on her feet to look across the room. The X-Ops agent who had tried to smother her was sprawled immobile near the connecting door and appeared dead.

Ed was lying face down on the floor just inside the hallway door. Kris' legs were too weak and wobbly to walk, so she dropped down on her hands and knees and quickly crawled over to him. He was still alive, but had a rapid, weak carotid pulse. She shook him and called his name, but he didn't respond. She saw a head wound above his right ear and blood on his right thigh. She was trying to roll him on his back when she heard garbled curses coming from the next room. She picked up her pistol and pointed it at the open connecting door. When no one appeared, she leaned over to get a better look, but all she saw was Flint's right foot move up and down. The swearing and slurred muttering were coming from him. It was obvious that both her friends desperately needed medical help, so she decided to take the chance that no X-Ops attackers remained. "We need help in here! Robby – Helmtrude – someone!"

There was only silence. The figure of a man loomed in the hallway door. Kris saw him in her peripheral field of vision and spun around, ready to fire her gun.

"Don't shoot. It's me, Robby."

"Thank God." She sighed with relief.

Paterson saw Ed lying on the floor. He switched on the overhead light and knelt down to start examining him.

Kris said, "Ed's been shot in the head and Cory sounds hurt next door."

"Are you okay?"

"Yes."

"Carmen and a soldier are dead by the nurses' station. Who are these men?"

"X-Ops agents – came to kill us." She pointed at Sanders' body. "I think he's dead. Don't know about the other one over there."

Paterson glanced at the bodies. "We'd better make sure." He got up to assess the downed X-Ops agents. When finished, he looked back at Kris. "Both dead. Any more of them?"

"Don't know. Hope not. Please help Ed – and what about Cory?"

Paterson glanced through the connecting door into the next room. "He's alive and moving. I'll get to him shortly. " He knelt back down beside her and had just pulled out his stethoscope to listen to Ed's chest when Sister Helmtrude appeared in the doorway.

Helmtrude was visibly shocked and upset. "Dr. Paterson! C-C-Carmen."

He looked up at her. "I know. Nothing we can do for her. Go check on Mr. Flint next door."

As she left to do so, they heard someone say, "*Madre de Dios,*" from out in the hallway.

Paterson said to Kris. "It's okay." He turned and shouted toward the hallway. "Guillermo – in here."

Moments later, the blue-coveralled engineer appeared in the doorway, crowbar in hand.

Paterson waved him in. "Help me get Dr. Beaufain up on the bed."

After they had lifted Ed onto the bed, Paterson picked up Sanders' gun. He handed it to Guillermo with instructions to make sure that the building and nearby grounds were secure.

Guillermo nodded as he took the handgun and inspected it. "I know how to use this."

"Good," said Paterson, who had already turned his attention back to Ed's airway and pulse. He examined the gunshot wounds as well as Ed's chest, and used the penlight to look at his pupils.

Kris thought she heard him whisper *shit*. "What is it?"

He sighed. "Not good. He's in shock from wounds to the thigh, mid-abdomen, and right temple. And he's got a fixed, dilated right pupil, which means there's likely an epidural hematoma that's putting pressure on his brain – needs a Burr hole to drain it." He paused. "And then I might have to explore his abdomen."

Helmtrude came to the connecting door. "Mr. Flint has a deep knife wound to his right neck. Awake and responsive with a blood pressure 100/60. He's lost blood, but he kept pressure on the wound with his right hand or would have lost more – and he's not moving his left arm or leg."

Paterson winced. "Give him a liter of saline and run it in wide open. I'll be right in to look at him. We need a nurse to start an IV and saline on Ed. And get someone to alert the OR staff for an emergency Burr hole and possible exploratory laparotomy."

Helmtrude nodded. "I'll start the IV. What about these bodies?"

"I'll have Guillermo handle it."

As if on cue, the engineer appeared in the doorway with gun-in-hand, having checked the building and nearby grounds. "I found no one except a dead man near the back door. Looks like a Colombian guerilla."

"That might be Carlos. They must've taken him out as they came in the back entrance."

Kris asked, "Who's Carlos?"

"A guerilla who guided Ed here, then stayed for a medical evaluation and was to return to the mountains this morning." Paterson turned to Guillermo. "Take pictures of the bodies with my camera for the *policia*, then cover them up and move them to the storage room we've used for a morgue."

"Wait a minute," said Kris. "How did X-Ops get here?"

"Good question. Helicoptered in, I imagine. The landing strip is about 200 meters from here." He motioned to Guillermo. "Go check out the landing strip before you do anything else." Paterson turned his attention back to Ed as Helmtrude brought in the supplies for the intravenous access and saline infusion.

Kris struggled to her feet. "How can I help?" She paused and grabbed the bedrail with both hands. "Woo – I'm still a little weak."

Paterson shook his head. "You're not in any shape to – " He stopped in mid-sentence when she started to topple over. He and Guillermo together caught her before she fell to the floor. "Let's put her in the bed across the hall," Paterson said to Helmtrude. "Start the IV while I get Kris' vital signs and check her for wounds."

Two hours later, Kris awoke to a commotion out in the hallway. Someone was shouting orders. Fearing another attack, she sat up and looked around for her gun but didn't see it. The door opened.

First into the room came a soldier with an American flag on his shoulder. She guessed he was Special Forces. He was followed by Paterson and a non-military man in plain clothes. The soldier strode to the foot of her bed and said, "Lieutenant Commander Jensen."

She wasn't used to being addressed by her U.S. Public Health Service rank. She was unsure of his rank and if she was supposed to salute him. She just nodded.

Instead, he saluted her and said, "Captain Joseph Parker, U.S. Army Rangers. We've come to take you home."

Kris grinned. "Thank you, Captain Parker. I'm ready to go." She looked to Paterson. "But what about Ed and Cory?"

"Their medics helped me with the Burr hole. Turned out we didn't need to open Ed's abdomen, and he's started to wake up. Mr. Flint is awake and stable, but unfortunately has suffered a stroke. His carotid artery thrombosed and we think a clot embolized to his brain. They've both been loaded into a Med-evac helicopter already. You're next up."

"So who called in the cavalry?"

The man in plain clothes stepped forward. "I'm Special Agent Roy Castillo of the FBI. Dr. Paterson called our U.S. office last night on his ham radio to report your location and to request an evacuation. We already had a search and rescue unit on stand-by in eastern Colombia. Just needed to know exactly where you were."

Paterson added. "I heeded your offhand remark to call the FBI and they were quite pleased to oblige. When it became clear that you were going to survive, I decided it was best to get you and Mr. Flint evacuated to a higher level of medical care."

"Yeah – I might still need a liver transplant, but I think we've gotten pretty excellent care here."

Paterson blushed. "Thanks. We do the best we can with our staff and resources."

Kris turned to Castillo. "So am I in custody?"

"Let's just call it protective custody. I have a lot of questions to ask you when you're up to it."

"And I have a lot to tell you."

Sister Helmtrude came into the room, followed by Sister Nita carrying a freezer box. The Lab Director held it out to Kris. "There was one more bag of Kurka's plasma. Want to take it along?"

Kris nodded. "I don't think I'll need any more, but we'll find a good use for it." She looked to Paterson, Helmtrude and Nita in turn and wiped away a tear. "I can't ever thank all of you enough for saving our lives. We've got to go now, but I promise I'll be back when I'm well to help you solve the hepatitis and control it."

As the Blackhawk HH60L Med-evac helicopter lifted off and started a climbing turn to the west toward Colombia, Kris had a good aerial view of the Santa Maria Mission compound and as they approached the mountains, she caught a glimpse of one of the Yachabo villages. She affirmed her vow to return. *There's still a lot more work to be done to figure out this hepatitis virus and to control it. I just hope any politics are settled and the paperwork for funding the investigation and lab support is done by the time I'm back on my feet.*

She looked over at Castillo, sitting nearby. *In the meantime, there's justice to be done and – some other unfinished business.* The FBI agent had just finished calling in a report using a satellite phone. She caught his attention and asked if she could use the phone.

"Sure," he said. "Want to talk to your family?"

"Yes, but not yet. I'd like to call the Medical ICU at Parish General Hospital in New Orleans."

"No problem." He dialed a number on the phone, relayed her request to an operator, and handed Kris the phone. "It's ringing."

"Good morning. Medical ICU. This is Lisa speaking."

"Hi. This is Dr. Kris Jensen with the CDC. I was up there a few days ago helping Dr. Schmidt with Homer Renk's hepatitis and B.J. Miller's needlestick exposure."

"I remember."

"I wanted to ask about B.J. Is she – ?"

After a pause, Lisa said, "I guess it's okay to talk to you. B.J. is still hanging on. On a vent in liver failure. GI bleeding and getting tons of FFP and other blood products, plus three different anti-virals. Not doing well at all. She's being considered for a liver transplant."

Kris was thrilled to hear B.J. was still alive. "Thanks for the info. I need to talk to her mother. Do you have her number?"

"She's visiting here in the unit right now. Want me to get her?"

"Yes. Please."

After a minute, Corrine Miller picked up the phone and said, "Hello? Dr. Jensen? I've been praying for you and your work."

"I appreciate that more than you know. Let me first say how sorry I am about the loss of your husband."

"Thank you. We buried Gary yesterday, and I'm about to lose B.J. too. I was afraid you had forgotten about us."

"Never. I've been away learning how best to treat this virus."

"Does the NIH have an experimental drug for B.J.?

Kris eyed the freezer box and said, "No, but I've got something much better." She covered the phone receiver with her hand and said to Castillo, "We're going to have to make an extra stop."

Epilogue

New Orleans - Four months later

The Gambino's hostess greeted Kris Jensen who was dressed in her US-Public Health Service khaki uniform, and showed her to the green checker-clothed table for four that she had reserved for lunch.

B.J. Miller was already seated sipping from a glass of sweet tea. When she saw Kris, B.J. got up to greet her with a hug and then stepped back in admiration. "Wow. In uniform. You look awesome."

Kris smiled. "I was just about to say how great you look."

They sat down and Kris ordered lemonade from the waitress. "Yeah, all my bruises are gone and just about all the swelling. I finally fit into my uniform, but I still stay tired. I just don't seem to have the quality of sleep that I used to get."

"I've been tired too," B.J. said. "I guess fatigue comes with having had a liver transplant, or maybe from the immunosuppressive meds I have to take."

"They tell me fatigue is common, even though all my tests are normal."

B.J. laughed. "I hear the same thing from my doctors. So tell me – is Dr. Beaufain going to join us for lunch?"

"I invited him, but he called earlier and backed out. Physically he's intact, but emotionally still a wreck. He's moody, irritable, depressive. Not sleeping well either, and tired all the time – never wants to go out and do anything. Still hasn't returned to work. I think he has PTSD."

"Post-traumatic stress disorder?"

"Yeah. But he won't go to get help. You know how men can be. That's especially true for Hispanic men."

A woman approached their table with her adolescent daughter, who asked for Kris' autograph. After Kris had written and signed a note for the girl, B.J. asked, "How are you dealing with your celebrity status?"

"Not well. It's just not me. I've declined almost every interview request, which makes the media even peskier. You wouldn't believe how much money I've been offered for the book and movie rights to the inside story."

"It *is* an unbelievable story."

Kris smiled. "I'm not sure I would believe it if it hadn't happened to me. For me, the true happy ending will be when Ed and everyone else have all healed their wounds and the Yachabo are protected by a vaccine against the yellow death virus. Then your dad and all my CDC friends and co-workers – " She paused to collect herself. "Then some greater good will have come out of all the suffering and loss of life."

"Are you headed back to Venezuela?"

"I'm going to go if for no other reason than to give something back to the mission hospital staff and the Yachabo who saved my life. But right now I'm still on medical leave, and the Venezuelan government is still balking at a collaborative research effort. They're miffed over our military coming into their country to evacuate us without their prior knowledge and consent. The State Department is working to repair the political damage. Plus I have to attend more hearings in the X-Ops trial in Washington over the next few months, even though Cory Flint is the prosecution's main witness. He still has left-sided paralysis from the stroke, but he's been fully able to testify."

The waitress came by and asked if they were ready to order. Kris said, "Not yet. We're expecting one more person."

B.J. raised her eyebrows. "We are? Who is it?"

"Someone I wanted you to meet. Here she comes now." Kris got up to hug a smartly dressed young woman with freckles and brown hair. Kris took her by the hand to bring her to the table and introduced LaDonna Fry to B.J. Miller.

When they were all seated, Kris told B.J. that after LaDonna's liver transplant, she moved to New Orleans and was taking classes to get her high school diploma and to learn computer science. "I'm proud of her."

Kris turned to LaDonna and explained that B.J. was also a hepatitis survivor who had gotten the Yachabo immune serum, followed by a new liver.

LaDonna said, "I been wantin' to know how come I didn't get that serum and still came out all right."

"It's because when you were transferred to Memphis, your doctors there decided to transplant your liver right away," Kris said. "I wouldn't have thought it would work, but turned out it was the right thing to do. The transplanted liver kept you alive long enough for your body's natural immunity to kick in and get rid of the virus before it had a chance to damage the new liver. In B.J.'s case, she was even worse off than you were. The Yachabo serum controlled the virus long enough for her doctors to find a transplant for her. In my case the serum got rid of the virus, but I still have so much liver damage that I might yet have to get a transplant."

"Okay, I think I understand it."

Kris smiled. "I can explain it more later."

B.J. looked at Kris and LaDonna. "It's Saturday. You two want to go out to a jazz club with me tonight?"

LaDonna said, "I'll go with ya."

Kris shook her head. "I'd love to, but after lunch I'm driving up to Corham to see Dan Stevens."

"Are you coming back to New Orleans?"

"Not this time, but I'll be back next month to see Ed Beaufain. From Corham I'll head east. On my way back to Atlanta, I'm going to stop at a little church near Heflin, Alabama to attend their Sunday morning service."

"Why?"

"I was driving to Birmingham right after the CDC bombing. At my darkest hour of grief, I happened upon the Mission Hill Presbyterian church just off Interstate 20. It was there I found peace and the strength to go on. I want to go back and thank the pastor."

When they had finished lunch and were having coffee, B.J. asked Kris, "How has this experience changed you?"

While Kris thought about it, LaDonna spoke up. "I can tell you about how I've changed." Both Kris and B.J. nodded for LaDonna to proceed.

"I understand now that big time trouble can come right out of your blind side and knock you into oblivion – or right close, anyway," LaDonna said. "A few folks, mostly men, had it comin', but most people, especially women like us, and other good people – like my mommy and daddy who were killed in a wreck – didn't do nuthin' to deserve it. But we three got us a second chance. For me, I know now that life here on earth is a gift. I aim to make the best of it – to educate myself and work hard but also to give back to make this a better world. All of us can, and we should. I will appreciate every little part of my world. Like the purr of a kitten, the full moon risin' through the pines and the delicious taste of this coffee. But even more, I'm going to appreciate the big important changes in my life – like my education and a new job, but most of all, my new friends." Ladonna raised her coffee cup toward Kris and B.J. "Cheers, ladies. Here's to us and the appreciation of life!"

As they clinked their cups together, Kris beamed at her. "Cheers, LaDonna, I couldn't have said it better myself."